THE MANTUARY

JULIE WASSMER

The Mantuary

Published by The Conrad Press in the United Kingdom 2024

Tel: +44(0)1227 472 874
www.theconradpress.com
info@theconradpress.com

ISBN 978-1-916966-66-6

Copyright © Julie Wassmer, 2024

The moral right of Julie Wassmer to be identified as author of this work has been asserted in accordance with the Copyright, Designs and Patents Act 1988.

All rights reserved.

Typesetting and Cover Design by: Charlotte Mouncey, www.bookstyle.co.uk

The Conrad Press logo was designed by Maria Priestley.

Printed and bound in Great Britain by Clays Ltd, Elcograf S.p.A.

For my friend, Paul McKenzie

*'Why should you love him whom the world hates so?
Because he loves me more than all the world.'*

Christopher Marlowe

CHAPTER ONE

Extract 1 from the transcript of a recorded interview with
Mrs Margaret Sheild
Date: 3rd April 2024
Conducted by: Officers of Marston Police
Location: Marston Police Station, West Yorkshire

I know I'm under caution and you warned me I don't have to say anything. But I do. I need to rewind and explain everything from that very first day, when it all began.

It was months ago but in my mind it's like it happened only yesterday. Sitting here, right now, I can hear the sewing machine needles clattering and some stupid pop song blasting out from the radio on the factory floor. The radio's a bit of entertainment for my girls; twenty-three garment workers on the payroll of Masters & Son. Phil Masters had been our boss until a stroke did for him last year and that's when Jason took over. Phil's son was the new master of us all.

From a window in my office, I could look down at my girls. I always called them 'girls', though some were older than me, and I turned fifty last birthday. I kept an eye peeled, making sure they were occupied but I looked out for them too. Why? Because over the years I've spent more time with some than I have with my own family and, yes, maybe that was part of the problem. But that afternoon I didn't see any of this coming. The girls were busy on their machines and Samira, my 'right hand' as I always called her, was walking down the rows making sure everyone had what they needed.

We'd been working on sets of pyjamas, fast-track orders for London, and I had the schedule pinned to the shelf above my desk, next to a postcard that had dropped through our door a few weeks ago.

On the front was a photo of our Lisa with a suntan, and her shiny dark hair falling almost to her shoulders. I kept looking at that photo because I'd never got used to my daughter as a brunette. She'd always been fair, with long blonde hair. As a kid, she was an angel, with the face of a cheeky cherub, because there was usually a bit of mischief in her smile, but now it was painted a shade of shocking pink, the same as the cocktail she held up in her hand – like it was some kind of trophy.

I used to search for signs of myself in our Lisa but she was always her father's child. They were that much alike, eyes the same bright blue as the heart-shaped swimming pool in that photo. The sign above it showed three words – *Hotel Miramar Tenerife*.

The Canary Islands is about as far as you can get from a parky Yorkshire afternoon but that photo warmed my heart and I'd let myself get distracted by it because I had Jason on the phone – his voice banging on above the sound of the sewing machines. He'd been giving me the usual warning about what would happen if we didn't meet our deadlines, but I'd heard enough for one day, so I stopped him right there and said, 'Jason, love, if your balls are on the line then you'd better get used to singing falsetto because we're doing the best we can.'

That's when I turned around and saw Samira in the doorway with two cuppas in her hand. She never said a word because she'd heard it all before. She just set the cups down among the fabric samples on my desk and I saw her glance at a little plaque the girls had given me for Christmas. It read: *If you want something done, give it to a busy person.*

She nodded and I smiled because we both knew Jason could have taken a lesson from that, but instead, he was wasting more time reading me the riot act. His dad might have left him the factory but you can't hand down common sense. Jason doesn't understand hard graft, or people, only profit, so I spelled it out to him. 'Look,' I said, 'I told you a fortnight ago, I needed more staff for this order but what did I get? One Kurdish refugee —and no,' I said sharpish before he had a chance to butt in, 'I don't care where she comes from. I just want *more* like her.'

Straight after that, I put the phone down because it never pays to let Jason go on. Besides, I had work to do, but then Samira piped up.

'You sure about that?'

I saw she was staring through the window down onto the factory floor where the new girl, Rona, was shaping up to someone. I could hear young Naila Akhtar spitting accusations and the girls were all getting up and leaving their machines to crowd around. Samira gave me a knowing look and I shot out of that office and down the metal staircase to the factory floor faster than a fireman down a pole.

No-one heard me coming above the music but I soon caught sight of Rona, bent double, her long brassy-blonde hair clutched in Naila's tight fists. The other girls were shouting from the sidelines and Naila was playing up to them, pulling Rona's head down to stop her fighting back.

'Go Naila!

'Watch her nails!'

I fought my way through a wall of bodies to see Rona's boot meeting with Naila's shin. A scream rang out and Naila lost her balance while Rona saw her chance. She grabbed Naila's work coat but it ripped and a cry went up, along with Naila's fist, but Rona blocked the punch with one hand while her other went straight to Naila's throat. It was all happening so quickly, but I saw the fear in Naila's eyes as Rona shoved her back.

Somehow I managed to force myself between them and I shouted out, demanding to know what the bloody hell was going on. Naila couldn't answer, she was gasping that much for breath, so I looked back at my girls and someone shouted something about 'the refugee' stealing Naila's fags. Rona was having none of it.

'That's not true!'

She was staring at me like a kid begging to be believed but Naila slapped her hand flat down on her work bench and ordered me not to listen.

'They were right here,' she screamed. '*She* took them. She's a liar as well as a thief!'

Everyone's eyes shifted to Rona, looks full of suspicion, but there was something else too, something folk registered whenever Rona opened her mouth to speak and let them know she was a stranger in our town.

'Okay,' she said. She was panting, her eyes darting around like she was searching for a way out – some way of escaping all the cold stares. Finally she found one. Turning to me, she flung her arms wide and gave me an order.

'You search me!'

I didn't even get a chance to reply before another voice shouted out.

'Don't do it, Mags. You might catch something!'

And that was it. I'd heard enough. I turned, quick as I could, and stared at every one of my girls in turn.

'Who said that?'

They must have known I meant business because the smirks suddenly faded. Music was still blaring from the radio, some DJ's voice prattling on in the background as though nothing had happened, but heads began to lower like they were burdened with shame. I waited, but no-one owned up so I strolled across to my girls, looked at each one in turn, and I stopped in front of young Tracey Tyler, who bit her lip, looking wary until I asked, 'How's young Caden doing? Still keeping you up at night, is he?'

Tracey blinked a couple of times then gave a smile like sunshine after rain. 'No, Mags,' she said, 'he's sleeping right through now. Good as gold.'

I nodded and moved along to Zara Ali who always sat next to Naila on the work bench.

'Is your nan out of hospital yet?'

She shook her head. 'Not yet,' she said, 'but they reckon she'll be home on Friday.'

'Good.' I said. 'No dancing on the table, all right? She doesn't want to go wearing that hip out too soon, eh?' I winked at her and Zara giggled. Then I turned to the girls and said: 'It's all over now. Let's get back to work.'

Everyone turned for their benches – everyone but Naila. She was still standing her ground, frowning at me, looking like I'd just betrayed her. She nodded to where Rona sat and spat, 'So, you're taking her word against mine?'

In that moment, I was suddenly taken right back, remembering a look that passed from one sister to another, with a question I'd never been able to answer properly because, after everything that's happened, I'll never understand the injustice that's played out in families. I took a deep breath and I repeated very calmly what I'd always said to my own girls – my flesh and blood – our Natalie and Lisa.

'I'm here for *both* of you.'

Then I looked away and yelled across the factory floor so that no-one could say that they hadn't heard me. 'We might not have a union any more, but we're a family – or we're nothing.'

No-one said a word so I took that as my cue to leave, before I saw something lying among the remnants beneath Naila's work station. I bent down to pick it up and I looked up at Naila and showed her the pack of ciggies in my hand. For a minute, she did nothing, then she shook her head and I could see she was struggling to find words. I waited for her to explain, but suddenly the factory bell was sounding. The moment had gone.

As usual, everyone behaved like Pavlov's dog and did what they always did when that bell rang: finished up at their stations and shrugged off their work coats. Naila was looking proper sorry for herself as she stared down at the ripped pocket in her own coat. We needed to talk but now was not the time so I put my hand on her shoulder and said, 'Go and get that clock punched.'

As I handed her the pack of ciggies, Naila looked relieved, until Rona walked by. I saw their eyes meet and I knew this wasn't finished, but Samira's voice kicked that thought out of my head.

'Mags?'

Samira was standing at the top of the spiral staircase, holding the cordless phone out to me. I wasn't in the mood to take a call.

'If that's Jason again,' I said, 'tell him I'll—'

'It's not,' she came down the stairs and handed me the phone. I could hear our Lisa's voice sounding from it.

'Mum...'

'Lisa?'

At the other end of the line she gave a long sigh. 'Now before you start fretting,' she said, 'nothing's wrong. I'm just calling to say I'm back.'

'You're what?'

'We've just touched down at Manchester.'

'But you're not due home for another—'

'I know,' she said, quickly, talking over me as usual. 'But something's happened and—' She broke off, then: 'Hold on a sec, will you?'

A million questions entered my head, filling the space she'd left on that phone line. *What's happened? Why are things not the way they should be? Why isn't my daughter where I'd imagined her to be... at that bar by the pool in the Hotel Miramar with a shocking pink cocktail in her hand...*

'Mum?' She was back on the line again but I was already one step ahead.

'You stay right there,' I said, 'I'll get your Dad to pick you up—'

'No,' she was adamant and our Lisa can be right stubborn – especially with me. 'There's no need,' she said, 'I'm all right. I'm just calling to let you know...'

I was straining to hear. 'Know what?'

'Can you hear me now?'

'Is it the job? Did you get your promotion?' She'd been in line for resort tour manager and I'd been waiting for news. I was still waiting – for too long.

'You're breaking up,' she said, 'I'll explain when I see you.'

'Lisa?'

'I'm on my way!'

And suddenly she was gone. All I could hear was the sound of a car engine starting up in the background. I listened hard but the phone went dead in my hand and I wondered if I'd just dreamt that, until another voice sounded – closer this time.

'Everything all right?'

Samira was buttoning her jacket, hitching the strap of her bag across her shoulder. I stared back down at the phone and I tried to remember every word our Lisa had just said. I ran the conversation back like a tape playing in my head, like the one you're recording me on right now, then I made a decision and heard myself say: 'Everything's fine.'

I nodded, convincing myself of that, allowing myself a little smile as I suddenly realised.

'Our Lisa's home.'

And that was the start of it all.

CHAPTER TWO

'So she didn't say why she's back?'

Jeff Sheild was staring at the glass in his hand, about to take a sip of wine when he saw his Jack Russell terrier looking up at him. He tossed the dog a peanut from a bowl on the coffee table and his wife's voice entered the room seconds before she followed.

'I told you,' said Maggie, 'there wasn't time before her phone went down. Maybe she's got some leave owed before this new job starts and—' She broke off at the sight of the wine glass at Jeff's lips. He gave a casual shrug.

'It's been in't shed for a while. I was just checking to see if it's all right.'

Maggie eyed him. 'And how many glasses did that take?' She took the bottle from him and noted half was gone.

Avoiding her stare, Jeff slumped down into his favourite Lazy Boy recliner. 'I've given up baccy *and* the beer, but a drop of red's good for yer.' The dog trotted over, sensing he needed support.

'Except you don't know what a "drop" is,' said Maggie knowingly. 'I've started so I'll finish.' She punched a few sofa cushions before fussing over a vase of irises.

Jeff stared down into his wine then offered another excuse. 'Well, we're meant to be celebrating, aren't we?'

At this, Maggie finally softened. 'Aye,' she smiled to herself. 'It's not every day your daughter goes from rep to resort tour manager, is it?' She paused then thought for a moment. 'And maybe now she'll give up that flat.'

Jeff sipped his wine. 'She likes the flat.'

'It's a waste of good money. She's hardly ever here—'

'Maybe. But she's only sub-renting and it's cheap. She paid up front, remember?'

'Aye,' said Maggie, ruefully, 'with her savings.'

Jeff sighed. 'She's twenty-one now. Old enough to do what she wants.'

'And still young enough to make mistakes.'

'You have to let her make them – or she'll never learn.'

Maggie shook her head. 'She doesn't need a flat while she's working abroad. And she's still got a room here.'

'It's not the same,' argued Jeff. 'And she didn't know how things were going to pan out with this job, did she? The agreement's up on the flat soon, so she can give it up then.' He held Maggie's look. 'She'll have to if she's got this promotion.'

'Aye,' said Maggie, placated by that thought before she quickly moved to her bag. 'What d'you think of this?'

Leaning in to Jeff she opened a small gift box to reveal a piece of jewellery nestled inside.

'I got it on the way home,' Maggie explained, before holding it up, allowing a silver locket to swing like a pendulum on its chain. 'What 'd'you reckon?'

Jeff's gaze shifted beyond the locket and spoke to his wife's uncertainty.

'I 'reckon' she'll love it.'

At the sight of Jeff's smile, Maggie relaxed and reached out to run her fingers through his hair. It was still thick, but white, and beginning to recede from his forehead like waves ebbing on a shoreline.

As a young man Jeff Sheild had been ruddy-skinned with a quiff as dark as the coal mine in which he had once slaved. Almost four decades on, it seemed as though he was now fading – together with memories of a previous life. His blue eyes were rheumy and his heart no longer beat as strongly as it once did. Maggie had to nag him to keep his medication on him at all times – pills – a permanent reminder of fresh frailty. Her husband was slipping away from her which made it all the more important for her to hold on to him, to secure the bonds that kept him attached to a future, while letting go of what might lure him back to a troubled past.

Jeff continued to smile, noting only the woman he had married thirty years ago – grateful for the kiss she was about to give him – when a car horn suddenly sounded outside. Bella barked at the racket while Maggie peered out of the window to see a sky-blue Renault turning off the road and on to her fake cobble driveway. 'She's here! Quick… you go and pay the cabbie while I sort this.'

Acting under orders, Jeff set down his glass and got to his feet, pausing at the living room door to look back at his wife as she carefully slipped the locket back into its box, before she began scribbling a message on to a gift tag.

A few moments later, Jeff opened the front door and saw the blue Renault was now parked on his driveway. The driver was opening the boot but Jeff's gaze remained fixed on his daughter. Lisa was facing away from him, dressed in an elegant blue trouser suit and looking much like a dark-haired stranger as she leaned back into the car to take her coat.

But after closing the passenger door, she turned to see her father and offered him the cheeky wink she always reserved for him. Hurrying forward, she fell into his arms and Jeff's eyes closed as he breathed in the scent of her perfume – and youth – before the dog began yapping, demanding attention. Lisa bent down and fussed over Bella as the creature turned excited circles.

'Who's been eating all the pies, then?'

''You talking about the dog or me?'

It was Maggie who had replied. Looking up, Lisa saw her mother standing at the front door and the two women moved quickly to embrace, when the moment was suddenly broken by the sound of the Renault's boot slamming shut. Remembering the driver, Jeff took out his wallet.

'How much do I owe you?' he asked cursorily. Taking out some notes he saw the amused look Lisa shared with the driver before they both began to laugh. 'What's so funny?' Jeff asked, confused.

Lisa took a step towards the driver. 'This is Bruce, Dad. And he's certainly no cabbie. We just flew back together – from Tenerife,' she gazed up at the man beside her as though inviting him to speak.

Bruce left a pause before he did so. 'Good to meet you both. I've heard a lot about you.'

Maggie eyed her daughter. 'Is that right?'

'Come on,' smiled Lisa. 'I'll explain.'

Minutes later, as they moved into the living room, Jeff caught the look on Maggie's face, a mixture of confusion and suspicion as she watched the stranger now depositing some Duty Free bags near Jeff's Lazy Boy. He was tall, well-built and somewhere in his early thirties, his smile still in place as he suddenly paused, reacting to the smell of food wafting in from the kitchen.

'Something smells good.'

'It's nowt special,' said Maggie guardedly. 'Just a casserole,' she eyed her daughter again – half knowing – half admonishing. 'But then our Lisa didn't mention she was bringing home company.'

'I didn't have time,' said Lisa, breezily. 'Signal went down,' she took a bright pink iPhone from her pocket – a twenty-first birthday present from her parents.

An awkward silence followed before Jeff turned his attention to the open bottle of wine. 'Well,' he said, rubbing his palms together. 'I reckon we could all do with a drink.' He turned to Bruce. 'Red okay for you?'

Bruce gave a nod. 'Actually I've got some Rioja here. Lisa said you might like this?'

From a Duty Free bag he produced a bottle caged in gold netting.

Jeff studied the label before looking up, impressed. 'Gran Reserva? You bet I bloody do!'

Maggie chided. 'Language.'

Jeff handed a glass to Bruce who quickly glanced around the room, noting as much as he could without appearing too intrusive; photos on a bookshelf; two young girls at play, one fair, one dark; a certificate marking twenty-five years' service at Masters & Son; a framed pencil drawing of Bella the dog and a commemorative plate on the wall above a selection of record albums. He stepped closer to them.

'That's Dad's mini shrine,' said Lisa, glancing back at her father.

'Aye,' said Jeff. 'Elvis at Gracelands.' He smiled proudly. 'All fully endorsed by the Presley estate.'

Bruce checked out the albums beneath it. 'That's an amazing collection of vinyl.'

'Yeah, Dad's got the lot.' Lisa winked again at her father who filled Bruce's glass as he explained.

'I know a lot of folk prefer the Rockabilly but for me nowt beats the ballads.'

'I think you're right there.'

Jeff looked surprised. 'Not too old fashioned for you?'

'Some things never go out of style.' Bruce smiled again.

Jeff eyed him for a second then raised a finger. 'See what you think of this!' He quickly moved to slip a record on the deck but Maggie lifted it from his grasp.

'Why d'you always have to play this when our Lisa comes home?'

Jeff snatched the record back. 'Cos it's *The Green Green Grass of Home.*'

'We don't have any green grass,' Maggie argued. You paved the front – *and* most of the back.'

'You know what I mean—'

'Aye, I do,' said Maggie. 'And I don't want Elvis Presley taking over, if you don't mind. Now,' she turned her attention to Lisa. 'How long are you going to keep us in suspense?'

Lisa gave a playful smile. 'About what?'

'What do you think?' said Maggie. Lisa's gaze shifted to her father but still she said nothing.

'Come on, love,' said Jeff, 'put us out of our misery. Have we got something to celebrate – or not?'

'All right,' said Lisa. 'You have!'

Maggie exclaimed. 'I knew it!' Picking up her own glass she shoved it in front of Jeff. 'Top me up!'

Lisa spoke. 'I handed in my notice last week.'

Jeff stopped pouring as Maggie stared back at her daughter. 'You… did what?'

Lisa thrust out her left hand and proudly showed the diamond ring on her finger.

'We're engaged,' she said finally, smiling at the man beside her before she looked back again at her parents.

Her smile began to fade as she saw their blank expressions. 'Well… I can tell by the jaws on your chests you're really pleased for me?'

A stunned pause followed which Jeff quickly filled. "Course we are, love.' Looking sidelong at Maggie, he then asked in an unsure voice: 'Aren't we, Mags?'

Maggie Sheild glanced between her daughter and the man beside her – the man who had just driven Lisa from the airport, who had taken a flight with her from Tenerife – a stranger to Maggie and Jeff but someone who had seemingly managed to change the course of their daughter's life. How could that possibly have happened without her knowing?

Lisa's voice nudged Maggie back into the room. 'Mum?'

Another moment's silence passed before Maggie felt able to speak. 'Dinner's burning.'

She turned and left the room.

A few moments later, Lisa entered the kitchen to find her mother staring through a glass oven door at a casserole bubbling inside.

'What d'you think you're doing?' asked Lisa in hushed exasperation.

Turning down her cooker Maggie turned slowly to face her daughter. 'I was about to ask you the same. You could've told us.'

'Told you?'

'Explained. Before this?'

Lisa took a deep breath. 'On Whatsapp?' Folding her arms across her chest she turned away, partly in frustration but also to escape her mother's searching gaze.

'If we'd have known,' said Maggie, 'we could've stopped you jacking in your job.'

Lisa turned slowly to face her. 'And is that all you can think about? A sodding job?'

Stung by the comment, Maggie felt conflicted on witnessing Lisa's clear disappointment. She heaved a sigh but pressed on. 'You were up for promotion, love.'

'So?'

'So,' said Maggie. 'How many other girls get a chance to work in a five-star resort in the Canaries?'

Lisa pointed to the ring on her finger. 'I'm getting married. Who cares about a friggin' resort?'

'*You* did. Once upon a time. You said you wanted to travel.'

'And I have. Been there – done that!'

'Aye. And you were having the time of your life,' said Maggie, tipping her head towards the door. 'Until him.'

Lisa steeled herself. 'His name's Bruce.'

'So you said.'

Unimpressed, Maggie turned towards the sink and began to rinse her hands.

Lisa shook her head. 'I should've known you'd be like this.'

'Then why act so surprised?' Maggie turned back to her, calmly picking up a tea towel before wiping her hands.

'Because I thought you might be happy for me.' Lisa turned for the door.

'Happy?' Maggie echoed, still clutching the tea towel in her hands. 'That you've got engaged to a fella you've hardly known five minutes?'

Lisa turned back to her. 'We've known each other long enough.'

'And is that a week or a fortnight?' Maggie held her daughter's gaze.

In the living room, a clock on the wall ticked its way towards 6.30. An uncomfortable silence had fallen broken only by the dog snuffling at the foot of the door. On hearing nothing on the other side, the animal slumped down and stared back at Bruce – the unexpected guest.

'Were you… on holiday?' asked Jeff, trying to make an effort.

Bruce looked back at him and Jeff clarified: 'When you met our Lisa?'

'Working,' said Bruce. 'At the same hotel.'

Jeff sipped his wine, then: 'Left your job too?'

Bruce shook his head. 'Contract came to an end. I'd been developing the management software.'

Jeff gave a nod but Bruce could see he was none the wiser. 'Computers,' he explained. 'That's what I do.'

'Fancy that,' said Jeff. 'You'll be a clever bugger then.'

Bruce looked back quickly but saw only Jeff's benign smile. He returned it, then noticed that the dog was still staring warily back at him.

Lisa's voice sounded sharply outside before she bustled into the room, addressing Maggie behind her.

'…It's a waste of time trying to explain,' she quickly positioned herself at Bruce's side before her mother followed her in.

'Try,' said Maggie.

On Lisa's silence, Bruce set down his glass and stepped forward.

'Look, Mrs Sheild, I—'

Jeff quickly put a hand on his sleeve: 'Call her Maggie, son.'

'No,' said Maggie firmly. Turning to eye Bruce, she heard herself announce: 'Mrs Sheild'll do just fine.'

A moment passed before Lisa quickly grabbed her coat.

'I've heard enough,' she said, turning to Bruce. 'Let's go.'

As Lisa moved to the door, Maggie heaved a heavy sigh. 'That's right. Turn it into a ruddy drama.'

Lisa turned to her. 'You're the one who always has to do that,' she said, holding her mother's look before nodding to Bruce. 'Are you coming or not?'

Bruce took a moment as he stared between Jeff and Maggie before deciding to join Lisa at the door. As they moved into the hallway together, Maggie quickly followed, calling out. 'You can't run away like this. We need to talk!'

Ignoring her, Lisa opened the front door and stepped outside. Bruce paused, waiting until she had reached the car before he finally looked back at Maggie and found his voice.

'I'm sorry,' he began gently. 'I can see this has come as a shock, but I promise we won't do anything without your blessing.' He waited for a response but Maggie ignored him, her attention fixed on Lisa as she got back into the Renault. Bruce looked to Jeff, who offered only a diplomatic shrug before he tipped his head towards the door. The dog began a low growl. Bruce got the message – and left.

After a few moments, the car's engine started up. Lisa stared resolutely ahead from the passenger seat as the Renault sped off the cobbled driveway. Jeff watched the car disappearing into the distance then stepped back into the house and closed the front door before addressing Maggie, gently, but with confidence.

'Don't worry, love,' he began. 'Our Lisa knows what she's doing. Like he said, it's all a bit of a shock… but that fella of hers seems nice enough—'

'Nice enough for what?' Maggie snapped, silencing him. She paused, suspicious now. 'Why hasn't she told us about him before?'

Jeff offered a helpless shrug. Maggie stared towards the door, trying to understand something. 'This is nothing,' she decided finally. 'A holiday romance, that's all. She'll come to her senses now she's home.'

She headed smartly upstairs, the dog scampering after her. After a moment, Jeff remembered the glass in his hand and stared down at it before knocking back his wine.

*

Ten minutes later, the sky-blue Renault parked up on a nearby street. Bruce pulled firmly on the hand brake and turned to Lisa beside him, registering her pretty features still taut with anger – but also disappointment. He spoke softly. 'It'll be all right.'

Lisa shook her head, her voice tense as she replied. 'You don't know my mum.'

'Not yet,' said Bruce. 'But I will.'

Lisa stared away and felt the anger draining from her, to be replaced now with uncertainty. 'I told you,' she said, 'we should have called from Tenerife… given them time to get used to the idea. They could have got to know you—'

'On FaceTime?' said Bruce.

Lisa looked torn. 'We did this all wrong,' she looked back at him and he laid a strong hand gently on hers, curling his fingers around her own. He said nothing, but offered a smile with which Lisa instantly connected. Leaning in, he kissed her, long and hard, and as they broke apart, he held her gaze and stroked her dark hair as he whispered. 'You do trust me, don't you?' His tone was as soothing as Maggie's had been abrasive.

Lisa smiled, grateful for it. ''Course I do.'

Still holding her look, he continued. 'It'll be fine. I promise. It's nothing we can't put right.'

'Are you… sure?'

'Certain.'

Lisa gave a long sigh, laden with remorse. 'Bruce, I'm so sorry—'

He put a finger to her lips, gently silencing her. 'It's not your fault.' He paused again then nodded towards the street. 'Go on. You go in and I'll bring the luggage.'

*

Lisa stepped from the car and pulled her coat tightly around her small frame to protect her from a biting wind. In contrast to the bustling tourist *calles* of Tenerife, the narrow cobbled streets were empty and, for the first time, the dark, weathered York stone walls of the local houses made the whole area appear bleak and uninviting, something to match the inhospitable reception from her mother, and far removed from the warm welcome given to all the guests at the Hotel Miramar – helped along by hot nights and Happy Hours.

Had she been right to leave it all behind? She hesitated, fraught with doubt, then looked back at the car – and Bruce. He gave a firm nod and an encouraging smile.

For all her bolshie Northern front, he knew, more than ever now, that there was part of her that remained raw, vulnerable – like a wound that had never properly healed.

He watched carefully as she headed towards the terraced house in which she sub-rented a tiny flat – a bolt-hole and symbol of independence – just a stone's throw from her parents. '*We're a close-knit family,*' she had once told him. '*Especially after what happened to our Natalie.*' Glancing back one more time, she then opened the front door and entered.

The tight smile that had remained frozen on Bruce's lips finally began to thaw. His hand snatched the key from the ignition and he gripped it firmly in his clenched fist, listening to Maggie's voice echoing in his head until he felt the key's jagged edge cutting into his palm.

The pain seemed to give some relief, allowing him to concentrate on something other than what he had been feeling about the woman who had shown him such disrespect – the woman who had ignored him, caring only about her daughter. Opening his hand he stared down at the key's edge imprinted on his palm, and as the impression began to fade, he could feel himself slowly regaining control. He took a deep breath, got out of the car and closed the door firmly behind him. Home at last.

CHAPTER THREE

The following day after the afternoon shift had ended, Maggie followed her workers out of the factory.

Masters & Son was based in part of the old canal warehouse that had once served local farms. More than a century ago, nearby Marston Mill had been the drop-off and pick-up point for a passenger packet boat, as well as the cargo ships that had ferried away worsted to be used as material for army uniforms.

Now the mill complex comprised mainly smart apartments overlooking the canal and towpath along which Maggie had walked to and from work for almost twenty-six years. She had never intended to stay long at the firm, especially after giving birth to Natalie a year after joining it, but by that time Jeff's health problems had already begun; the persistent debilitating cough that miners and their families feared as pneumoconiosis – 'black lung' – necrosis caused by exposure to coal dust. In fact, Jeff had been given a reprieve from this, only to receive instead an early diagnosis of obstructive pulmonary disease which had led to an early retirement shortly after his fortieth birthday.

Even without Jeff's health issues, the insecurity had always been there as he had joined the local colliery only a few years after the defeat of the Miners' Strike. What followed had been a sense of time running out, not only for the industry but for all those who worked within it, though Jeff's fellow miners had continued on until the pit's final closure had signalled the end of deep coal mining in England.

A week before Christmas 2015, 450 local men had been made redundant, with thousands marching the next day beneath banners proclaiming 'Coal not Dole' in order to commemorate Marston Colliery's last shift. Jeff and Maggie had been among them, with Natalie and Lisa, all marching in time to the town's silver band on the mile long stretch from the town hall to the pit where a pair of miner's boots had been left, two dates painted in white on the toes, marking the colliery's birth – and its death.

The event had been a fitting memorial to the local industry led by a grim reaper in a black cloak, with scythe in hand, while the marchers ended the day at Marston's Social Club – where many still chose to spend their time, reviving memories of a working life, as life itself moved on without them.

Maggie sighed to herself, unable to shrug off the hangover she felt she was suffering from a further conversation with Jason Masters – another reminder of time moving on – not just about the deadline for the new order but business in general. Jason had confided that he was off to Bradford on business, seeking loans to undertake improvements, ways of moving forward, of 'making progress'.

Maggie questioned why 'progress' was always seen in terms of 'improvements' when so often things seemed to be made worse with the passage of time? After becoming supervisor at the factory, she and Jeff had begun buying their terraced house with a mortgage funded by the council.

It had cost a sum that neither could imagine ever increasing further and yet a similar neighbouring property had recently sold for almost four times the amount. Marston's houses were no longer homes but 'assets' and development opportunities – unaffordable to young people from local families.

Maggie resented the rent that Lisa was paying on the sub-rented flat, particularly as her daughter had been home so little during the last few months, and then there was the outstanding student loan, another debt that Maggie begrudged, especially as she remembered a time when tuition fees had been financed by the state – long before education had become the industry it appeared to be today.

Maggie despised the fact that young people were not only expected but encouraged to enter adult life burdened with debt. Why were they not out on the street, protesting that standards of living should exceed those of past generations instead of slipping far behind them? Surely that was what 'progress' was meant to be?

While thinking about this, Maggie wondered if perhaps she really was the dinosaur she knew Jason Masters considered her to be – unable to accept the way things were moving or her new boss speculating with his father's factory – a business that had been built on sound foundations – not on Jason's idea of 'progress'. Of one thing Maggie was certain – her relief on hearing the factory bell sounding that afternoon to put an end to Jason's call.

*

The 'girls' were already walking far ahead of her, swarming together in groups as they set off for home.

Maggie observed them, noting how different they looked once they were out of their work coats, when their pinned-up hair came down and the lipstick and mascara went on as they re-assumed identities beyond the factory walls. They were a good mix, as the town itself had become, with almost a third of the workers, like Samira and Naila, coming from British Pakistani families, though the connection ended there.

The women themselves were totally distinct; Samira had always been a faithful ally while Naila was a natural rebel – a loose cannon among the work force. Maggie admired the girl's spirit but Naila's attention-seeking complaints often wasted valuable time and the recent fight with the new Kurdish worker raised fresh concerns.

Maggie buttoned her coat and walked on, distracted by other worries, this time much closer to home. Words began to echo from last night's exchanges with Jeff about their daughter's new relationship: '*It's a holiday romance… She'll soon come to her senses…*'

Throughout the day it had been easy to cling to that thought, to allow work to banish anxiety and to trust that Lisa would consider what her mother had said and pick up the phone so they could talk sensibly about the future. But now, with the dregs of the day, things seemed more uncertain. Maggie pulled a scarf from her bag and was about to slip it around her neck when a voice sounded close by.

'Thank you.'

It was Rona who stood behind her, peering out from the hood of a pink nylon anorak trimmed with fake fur.

With hands thrust deep into her pockets, she appeared to brace herself before stepping forward. 'What she said about me,' she began, 'you know it wasn't true,' she nodded her head in the direction of Naila who was walking ahead, chatting animatedly to her workmates as they neared the local bus stop.

Maggie chose her words carefully. 'She made a mistake.' Wrapping her scarf around her neck, Maggie hoped this explanation would suffice.

Rona shook her head slowly. 'No.' Her gaze was fixed on Naila in the distance as she explained. 'These people don't like me. They know I don't belong.'

A bus pulled up ahead and Maggie watched Naila mount it with her friends. 'Not so long ago, Naila's parents were saying the same, but now they're part of this community. And you'll be the same. People need time.'

'Time?'

'To get to know you.' Maggie held the young woman's look, willing her to believe this. 'Trust me,' she went on. 'Keep your head down, get on with your work and they'll accept you soon enough.'

'Like you do?' In that instant, peering out from her anorak hood, the young woman looked to Maggie like a child seeking reassurance.

'Aye,' said Maggie. 'Like I do.'

The ghost of a smile appeared on Rona's lips. Maggie went to return it – then froze as she focused on something else. A short distance away, a young woman was standing back, hesitant, as though wary of intruding.

'That's my daughter,' Maggie explained. 'She's just come back from abroad so…' She trailed off, feeling torn. 'I have to go,' she said finally, 'but we'll talk. Soon.' She placed a hand on Rona's shoulder, an apology, but also an act of solidarity, before she moved quickly off.

Left alone at the factory gates, Rona continued to look on, watching as Maggie headed towards Lisa, observing carefully as she witnessed an awkward pause between the two women before they finally embraced.

A moment later, Rona zipped up her anorak against the cold wind – and walked on.

Breaking apart from their embrace, Maggie smiled at her daughter and spoke softly, in a conciliatory tone. 'I'm glad you came.'

Walking together along the old canal tow path, Lisa said nothing but stared towards a group of ducks brawling in a feeding frenzy on the canal bank. A drake squawked loudly, fighting the other birds for a piece of bread before quickly guzzling it.

Amused, Maggie asked: 'Remind you of anyone?'

'Who else?' said Lisa. 'Dad never knows when enough's enough.'

Her smile acted like a fragile bridge between them before a brief silence fell again.

'Look,' said Maggie, 'about last night, maybe I was unfair but it was—'

'A shock,' said Lisa breaking in. 'I know that, and I know that you and Dad would prefer for us to wait but…'

'Lisa—'

'I can't,' she said bluntly. 'And I don't want to.' Her explanation followed quickly leaving no time for argument. 'Bruce is special. You'll see that yourselves if you'll only give him a chance. And I know how you feel about me giving up my job, but at the end of the day – that's all it was.'

Maggie stopped in her tracks. 'After all that study you put in?'

'A few years at college—'

'Education's not for wasting,' said Maggie sharply. She stared away to gather her thoughts. 'In my day you had two choices – if you had half a brain they'd put you in for shorthand and typing and if you couldn't manage that, it was Layette.'

Lisa looked confused. 'Layette?'

'Planning what to dress your baby in.'

Lisa scoffed. 'Times have changed.'

'Tell that to the girls on my factory floor,' said Maggie. 'I never wanted a daughter of mine sewing pyjamas for a living.'

'And I won't have to,' said Lisa boldly. 'Bruce earns good money.'

'Don't you want to earn your own?'

Lisa stared away in frustration. Why was it proving so difficult to explain? 'Of course,' she began again. 'And I'll find some work after we're wed. Maybe at a hotel closer to home, but it's going to be a busy few weeks before then.'

'Weeks?'

'Aye,' Lisa nodded. 'I called up this morning – and booked a date for the twenty-eighth.'

Maggie stopped in her tracks. 'You did what?'

'I just told you,' said Lisa. She spelt it out: 'I don't want to wait.'

Maggie closed her eyes for a second, unsure if she had heard correctly. 'And just how d'you expect a wedding to organise itself in that time?'

'I don't want a fuss. Just you and Dad and a few mates—'
'And Bruce's family?'

'He doesn't have any.' Lisa heaved a sigh. 'His parents are dead and most of his mates are still in the army. He was in the Guards but he's been out for a few years now, and he's done really well for himself. As long as you and Dad agree, he's happy to do things my way.'

'You mean,' said Maggie, 'get wed in a... register office?' Her tone made the notion seem execrable.

Lisa shrugged. 'It was good enough for you and Dad.'

'It had to be,' said Maggie, 'we couldn't afford anything else. But your dad and me have got a bit set by for—'

'Keep it,' said Lisa quickly. 'Or spend it. Life's too short,' she began to turn away.

Maggie instantly reproached her. 'Don't talk like that.'

'Why not?' asked Lisa, looking back. 'Why shouldn't I say it – after what happened to Nat—'

'Your sister was ill.'

'But none of us knew, did we? Least of all her,' she looked searchingly into her mother's eyes, seeking a connection. 'It's been six years but... every time I come home I still expect to see her, sitting in the kitchen, dog on her lap, nose in a book.'

'Lisa...'

'She's dead, Mum. She's *never* coming back.'

For a second, Maggie felt physically struck by a terrible truth but Lisa summoned her resolve and continued. '*I'm* alive. And I don't want to waste time, making plans when I know what it is I want – and *who* I want.'

Scanning her daughter's features Maggie saw she was staring at the confidence of youth – and the certainty of first love. But was it misplaced? It was the question she needed to ask but only a passage of time could answer it. Instead, she took a deep breath before reaching into her bag.

'I… meant to give you this last night,' she said gently, handing a gift bag to Lisa. Inside it, Lisa found the silver locket and chain. A moment passed before she gently prised open the heart to find two photos inside: Maggie and Jeff on one side and the delicate smiling features of another young girl on the other. Gently tracing the image with her finger, Lisa remained silent.

'I put those in last night,' Maggie said softly, 'after you left?' She paused, then: 'She might not be here, Lisa, but… we'll always be a family.' Her voice dropped to a whisper. 'You have to understand, love. All I've ever wanted is the best for you.'

Lisa closed the locket in her hand and nodded slowly. 'And I've got it.' Convinced of this, she smiled and stepped forward to kiss her mother's cheek. Laying her head on Maggie's shoulder, she felt the familiar warmth of her embrace – but failed to see the look of uncertainty on Maggie's face.

CHAPTER FOUR

Half an hour later, in his garden shed, Jeff gave a loud hiccup – followed by a wry smile.

'Want to know the secret to a happy marriage?' He glanced across at Bruce who was sitting in a deckchair that matched Jeff's own.

'Tell me,' said Bruce taking a swig of beer from the can in his hand.

'A shed with a strong lock.' Jeff raised his own beer as a salute to the space surrounding them. 'A man cave,' he announced.

'Is that right?' Bruce smiled, grateful for Jeff's easy manner, while noting that the dog, sitting close to Jeff's feet, was still staring back towards him as though he was an intruder.

'You bet,' said Jeff, opening his arms in an expansive gesture before he went on. 'A bloke's got to have his privacy or he'll go doolally.' He went to sip his beer then added, '*And* a hobby.' Gesturing to rows of trays containing seedlings labelled with tiny white flags, he went on. 'This is mine,' he said wistfully, 'and it might not look much but once upon a time I had my own allotment, you know. Nigh on a quarter of an acre. I built a rockery and diverted a bit of stream.' He took a deep breath, closed his eyes and allowed a rush of images to flood his mind: two little girls sowing seeds with plastic shovels; watering flowers on a hot summer's day; paper boats set upon water, carried away downstream… Then a cold draft whistled its way into the shed and ushered him back to the present.

'Heart attack put paid to all that,' he said with finality.

'I'm sorry,' said Bruce, his smile fading.

Jeff shrugged and took a hefty slug of beer as consolation. 'Could have been worse. I'm still here – and I've still got my man cave – *and* a hobby.'

Bruce paused before responding. 'Maybe I've got one too.'

Jeff looked at him. 'Oh aye? And what's that?' Jeff waited for a response but Bruce failed to answer, hearing footsteps approaching on the path outside. Bella began a low growl until Maggie's voice finally sounded.

'Jeff? Are you in there?'

Glancing quickly at Bruce, Jeff pressed a finger to his lips before grabbing the beer cans and hiding them behind his deckchair.

The shed door suddenly rattled: 'Jeff!'

Maggie's face suddenly appeared at a dusty window while Jeff called back innocently. 'That you, love?'

'No, it's the Ghost of Christmas Past, who the ruddy hell d'you think it is?'

Bracing himself, Jeff opened the door to find his wife eyeing him suspiciously. 'What're you doing in there?' The dog scampered out to join her.

'Door must've come off the latch.' Jeff lied, offering an innocent shrug, but Maggie's gaze was now fixed on the figure standing beyond him.

Bruce stepped forward. 'Nice to see you again, Mrs Sheild.' He gave a warm smile.

Maggie glanced back at her husband and saw Jeff's unease, then she remembered Lisa's words: *Bruce is special… you'll see that for yourself if you'll only give him a chance…*'

'Call me Maggie,' she said finally.

On her words, a look of relief passed between the two men.

'Right, let's go in for a cuppa,' said Jeff, slapping Bruce on the back.

The younger man's smile was still in place but his eyes remained trained on Maggie. 'I'd love to,' he began, 'but I really only popped by. Another time?'

Jeff decided not to press him further. 'Any time.' he said. 'Come on, I'll see you out.'

With a hand still on Bruce's shoulder, Jeff steered him down the garden path while Maggie observed the two men from a distance as they said goodbye at the garden gate, shaking hands like two old friends.

Bruce raised his palm in a friendly wave to Maggie before disappearing, leaving Jeff to lock the gate after him. As he walked back to Maggie, Jeff offered another smile.

'Nice fella.'

'So you said last night,' Maggie reminded him. 'Why d'he 'pop by'?' She moved into the kitchen.

'Why d'you think?' said Jeff. 'He wants us all to get along.' He gave her a sidelong look. 'Seems reasonable enough,' he added, before taking his phone from his pocket and explaining.

'Gave me his phone number too. He's responsible. Used to be in the Army.'

Sitting down at the kitchen table, Jeff set his mobile on the table and plucked a newspaper from Maggie's shopping bag. 'Welsh Guards. No rubbish.' He gave a frown and paused for a moment before looking up again. 'Now I come to think of it, there's someone down the club who's got a "relly" in the Guards... or is it the Fusiliers?' Unsure, he looked back at Maggie.

'Am I meant to be impressed?' Maggie asked, as she began unpacking her shopping. Jeff offered an admonishing look and in response to it, Maggie heaved a sigh. 'All right,' she said. 'He's got balls, I'll give you that. Because if you hadn't been home, he'd have run into me and—'

'No,' said Jeff, casually turning a page of his newspaper. 'He knew you were out with our Lisa.'

'Oh?' said Maggie, brought up short.

'He mentioned she was meeting you from work.'

Maggie considered this, a packet of cornflakes still in her hand. 'I see,' she commented. 'A two pronged attack.'

'Well, would you rather neither of them made an effort?' Jeff gave her a reproving look, then added: 'They don't need our consent, you know? But like I say, he's a nice enough fella.'

'So you say. But nice enough for what?'

'For our Lisa. At least she seems to think so.' As he eyed her, Maggie turned from him and began stacking eggs in the fridge.

'And what does she know about fellas?'

'She knows what she wants,' said Jeff. 'Same as you did at her age.' Jeff gave her a knowing glance.

Maggie threw one straight back. 'And that doesn't include

a proper wedding.' Jeff frowned at this. Emboldened, Maggie went on. 'He didn't tell you that, did he? A rush job at a register office, that's all she's going to get.'

Jeff set down his newspaper as he considered this. "Think she could be expecting?'

Maggie sniffed dismissively. 'That's no reason to get wed these days.'

'Well,' said Jeff. 'What does it matter where they're wed? You've seen them together – they're in love. Just like you and me were all them years ago.'

Maggie slowly looked back at him. 'You mean, you're not any more?'

At this, Jeff slowly folded his newspaper, set it to one side and got to his feet. Holding out his arms he nodded for Maggie to come to him. 'Come here.'

As she did so, Jeff leaned in to kiss her but before their lips met, Maggie drew back and eyed him. 'You smell of beer.'

Less than half an hour later, Bruce was sipping from a can of beer, his arm around Lisa as they sat on the sofa together. He turned the can in his hand as he considered something.

'Doesn't miss much, does she?'

Lisa gave a smile. 'She nags him – but Dad loves it. It keeps him going.' She nestled closer and asked: 'Think we'll be like that one day?'

Bruce winked at her. 'No chance.' He paused then went on. 'But... on the way home I got to thinking. I *could* give him a hand.'

'Dad?'

Bruce nodded.

'With what? Advice on how to handle Mum?' Lisa smiled but Bruce sipped his beer.

'He could do with a rockery in that garden. I could build it for him?'

Lisa gazed at him. 'That'd earn you some Brownie points.'

'Think I need them?'

'Not with me.'

She stretched up to kiss him but her phone suddenly signaled an incoming text. Picking it up from the coffee table, she checked the message and set the phone back down, before noting Bruce was still staring down at it.

'Just a friend,' she said casually. Bruce's silence prompted her to explain. 'Now that Mum and Dad know, I left a message telling her all about us. But it looks like she may need convincing,' she picked up her phone again and this time showed the text to Bruce.

Pull the other one! Dee ☺

Lisa smiled. 'I'll ring her tomorrow,' she went to set the phone down but Bruce held her hand.

'Why not do it now?' He got to his feet. 'I was just going to make us something to eat—'

'But you cooked last night.'

'So?' He moved on towards the kitchen then looked back from the door. 'Go on. Call her.' He offered a quick smile before disappearing into the kitchen. Lisa considered the phone in her hand – and dialed.

In the kitchen, Bruce opened the fridge, taking out a carton of eggs and a bag of prepared salad as he listened for Lisa's voice in the other room. Her call connected.

'Dee?' A pause. 'Yeah, it's me. No, I *swear* I'm not kidding!'

Silence followed. Bruce craned his neck to hear as Lisa continued on the phone.

'And no. He is *not* desperate. 'Matter of fact, he's drop dead gorgeous.'

Bruce cracked eggs into a bowl before taking a frying pan to the hob. Lisa's voice sounded again from the other room.

'Course you'll meet him. At the wedding.' A pause then: 'Yeah I know.'

Another pause as Bruce waited for Lisa's response, then: 'I've missed you too.'

Staring down at the bowl in front of him, Bruce grabbed a fork and punctured the egg yolks before pouring oil into the pan. Hearing Lisa giggle in the front room he turned down the heat and called out. 'Cheese and ham?'

'Sorry?'

Bruce peered around the door. 'Your omelette.'

Lisa smiled sweetly. 'Both, please.'

He returned her smile and watched her for a moment until she gave her attention again to the mobile. 'Yeah, he cooks too.' Her eyes moved playfully back to Bruce before she held out the phone. 'Dee wants to say hi.'

Bruce hesitated for a moment, then took the mobile from her. On the other end of the line a young woman's voice sounded in a confident tone: '*You're making a big mistake, mister.*'

Lisa looked on as Bruce replied: 'Is that right?'

'*She's a slut around the house and she can't cook to save her life.*'

'Tell me about it.' Bruce smiled then looked back at Lisa who mouthed in suspicion.

'What?'

Dee continued on the line. *'You must be pretty special though – because our Lisa's nothing if not choosy.'*

Bruce held Lisa's look. 'Pleased to hear it.' As he smiled again, Lisa reached out and grabbed the phone from him.

'Back off,' Lisa warned Dee quickly. 'I found him first!' She winked at Bruce who returned to the kitchen to see the frying pan spitting oil. Pouring the eggs into it he continued to listen at the door as he loaded a tray with cutlery and two plates.

Lisa continued to Dee. 'I'm not sure. We've only just got back, and I...'

Silence.

Lisa called down the line: 'Dee? Are you still there?'

Bruce entered the room with the tray. Setting plates on the table, he saw Lisa switch off her phone. 'What's up?' he asked casually.

'Nothing.' Lisa shrugged. 'She was on a train. Signal's lost, I guess.'

'And... what were you not sure about?'

Lisa paused before explaining: 'They want to take me for a drink next Friday.'

Bruce handed her some cutlery. '"They"?'

'Dee and the girls. My old school mates. The Witches of Ilkley,' she gave a smile that faded as she added: 'And it won't be just one drink either.'

'Well,' said Bruce, sensing she was vaguely troubled, 'if you don't fancy it, you could always tell them you're busy. The wedding?'

Lisa looked torn. 'Yeah but... well, they've got a big trip coming up soon – they're off to the States. They'll be gone for weeks so… this could be our last girls' night out – for a while anyway,' she stared down at her meal.

Bruce took time to consider this. 'So, what's the problem?' he asked softly. 'Every girl deserves a hen night. And like you say,' he went on, with an easy smile. 'It's a last chance for a girls' night out?'

'Yeah,' Lisa nodded. 'As a single woman,' she mused on this while Bruce sat down beside her and picked up his own cutlery before broaching something. 'I've been thinking,' he began. 'Your folks. How about we take them out tomorrow night?'

'Where to?'

'Somewhere local. A nice meal. A good red wine for your dad?'

Lisa met his gaze and returned his smile. Leaning closer, she kissed him, keeping her face close to his as she asked: 'What did I do to deserve you?'

Bruce watched as she tucked into her meal, then his eyes shifted to the phone lying on the table between them – his thoughts on a girl called Dee – and the Witches of Ilkley.

CHAPTER FIVE

Maggie considered her reflection in her bedroom mirror.

The red suit she wore was far tighter than she remembered but she had failed to notice that until now because she'd had scant opportunity to wear anything smart since the works outing to Skegness last summer. She reminded herself that it was high time she organised something for the girls, perhaps in the spring, around May Day, though she knew her workers wouldn't be too interested in the folklore surrounding the date or, for that matter, its association with labour rights.

Nevertheless, an outing was always good for morale and she recognised that morale needed boosting right now, especially with the friction between Naila and the new worker, Rona. It was worrying that one of her girls should have taken against a refugee in this way. Could it really be that Naila was unwilling to accept a young woman granted asylum from conflict in her own country – or had she actually convinced herself that Rona had stolen her precious cigarettes? Of one thing Maggie was sure; the incident had to be forgotten because allowing the girls to dwell on disharmonies only ever resulted in exacerbating them.

Reflecting on this, Maggie was suddenly struck by parallels with her own feelings towards Bruce. Was she justified in blaming him for tensions that existed between herself and her daughter – or had she simply transferred her own frustrations with Lisa to the new man in her life – her fiancé?

While she couldn't be sure, it seemed even more important to make an effort this evening – to do the right thing and give Bruce Carter a fair chance – as she hoped her girls would one day give Rona. Patting down the front of her jacket, she realised she must have gained at least a stone since turning fifty. Unless she soon took herself in hand, most of her smart outfits would be destined for the local charity shop.

Closing the wardrobe door on them, she reached into a jewellery box and took out a delicate gold chain – an old Christmas gift from Jeff. Slipping it around her neck she suddenly thought of the present she had given to Lisa. Her daughter might not choose to wear the locket but the important thing was that she had witnessed the look on Lisa's face as she had opened the silver heart to find the photos inside; a reminder of an unbroken connection to family. Not that Lisa had needed such a reminder because Maggie was sure Lisa had always understood what she had impressed upon her factory workers and her daughters alike, that they were stronger together than apart so must always be there for each other. *We're family or we're nothing.*

*

With that thought in her mind, Maggie found herself struggling with the clasp of her gold necklace – until she felt Jeff's hand on hers. In the reflection of her dressing table mirror she caught sight of him standing behind her, leaning forward to secure the chain before laying his hands firmly on her shoulders as he stared back at her.

'You look a million dollars.'

Maggie smiled. 'Not that you or I will ever know what a million dollars look like.'

Jeff planted a gentle kiss on her neck, on the soft spot that he knew always caused her to tremble. In spite of his wife's tough exterior – the carapace she had assumed long ago – he knew Maggie was vulnerable, more so than anyone else because she chose to suffer alone. It was the way she had been brought up, trained from an early age never to show weakness but to endure; a lesson passed down from her own mother, a woman who had known she would never live long enough to protect her daughter.

Maggie got to her feet and surveyed Jeff's choice of clothing as he asked: 'Will I do?' He was wearing his best suit, smiling benignly, aiming to please, and as she considered him, Maggie realised that since his heart attack Jeff had become more like her child than her husband – or was it that he was simply trying to fill the void created by Natalie's death?

'Aye,' she said. 'You'll do,' she began brushing down his jacket with the palm of her hand. 'But I don't know why we're making such a fuss about The George on a Thursday night,' she turned and grabbed her bag.

'Because we're not going to The George.'

Maggie looked back at him.

'Didn't Lisa tell you? We're meeting them at that swanky place in Ashton.'

'The Grange?'

Jeff nodded.

'You're kidding.'

'Cross my heart.'

Maggie took a moment to absorb this then slipped the strap of her bag across her shoulder. 'Then I hope someone else is paying.'

'Don't worry,' said Jeff, opening the door for her. 'They are.'

The Grange Hotel was set in twelve acres of picturesque grounds. Built two centuries ago as a country mansion, it enjoyed a long-established history in the neighbouring town of Ashton but its recent refurbishment had provided new additions; an indoor swimming pool and gym, a champagne bar and an award-winning restaurant in what had once been a Victorian orangerie.

Seated at a table beside the window, Maggie stared out at fairy lights strung like stars among the trees.

Lisa tried to gain her attention. 'So what d'you think?'

'It's grand all right.'

Lisa smiled. 'We'll have to come back some time for a package.'

'Package?' Maggie looked back to see her daughter using a glass stick to stir an Espresso Martini.

'A spa day,' Lisa explained. 'They've got a steam room and saunas as well as a pool. We could have afternoon tea afterwards.'

'And undo all the good work?' said Jeff. He winked at Bruce who was sitting close to Lisa.

'More calamari, Maggie?' Bruce offered the dish to her but Maggie hesitated.

'Go on, Mum,' Lisa urged. 'It's your favourite.'

After a moment, Maggie accepted, serving herself as Jeff commented. 'Nice idea, this tapas for starters.' He helped himself to *patatas bravas*.

Bruce topped up Maggie's glass with wine. 'Good to see a traditional venue like this moving with the times.' His eyes met Maggie's, prompting a reply, just as Jeff's hand wavered and dropped a dollop of tomato *frito* on to his shirt cuff.

'You're meant to be eating it not wearing it,' Maggie scolded, pouring water from her glass on to a napkin before dabbing at the stain. 'It's your best shirt as well and we haven't even got through starters.'

'Have you checked out the mains?' asked Bruce as a distraction, handing the menu to Jeff who glanced at it then looked up again sheepishly.

'Have I got the right glasses on?' Jeff passed the menu to Maggie. Her face set at the prices.

'Maybe we'll just stick to tapas.'

'Don't be daft,' said Lisa. 'It's our treat.'

'*My* treat,' said Bruce. 'You have whatever you like.'

Maggie peered across her glasses at Bruce. His dark hair was slicked with a shiny gel and his sleek grey sharkskin suit contrasted with his suntan. He was wearing a strong citrus aftershave but now she noticed silver cufflinks and what appeared to be an expensive designer watch on his wrist.

'You know, you really should be saving your cash if you're planning on getting wed.'

'We *are* getting wed.' Lisa insisted.

A waitress suddenly appeared and began clearing away plates. Bruce used the moment to pass the wine list to Jeff.

'There's a nice Beaujolais there. Should go well with the ribeye?'

'Jeff's keeping off red meat,' warned Maggie.

'Gone vegan, Dad?' asked Lisa, amused.

Jeff eyed her. 'It's your mother and her health fads.'

'*Not* fads,' said Maggie, with a look intended to keep him onside.

'Well,' Jeff continued, 'I'm not sure staying off meat and booze will make me live any longer.'

'Might make it seem that way though, eh?' Bruce smiled and topped up Jeff's glass. 'I'm going to have the lobster. How about you, Lise?'

Maggie saw Lisa was musing, menu in hand. 'I fancy the linguine,' she set down her menu then noted Bruce was looking at her. 'Or,' she began again, 'maybe the chicken salad.'

Jeff spluttered. 'You don't come to a place like this for salad!'

'Are you dieting, love?' asked Maggie.

'I had a big lunch.' Lisa offered a smile as the waitress took their orders.

Bruce asked: 'And how about you, Maggie?'

Maggie remained silent, still staring at the prices on the menu, having calculated that the bill would probably amount to a week's take home pay for one of her girls.

'Mum?'

Maggie finally looked up and viewed Lisa's expression: expectant, encouraging, hopeful. The waitress lingered, notepad in hand. Bruce's smile was still in place but there was something about it that unnerved her in that moment.

'All right,' she said quickly, handing the menu to the waitress. 'I'll have the ribeye. *And* so will Jeff,' she added. She picked up her wine glass, took a sip and produced a smile for Lisa.

A few moments after the waitress moved off, Jeff loosened his shirt collar and set his glass down on the table. Maggie caught the wink he gave Bruce and recognised that a good Beaujolais would only reinforce Jeff's acceptance of the man who was sitting across the table from them – his hand clasped over Lisa's – protective, or was it perhaps proprietorial? The smile was still there but Maggie now realised what it was that had unnerved her; something in the man's dark eyes failed to follow suit. His mind seemed elsewhere.

Tapping her glass idly with her finger she decided to broach something with him. 'Your folks,' she began. 'Lisa mentioned your parents are—'

'Both dead,' said Bruce. 'Mum passed when I was twelve. Dad when I was twenty. I was away in action.' His sipped his wine. 'Afghanistan.'

Jeff's face clouded. 'Sorry to hear that,' he said quickly. 'Losing family's bad enough but when you're overseas, fighting for your country…'

'No brothers or sisters?' Maggie fixed her gaze on Bruce.

He shrugged, then: 'Only child.'

'An orphan,' said Lisa, smiling sympathetically.

Bruce gave a small shrug. 'It could have been worse, but the Army teaches you to be resourceful… find a way through.'

'The Guards, right?' said Jeff.

'Welsh Guards,' said Lisa proudly.

Bruce took another sip of wine. 'I grew up in a little place called Aberaeron, but we moved to Swansea after mum died. That's where I grew up—' Breaking off, he set down his glass. 'Look,' he paused before beginning again. 'I'm sure you don't need my life story so why don't we get to the point? We all know there's a ruddy great elephant in the room. The wedding? And I know me and Lisa could wait—'

'No we can't,' she insisted.

'Well, what's the hurry?' asked Maggie gently. 'If you give it a bit of time you could get yourselves properly settled,' she eyed Bruce. 'Lisa needs to find a new job.'

'No,' said Bruce. 'With all due respect, she doesn't 'need' to.'

Jeff frowned. 'You mean… you could manage on—'

'What I earn?' said Bruce. 'Easily.'

'But you're freelance.' Jeff argued. 'Computer work can't be that reliable?'

Lisa leaned forward. 'Bruce has lots of clients and plenty of work.'

'Doing what exactly?' asked Maggie.

Bruce sat back in his seat. 'Cyber security.'

Jeff looked confused. 'Cyber…?'

Lisa glanced at Bruce as she explained: 'Dad doesn't even do online banking.'

'Because he doesn't need to,' said Maggie proudly. 'I take care of our finances.'

'And she always has,' said Jeff, sipping his wine.

Bruce took a moment to process this then offered a smile for Maggie. 'And I'm sure you do that very well,' he began, 'but my client base consists of the kind of businesses that can't afford to have their production systems locked, or backups destroyed. A ransomware attack, for example, can potentially cripple a company's entire infrastructure.'

'You're... losing me,' said Jeff.

'Ransomware,' Lisa repeated carefully. 'It's used to block a computer system until a ransom is paid.'

Jeff frowned. 'You mean... a virus of some sort?'

'Malware,' Bruce explained. 'Malicious software. It's used against individuals as well as companies. Basically, a company's data becomes encrypted so it can't be used. A demand is then sent to the user, usually to be paid in a cryptocurrency like Bitcoin, in return for the necessary decryption that's needed to restore the locked files.'

Jeff took a moment to absorb this. 'And... there's a lot of this going on, is there?'

Bruce picked up his wine glass. 'In America, hundreds of millions of dollars a year are paid out in ransoms.'

Jeff whistled. 'And you know how to stop it?'

Bruce gave a smile. 'I've come up with a few solutions for clients but usually I just advise on how to keep systems protected so things never have to reach that stage.'

'Cyber security.' Jeff repeated as the penny dropped. He turned to Maggie. 'Did you know about this?'

Maggie gave a small shrug. 'I use a computer at work, don't I?' She glanced back at Bruce and found herself compensating for Jeff's ignorance. 'I know all about *pfishing*,' she said defensively, 'that's when you're tricked into giving out information like your credit card details,' she met Bruce's gaze. 'And I also have to be careful of insider threats.'

'Insider...?' said Jeff.

Bruce explained. 'It's a term for when someone abuses their access permission.'

Maggie sipped her drink. 'Then there's man-in-the-middle attacks.'

Lisa leaned forward and explained to Jeff. 'That's when someone eavesdrops to send messages between two parties, say, if you've got an insecure Wi-Fi network?'

Jeff picked up his glass. 'How come *I* don't know anything about this?'

'Because you don't need to,' said Maggie bluntly, 'you've got me,' she smiled at Jeff, lightening the atmosphere before the waitress returned to set their main courses before them.

Jeff eyed his steak. 'That looks champion.'

Lisa's look prompted a response from Maggie. 'Very nice,' she agreed.

Bruce topped up wine glasses and spoke again. 'Look I… know we didn't get off to the best of starts,' he began, 'but hopefully we can put that right – from now on. One thing I can promise you is…' He looked at Lisa. 'I do love your daughter.'

'And the feeling's mutual,' said Lisa before turning to her parents. 'We know what it is we want.'

Maggie paused. 'A quick register office do?'

Lisa sighed. 'How long did you and Dad wait before you were wed?'

'That's not the point.'

'Oh? One rule for you and another for—'

Bruce broke in. 'Lise. Your mum and dad just want the best for you. I understand that. And I respect it.' He looked again at Maggie, silencing her by taking the very words from her mouth. Of course it was only to be expected that she and Jeff would want the best for their daughter – an only daughter on whom all expectations now fell – but the question remained; was Bruce the best partner for Lisa? A moment passed before Jeff made his own decision. 'Well, we can't ask for more than that,' he said, raising his glass. 'I'd say it's time for a toast.' He paused before announcing: 'Here's to you two.'

Bruce and Lisa raised their own glasses, then waited for Maggie to follow. Jeff eyed her. No-one spoke. Maggie took her time, as though making peace with herself before she finally offered a smile for her daughter.

'You'll be needing a wedding dress,' she began. 'How about I give you a hand tomorrow?'

Lisa exchanged a look with Bruce before returning her mother's smile.

'I'd love that.'

'Good,' said Maggie, finally raising her own glass. 'Then it's a date.'

A few hours later, Marston's parish church bell was sounding midnight as Jeff climbed into bed. He lay gazing up at the ceiling for a moment, before glancing at his wife beside him. Maggie was wearing her reading glasses as she studied some paperwork.

'How d'you know all that stuff about... ransomware?'

Maggie licked her index finger and turned a page. 'I told you, we've got computers at work.'

'Aye,' said Jeff, 'and we've got a laptop downstairs but all I know is how to switch it on and off.'

She turned to him. 'I have to deal with orders, shipping, *these* things...' She waved the spreadsheets in her hand.

'All right... all right.' Jeff paused, then: 'Rather you than me.' He eyed her. 'I might not know much about business – but I know you.' As Maggie turned to him. Jeff went on. 'And I know that were all for his benefit tonight – not mine. I'm right, aren't I?' Jeff went on. 'You wanted to let him know you're no fool?'

Maggie gave a small shrug. 'Maybe.'

Jeff smiled as she returned to her paperwork.

'You did well tonight, love. I'm right proud of you.'

'For?'

'You know what for.' He turned to meet her gaze and leaned over to kiss her. Straight after – he gave a hiccup.

Maggie smiled. 'You'd best have one of your indigestion tablets.'

Jeff gave a nod and then reached into a drawer in his bedside cabinet to retrieve a pack of pills. Pushing one from a blister pack he took a sip of water and downed the tablet before settling back, head on his pillow, watching his wife for a few moments more until his eyelids grew heavy and finally closed. The sound of Jeff's gentle snoring filled the silence that followed. Maggie set down her spreadsheets and sighed to herself. 'Aye,' she whispered. 'I did well.' Then she turned out the light.

At exactly the same time, Bruce lay on Lisa's bed, a bath towel around his waist, his hair still damp from the shower as he idly watched TV.

Lisa's voice sounded from the bathroom. 'It was a good idea.'

'What was?'

'Tonight,' she replied just before entering. 'Taking Mum and Dad out to dinner?'

Bruce turned to see she was wearing a red silk pyjama camisole top and matching cami-knickers. She gave a smile but he failed to respond.

'What's wrong?'

He shrugged. 'Nothing.' He looked back at the TV. Unsettled, Lisa moved closer.

'Bruce?'

Sitting down beside him on the bed, she leaned in and gently kissed his temple. He turned to her then reached out to pull her towards him, kissing her hard on the lips. As they broke apart, he gave an amused smile and patted her waist.

'What?' asked Lisa.

'Nothing.'

'Then what're you smiling at?'

He gave a shrug. 'You.'

'Me?'

'Still a bit cuddly?'

"Cuddly'?' Lisa echoed. 'I'll have you know I lost three pounds last week.'

'Must be what you're wearing.'

Lisa glanced down at the silk camisole. 'What's wrong with what I'm—'

'Try this,' said Bruce quickly. Reaching beneath his pillow, he produced a package wrapped in pink crepe paper. Taken aback, Lisa eyed him then quickly tore the paper to find white satin lingerie inside. She looked back at him. 'For… me?'

He smiled. 'Who else?' Nodding towards the bathroom he winked at her. 'Go on, surprise me.'

Staring down again at the delicate white silk items, Lisa returned Bruce's smile before she hurried into the bathroom. After a moment, her voice travelled back into the room. 'This… must have cost a fortune.'

'It did. But guess what? You're worth it.'

Getting up from the bed, he moved to his jacket, hanging on the back of a chair, and took a small black object from a pocket. Quickly positioning it between some books on a shelf on the opposite wall, he checked it then returned to the bed before calling out: 'Well?'

After a moment, Lisa entered slowly, wearing a white satin baby doll nightie and glossy white hold up stockings. She spoke softly. 'How do I look now?'

As she stood in front of him, Bruce's dark eyes slowly scanned her body – then locked with hers. Reassured, Lisa smiled and allowed herself to be swept up into his arms, before he laid her gently down upon the bed.

Still smiling at him, she noted his breaths becoming deeper as his hands traced the floral appliqué lace covering her breasts. Leaning forward, his mouth slowly closed on hers in a deep kiss after which he whispered: 'You know what comes next?'

Lisa nodded slowly. A moment passed before Bruce's hand came forward – a long snake of black silk fabric in his palm. He draped it across her closed eyes and Lisa pushed her head towards him, her lips parting in expectation as she allowed him to secure this in a tight knot behind her head, then she lay down once more, waiting until he began to trail the fabric across her face, its tip gently brushing against her lips.

He watched carefully as her mouth opened wider, her tongue trying to capture the scarf as he raised and lowered it, toying with her like a kitten. She craned her neck towards him but he failed to kiss her and instead continued to observe her, his palm hovering above her body as he noted her pink nipples growing tight beneath the lace.

'Bruce…?'

'What is it?'

'Please?'

She gave a small frown, her body beginning to arch beneath him. Carefully, he slipped his hand deep between her thighs and fingered the soft mound of warm flesh bulging slightly above her tight white stockings. She moaned gently beneath his touch and he parted the panels of sheer white satin and took in the sight of her suntanned body beneath him. She had been telling the truth – she had lost more weight – and all because of him. She spread her legs wider but his strong hands now reached for her slim throat and tilted her jaw up towards him as she gave a small cry.

'Bruce?'

After a long pause, he glanced back towards the dresser and checked for a tiny red speck. Reassured to see it, he turned back to her. 'Whose little girl are you?' he asked softly. He watched her frown transform into a smile before he gripped her jaw and turned it towards his own, kissing her hard, pushing her legs wide beneath him before he penetrated her.

'*Whose* little girl?' he asked breathlessly, savouring her small screams as he thrust deep inside her. This time she exhaled loudly, happy to finally give him the answer he needed to hear.

'Yours.'

CHAPTER SIX

'What do you think? Can we do it, Mags?'

Samira waited for an answer while her boss studied the new schedule in her hands. Maggie finally took off her glasses and pinched the bridge of her nose before tossing the paperwork on to her desk. 'With overtime,' she decided. 'But I'll be hard pushed to get any bonus payments out of Jason.'

At this, Samira glanced down through the office window to the machinists on the factory floor. 'There's some that won't be too bothered about that.'

Maggie followed Samira's gaze to see Rona working below, deftly pushing fabric beneath the needle of her machine, turning it in a neat circle before she hesitated as though suddenly aware that she was being watched. Looking up from her work she caught sight of Maggie at the office window and offered a reserved smile before she quickly returned to her machining. Maggie's eyes remained trained on the young woman as she commented. 'She's a bloody good worker.'

'Aye,' said Samira. 'And is that why the others don't like her?'

Maggie turned to meet her gaze but Samira broke the moment with an unexpected smile and said, 'Ruddy asylum seekers, coming over here with their work ethic?' She gave a wink.

Maggie returned her smile. 'She's a refugee not an asylum seeker, so she's legally entitled to work here. It's only Naila who's taken against her and you'd think she'd be a bit more accepting of strangers.' Maggie turned to pin her schedule to the wall.

'And why's that?' asked Samira knowingly. 'Because Naila doesn't belong here either?'

Maggie looked back sharply at her. 'You know that's not what I meant. Naila's family didn't exactly have it easy when they first arrived, did they?'

Samira shrugged. 'True. But Naila's third generation. She's never been further than Bradford – let alone Pakistan. This is *her* world and Rona's barged into it. Besides,' she added, 'maybe Rona *did* steal her fags. Have you considered that?'

'No,' said Maggie firmly. 'Naila made a mistake.'

'Sure?'

Maggie sighed. 'When have I ever been wrong about someone?' She gave a smile. 'Trust me. Once we get this order finished, we'll all be one big happy family again.'

'Oh aye?' said Samira, unconvinced.

'Aye,' said Maggie, confirmed. 'I'm going to organise a 'do' for us. It's been far too long since the last one.'

Samira gave a cynical look. 'And Jason's going to pay for that, is he?'

'He'll pay some,' said Maggie, 'and I'll pay the rest. I've got a bit put by.'

'Which you'll need for your Lisa's wedding.'

'No,' said Maggie, looking away as she tidied her work space. 'Lisa doesn't want a fuss, register office.'

Samira came closer. 'You're kidding.'

As Maggie shook her head, Samira read her disappointment, but before she could comment the factory bell sounded for lunch. Grateful for the distraction, Maggie sprang to her feet and quickly shrugged off her work coat. 'I've got to get off.'

Samira gave a mischievous smile. 'Don't tell me – Jason's buying you lunch?'

Maggie grabbed her jacket and scarf. 'Meeting our Lisa. We're going shopping – for a wedding outfit. She'll be needing one – if only for a register office.'

'Tell her congratulations from me?'

'I will,' said Maggie, moving to the door.

Samira's voice sounded again before she opened it. 'You haven't said what he's like.'

Maggie turned back to face her.

'Your future son-in-law?' said Samira.

'Well, he's...' Maggie suddenly found herself lost for words.

'Tall, dark and handsome?'

Maggie gave a nod. 'Aye,' she admitted, 'I s'pose he is.'

'Then your Lisa's got good taste. Like her mum,' Samira gave another wink and Maggie left, pausing for a moment on the other side of the door as she considered this – before heading off.

Lisa stood outside Marston's department store, Jessop's, listening to the final chimes of the stylish clock that had been added to the building to celebrate the Millennium, and the store having remained in business for a century.

Jessop's was part of the local landscape; the emporium to which Maggie had brought her daughters twice a year to buy summer and winter wardrobes, school uniforms – and to pay an annual visit to Father Christmas when Lisa and Nat had still believed in him. These days the store sold contemporary furniture, carpets and clothes while still providing funeral teas and Rotary Club lunches. It was now the place to which Lisa was coming to choose her wedding outfit.

Glancing up and down the crowded pavements, Lisa spoke quickly into the phone in her hand, explaining to Bruce: 'No, she's not here yet. She only gets off at twelve.'

On the other end of the line, Bruce glanced down at a leaflet in his hands which showed the name of a local estate agent, Wentworths, and a colour photograph of a detached house with the words 'To Let' above it.

He paused for a moment then spoke firmly. 'Well, I think we should go and see it.'

Lisa sighed at his impatience. 'Can we talk about this when I get back?'

'It could be too late then,' Bruce argued, his eyes scanning the leaflet in his hand once more. 'This is just what we're looking for.'

Lisa glanced down the road, wishing Maggie would arrive soon so she could end this call and get on with her shopping. 'But... you just said this place is out of town?'

'Not that far out. It's got space... views. Everything we want.'

Lisa chewed a fingernail before making a decision. 'All right. Then why don't you make an appointment for later?' She quickly checked her watch. 'I should be back in time.'

'And if you're not?' Bruce calmly spelled things out for her:

'Look, I'm at the estate agent's right now. *I* could go and view it.' He turned around and offered a smile for the estate agent seated at her desk behind him; a pretty blonde in her early thirties, waiting patiently for a conclusion to this conversation while trying to look busy on her computer screen. She returned his smile, ever hopeful.

'Without me?' asked Lisa on the end of the line.

Bruce recognised that Lisa was putting up a good resistance but she was also sounding increasingly stressed. He took a deep breath and went on. 'Lise, I know what we want. We've discussed it enough. Or...' he paused, 'don't you trust me?' He waited for her reply but at that moment Lisa saw Maggie approaching from a distance, waving as she made her way through a sea of shoppers.

'Of course I do,' said Lisa quickly, feeling increasingly pressured.

'Then what's the problem?'

'All right,' Lisa said finally. 'Go and view it but don't do anything until I've seen it?'

'Of course I won't.'

'Promise?'

'I promise.'

Bruce ended the call and glanced back at the estate agent. She gave a nod of her head, knowing she couldn't have done any better herself.

Outside the department store, Lisa slipped her phone in her pocket as Maggie approached.

'Everything all right, love?'

Lisa nodded, covering her distraction with a smile.

'Good,' said Maggie. Glancing up at the grand façade she took a deep breath. 'Then what're we waiting for?'

Taking hold of her daughter's arm, she steered Lisa towards the store's revolving doors.

CHAPTER SEVEN

Forty minutes later, in the bridal department of the store, a pile of discarded gowns lay draped across a row of brocade chairs.

Maggie stood waiting outside a changing cubicle, checking the time on her watch before she stared across at a young sales assistant who failed to stifle a yawn. It was clear the young woman had long since given up on the chance of making a sale. Maggie leaned in closer to the cubicle and hissed in a loud whisper: 'Lisa, love. What're you doing in there?'

'What d'you *think* I'm doing?' said Lisa tersely, 'I'm trying it on!'

A moment passed before the curtain was suddenly drawn back to reveal Lisa in a fussy pale pink mid-length wedding dress with a pill box hat, topped with fabric fruit and net, perched on her head.

'Well?' she asked unsurely.

Maggie's jaw dropped slowly open. 'You look like a Raspberry Pavlova.'

Lisa swiped the hat from her head. 'This is hopeless…'

Maggie took the hat from her and handed it to the sales assistant who calmly moved off and replaced it in a box. Once Maggie was sure the young woman was out of earshot she leaned in to Lisa and whispered: 'You've only tried on a few.'

'I've tried on half the store!'

Maggie failed to find words to disagree but another voice did so.

'Not this one?'

Turning, they saw the sales assistant had reappeared with a white dress carefully draped across her forearms. Lisa took a cursory look at it before shaking her head. 'I don't think so.'

Maggie looked back at her. 'What d'you mean, 'you don't think so'? What's wrong with it?'

Lisa frowned at the gown's deep 'V' neckline. 'Bruce won't like it.'

The store assistant started to move off but Maggie quickly stopped her as she explained to Lisa. 'Bruce doesn't have to wear it, does he?'

'I'm telling you,' said Lisa. 'It's not right.'

Accepting this, the sales assistant went to leave once more. This time Maggie snatched the dress and told her: 'Just give us a minute, will you?'

Once the young woman had moved off, Maggie looked back at Lisa and framed her thoughts carefully before she began. 'They say your wedding's a day to remember, and it will be if you walk up the aisle of that register office in the altogether. So just try it, will you?'

She held out the dress. Lisa looked stubbornly at her mother, preparing to argue, when she saw the sales assistant looking across. She heaved a sigh. 'All right,' she said, reluctantly snatching the dress before she re-entered the cubicle.

Relieved, Maggie heaved a sigh and approached the curtain, speaking through it, calmer now.

'Look,' she began, 'what you've got to remember is: it's *your* day. *Your* wedding. And you can wear whatever you like. Why? Because you're a grown woman, that's why – though you might not always behave like one.'

Lisa's voice answered back: 'Full of compliments today, aren't we?'

'I'm just saying,' Maggie went on, 'you could stick a ruddy lampshade on your head if you wanted – it's up to you. Bruce won't see this dress until you're walking down that aisle. And when he does, I guarantee he'll think you're—' She broke off as the curtain drew sharply back and Lisa stepped out of the cubicle. Maggie was further silenced at the sight of her. Lisa's trembling hands moved uncertainly to the plunging neckline before she considered her own reflection in the mirror. Finally she turned to Maggie.

'Maybe it's… *not* too low?'

Maggie smiled before she whispered: 'It's ruddy perfect.'

At exactly the same time, across the other side of Marston, Bruce entered the hallway of an empty house. The blonde estate agent closed the front door behind them and produced a professional smile before indicating the way ahead. 'As you can see, the hallway's quite spacious,' she began, 'and the kitchen's been recently re-modelled. If you'd like to take a look?' She set off confidently but Bruce suddenly spoke.

'Your… leaflet says it's got a basement?'

The agent turned back to him, her tight smile indicating that she wasn't accustomed to being interrupted like this. But Bruce was holding up the leaflet, pointing to it, waiting for an answer.

'That's right,' she said finally. 'It was converted by the current owners but if you'd like to follow me, we can take a look first at the—'

'Can we start with the basement?'

The estate agent turned again, recognising he was used to taking control. She gave a small shrug. 'Of course.'

A few moments later, Maggie and Lisa entered the George and Dragon pub across the High Street from Jessop's. The place was full of office workers perched on stools at the bar but Maggie managed to claim a vacant window table and dumped several store bags on the floor.

'We've done well,' she began ticking off items in the notebook in her hand.

'Dress... shoes... underwear... all bought.'

'And flowers ordered.' Lisa reminded her.

'Aye,' said Maggie. 'I've even got an outfit for myself – *and* you've got the club if you want it?'

Lisa eyed her mother and Maggie explained: 'I know you don't want a fuss,' she began. 'But Marston Social is hardly the Ritz, and you'll get nowhere else at this short notice,' she paused for a moment, then: 'If you *did* want a bit of knees-up, me and your Dad'll pay, but... it's up to you.'

Lisa took a moment to consider this – then smiled. 'Thanks Mum, that'd be great.'

Maggie watched Lisa's smile begin to fade. 'Not still fretting about that dress, are you?'

Lisa failed to answer.

'Oh come on,' said Maggie, 'if you've got it – flaunt it. Bruce should be proud of you—'

'He is,' said Lisa quickly, 'it's just…' she trailed off, troubled.

'What is it?' asked Maggie, concerned.

'Just… something he said once.'

Maggie tried to read her daughter's expression. 'About you?'

Lisa shook her head. 'About some girls in Tenerife. They'd got steaming drunk down in the town and were letting it all hang out and…' she broke off for a moment, then: 'I saw the look in his eyes, how disgusted he was…' She paused. 'He said he was glad I wasn't like that and… he could tell from the way I dressed that… I had class?'

She looked at her mother. Maggie took a moment to consider what she'd just heard.

"Class'?'

Lisa nodded.

'Well, he's right,' said Maggie finally. 'You take after me,' she winked but saw Lisa was still distracted. 'You *are* sure,' Maggie began, 'that he's the one?'

Lisa paused before she nodded. 'Of course I am. Why d'you even ask?'

'Why?' Maggie echoed. 'Because he's a good looking fella. But it's not like you've been out with many others, is it?' She hesitated, suddenly unsure. 'Or… is it?'

'I've been out with a few,' said Lisa. 'But no-one like Bruce. I told you, he's special. He's the one I knew I was waiting for… even before we met?' She paused. 'We… understand each other. It's easy.'

'Easy?'

Lisa nodded. 'We need to be together, Mum. We... fit.'

Maggie considered this. 'Fit?'

Lisa nodded, still thinking of last night, of the bedroom games Bruce had been introducing her to. She was enjoying it all; the lingerie, the role play, being allowed to tease him before responding to his power.

It was all harmless enough. She loved the blindfold, submitting to it, succumbing to the element of surprise. Bruce had always been gentle with the scarf, especially when he had used it to tie her wrists above her head or behind her back.

None of her previous lovers had ever engaged in the kind of games that Bruce had introduced her to. Maybe she should have hinted to them, explained what she liked – though Bruce had never needed an explanation – instinctively he had known what it was she would enjoy – what she needed. How could she possibly explain this to anyone – especially to her mother? She took a deep breath, reached forward and held Maggie's hand.

'Trust me,' she whispered. Then she gave a smile – a smile with which Maggie knew she couldn't argue.

An hour later, Lisa was still smiling to herself as she entered the living room of her flat and set down her store bags. The phone was blinking an alert. Moving across to it, she tapped the button and took off an uncomfortable shoe as a voicemail message began to play.

'Hi there. This is Kate Jackson from Wentworth's for Mr Carter. Just to let you know I've spoken to the owner of Woodside and he's confirmed that you and your fiancée could move in as early as the 15th...'

Lisa frowned at the machine and slipped her shoe back on as the voice continued. *'...I've also left a message on your mobile number so if you could give me a call tomorrow we can confirm the details then. Have a nice evening.'*

A tone signaled the end of the message but Lisa continued to stare at the machine until she heard the soft click of the door behind her. Turning, she saw Bruce had entered, his key still in his hand. He followed Lisa's gaze to the phone as she pointed to it. 'Message from an estate agent. But there must be some mistake?'

Bruce hesitated only for a moment then spoke flatly: 'No mistake.' He took something from his pocket. 'I just signed the lease on a great house for us.' He offered her the paperwork in his hand.

'You... did what?'

'Lisa—'

'I haven't even seen it.'

He held up the estate agent's leaflet. Lisa snatched it from him.

'Trust me,' said Bruce. 'It's perfect.'

Lisa glanced down at the photo on the leaflet then back at Bruce – her eyes narrowing. 'Why did you do this,' she asked confused, 'when I told you—'

'I know what you told me,' Bruce said, cutting in. 'But someone had to make a decision.'

'You mean... you?' She shook her head. 'This is something we should have done together. It's important.'

'Look—'

'No,' she said firmly. 'We're talking about our first proper home together. Don't you think I should at least have been allowed to give my opinion?'

'Of course you should.' Bruce glanced across at the department store bags. 'But you were out shopping.'

Lisa frowned in exasperation. 'Oh come on…'

Bruce plucked the estate agent's leaflet from her hand. 'All right. If you don't like it—'

'How do I *know* if I don't like it? I need to see it!'

'And you can do that tomorrow.'

'*After* you've already signed the lease?'

Bruce turned to face her. Confounded, Lisa moved to him, feeling more hurt than angry. 'You promised.'

'I know,' he said smoothly. 'But the agent said someone else was interested…'

'Agents always say that!' She was staring at him challengingly. He considered her then turned his back on her and began moving towards the door.

'Bruce?' She grabbed his arm. He failed to look at her and suddenly she felt as though she was re-enacting a million family conflicts, struggling for her own voice to be heard. 'Is… this our first fight?'

A moment passed before Bruce looked slowly back at her. He spoke softly, aware that if he remained calm, only one of them would appear irrational. 'I don't know why you're so angry about this,' he began coolly. 'I don't want to fight with you, Lise. I never want to do that.'

As though trying to regain composure, he rubbed his brow but Lisa reached up and took his hand from his face, forcing him to look at her, shocked to see his pain. 'Bruce…'

'No,' he said. 'You're right. I'll call the agent in the morning. Tell her there's been a mistake and that I shouldn't have jumped the gun.'

Lisa blinked, realising that she had managed to do what Maggie always did to Jeff – hectored him into submission

– something she had always promised herself she would never do with her own partner. She shook her head slowly and made a decision. 'No,' she said softly. 'No, it's fine,' summoning a smile she reached out, trying to breach the gulf between them. 'I'm sorry.'

Bruce responded by leaning in and kissing her, holding her tightly, as the estate agent's leaflet fell from her hand to the floor. It had been a battle – and more of a challenge than he had expected – but he had won.

CHAPTER EIGHT

A week later, Maggie was on the speaker phone in her office at the factory, sifting through print-outs as she spoke to Lisa. 'So I put the order through to the catering company – the full cold buffet – but without those *sate* things just in case anyone's allergic to nuts. You've got to be really careful these days.' Lisa failed to respond. Maggie checked she was paying attention.

''You still there?'

On the other end of the line, Lisa struggled to take off her coat, juggling the phone in her hand before she managed a reply. 'Yeah. Thanks, Mum.'

Unsettled by her daughter's stressed tone, Maggie asked: 'You sure you're all right, love, because if you need a hand with moving—'

'No, it's all sorted.' Lisa said quickly. 'Everything's booked for Thursday morning.'

Maggie took a moment to absorb this. 'As if you haven't got enough to do.'

'I said it's fine,' said Lisa, tersely.

Maggie heaved a sigh. 'Well, at least you don't have a lot to move, but why you've decided to move so far out, I don't know. You could've rented closer to town.'

'I told you; we want somewhere with a bit of space.'

'Don't we all? But you don't need to be paying rent on such a big place.'

'Mum,' said Lisa, 'why d'you always have to tell me what I do and don't need?'

'I'm just saying,' Maggie began calmly, 'if you'd waited a bit longer and found yourself a new job you might've been able to buy somewhere. Your Dad and me would have helped—'

'Please,' said Lisa, breaking in. 'Not now, Mum. I don't have time.'

Maggie was brought up short. 'Why?'

'Because I've got to get changed. I'm meeting Dee and the girls.'

Maggie felt a sudden surge of relief. 'Well, why didn't you say? Go on. Forget about weddings and get yourself ready. Have some fun – and say hello to Denise,' she added, remembering Lisa's old school friend. 'I haven't seen her in ages.'

'No,' said Lisa, realising something: 'neither have I.' After ending the call she took a deep breath before turning to check her reflection in the mirror, then she glanced down at her watch – and saw it was already 5.20 p.m.

At the factory, straight after the call, Maggie was just getting up from her desk when her door opened. She turned to see Naila. 'Didn't hear you knock,' said Maggie as she pinned a new work schedule to her board. 'What is it?'

Naila summoned her resolve before explaining: 'I need to talk to you – about the refugee.'

Maggie paused for a second before explaining. 'She's a new member of staff, and her name's Rona.'

'Aye,' said Naila, 'whatever it is, it spells trouble.'

Maggie saw Naila's implacable expression, her mouth set, chin jutting forward.

'Look—'

'No, Maggie, you need to listen to me.' Naila took a step forward. 'Stuff's going missing.'

'Like your fags?' said Maggie wearily.

Naila nodded towards the window onto the factory floor. 'She took 'em all right.'

Maggie noted Naila's brooding look as she continued to stare down through the window.

'And that's why they were under your work bench, was it?'

Naila looked back sharply. 'She got 'em back under that bench just in time – to fool you.' Lips pursed tight, she now waited for Maggie's response.

'And you expect me to believe that?'

'She took my fags… and *now* she's got Tracey Tyler's ring.'

Maggie frowned. 'What're you talking about?'

'Tracey just told me. She took her engagement ring off and left it on the sink in the toilets. Now it's gone. And *I* know where.' Naila held her head high as she announced: 'Your refugee went in straight after her.'

'She's not *mine*,' said Maggie, irritated by the inference. 'And why isn't Tracey here telling me this herself?'

'Why d'you think? Because she knows you won't listen.'

'That's not true,' snapped Maggie, looking away to avoid Naila's unflinching gaze. 'I've spent a lifetime listening – to every single one of you—'

'And I'm telling you – that girl's *not* one of us.'

Maggie nodded, finally agreeing. 'Aye,' she said, 'you're right there. She's kept her head down and worked her arse off, which is more than I can say for some.' Crossing the room, she grabbed her coat while Naila frowned and stepped forward. 'I'm *telling* you, Mags,' she said urgently.

'Telling me what?' said Maggie turning to her. 'Doing disappearing tricks, is she? Member of the Magic Circle?'

Naila's expression set. 'She took 'em. *My* fags… Tracey's ring.'

'So you say.'

'And so much for listening!' spat Naila bitterly.

Maggie stared away again – a final act of betrayal for Naila who turned quickly for the door. Maggie watched her, suddenly stabbed by a pang of remorse. 'All right!'

At the door Naila hesitated and turned back slowly to face her boss. Maggie finally gave a nod. 'Tell Tracey I'll deal with it.'

The factory bell began sounding for the end of the day. Naila's slow smile was one of triumph as she turned again for the door and left.

Alone now, Maggie moved to her desk and stared down through the window onto the factory floor below. The girls were already leaving, Rona deserting her machine, hitching a bag across her shoulder as she headed for the exit. Maggie looked away, remembering what she had said to Samira only recently – and with such certainty: '*when have I ever been wrong about someone?*' Now she allowed herself to consider the impossible – could she have been wrong about Rona, after all?

Later that same evening, Lisa leaned closer to the mirror in her living room as she applied a slick of lip gloss then primped her hair and straightened the tight fitting red dress she wore. Her hands smoothed the fabric over her hips before her palms glided smoothly across her abdomen.

She turned sideways, standing up straight, sucking in her stomach before she was finally satisfied with her reflection. She had lost a few more pounds, not enough for Bruce to have noticed, but knowing that if she continued he was bound to comment soon – positively this time. Replacing the lipstick in her bag she then grabbed her coat and went to unplug her phone which had been charging on the table, when she suddenly noticed that the cable wasn't connected properly to the power point.

Checking the phone's screen, she saw it was almost out of battery but it suddenly rang in her hand and she quickly replied to the caller's question.

'Hi. No, I'm Lisa. Mrs Sheild is my mother – the one who placed the buffet order?' She listened further. 'Does it... have to be in writing?' She frowned at the response. 'Well surely...' Then she broke off as the caller went on. 'Okay,' she said, 'I realise it's a late booking, it's just... my phone's about to run out of battery and...' She glanced across the room and suddenly noticed Bruce's silver laptop on the dining table. 'Could you give me the address?' Moving to laptop, she switched it on then took a pen from her bag and scribbled down an e-mail address from the caller. 'Got it. Bye.'

Quickly ending the call, she waited for the laptop to start up, then braced herself and tried to bring up an e-mail programme. A warning appeared on the screen. 'ACCESS DENIED'. Hitting the shift key – a new message appeared: 'USER IDENTITY REQUIRED'. Frustrated, she tried again.

Another message appeared – 'REQUEST FINGERPRINT I.D.'. Lisa frowned at the screen. A voice sounded behind her.

'What're you doing?'

Startled, Lisa turned quickly to give a sigh of relief on seeing Bruce standing at the door. She smiled. 'That's right. Creep up on me,' she pointed to the laptop. 'My phone's about to die and the caterers want written confirmation of the order – right now – and you'll get the prize for Geek of the Week if you can get this thing to work?' She nodded to Bruce's laptop. He glanced at it and stepped forward.

'It's just standard.' He tossed his keys on the table.

'Oh yeah? Who for? James Bond? It's asked me for my ruddy fingerprints.'

Bruce pointed to the computer. 'I use that feature when the laptop's out of my hands. D'you know how many client passwords I've got stored on here? I need reliable encryptions—'

'All right, all right.' Lisa indicated the address on the piece of paper in her hand. 'Can you just e-mail this address for me? Confirm the order and let them have whatever else they need?'

Bruce considered her helpless look – and smiled. 'Sure.' He took the address from her then glanced at his silver laptop as he added: 'After I've done this, I'm going to get a few things over to the house.'

Lisa glanced back at him. 'We can do that on Thursday, can't we?'

'No,' Bruce said starkly. 'Until I get a new system up and running there, I don't want anything going missing in the move – especially from here.' He threw a look back to his laptop.

Lisa shrugged. 'All right. Mr Security,' she smiled then leaned in and kissed him. A car horn sounded outside. She quickly looked out of the window. 'That's my cab.'

'I can drive you if you hold on?'

She shook her head. 'I'll be late. The car's here now.' The cab's horn sounded again. This time she moved quickly to the door.

'Lise?'

Turning back, she saw Bruce was looking concerned. 'Be careful.'

She shrugged. 'Of what?'

He moved to her and laid his hands on her shoulders. 'Don't drink too much. You're vulnerable if you do. Remember the girl in Tenerife?'

Lisa shook her head slowly. 'I'm not that girl, Bruce. And I'd never put myself in a situation like that either. This is just a night out with the girls. We'll go for a meal and probably end up in the pub in the High Street – the George and Dragon? I promise you, I'll make it back in one piece,' she smiled.

Bruce appeared to relax. 'Good,' he said. 'You'd better.' He returned her smile then leaned in and kissed her again. A car horn sounded once more and Lisa broke away to move to the door, adding: 'Don't forget that e-mail!' Blowing him a kiss, she left. Bruce waited for the sound of the front door closing then looked back at his laptop and the e-mail address in his hand.

Twenty minutes later, Lisa was waiting patiently outside a small bistro in town. Young couples bustled past her into the busy interior. Lisa stared after them before glancing up and down the street, feeling the cold – something she had long forgotten during the warm evenings in Tenerife. It had been some time since she had found herself in the centre of Marston on a Friday night and she took a moment to remember how her teenage years had been spent living for weekend nights on the town like this – out with her girls after they had plastered on some make-up and slipped into new outfits bought with pocket money saved from Saturday jobs; lying about their ages to get a few drinks in at the George and Dragon before heading off to dance the night away at the local clubs.

It had been a ritual – but one in which Lisa's sister, Nat, had never taken part, preferring instead to stay at home, studying, or watching films on TV. Nat was the quiet one, the studious one, the academic sister who would have gone to Leeds University and graduated with a good degree in English and History – if only her heart had been strong enough.

Lisa heaved a heavy breath knowing that her sister's death had been so much more than a family tragedy because it had brought about a deep and fundamental change in the way Lisa viewed herself. While Nat was alive, Lisa had remained an easy reference point for everything her sister wasn't. She had come to relish being the opposite: the chatty one, the funny one, the extrovert. But some months after Natalie's death, Lisa had begun to wonder if she really needed to be any of those things at all.

On witnessing Lisa's lack of focus, Maggie had attempted to deal with things by taking control and persuading her daughter to apply for a diploma in hotel management – something she would never have done if Nat had been alive – but it was incumbent on one of Maggie's daughters to go to college – even if meant Lisa finishing a practical course without gaining any letters after her name, or producing a photograph of herself, dressed in mortar board and gown, to display on her mother's sideboard.

Lisa hadn't regretted taking the course because apart from pleasing her parents, college had provided an escape route from home so she could forget what she wasn't – and find out who she really was. Now she knew – and not because she had travelled – but because she had met Bruce.

In Tenerife, Bruce had helped her to discover herself, had shown to her, in his reflected gaze, a new Lisa. She was sure he could have had any one of the pretty young women working in the Miramar in Tenerife – but he had chosen her. Why? Because, as he had told her so many times; she was 'the one'. He never tired of telling her that. He loved her, cared for her, protected her and had introduced her to the kind of sex she had never experienced – either here in Marston or while repping abroad.

What she had told her mother was true: she and Bruce were a good 'fit' – and now she was sure nothing could ever be the same again. Bruce had entered her life and taken control of almost everything. He liked organising things – organising her – and in doing so he had taken a weight of responsibility from her shoulders. Now she was about to become his wife. They would be together forever, just like her parents, though Lisa had already vowed to herself that she would never treat her husband the way that Maggie treated Jeff; bossing him around and nagging him until he retreated into the garden or his shed. Bruce had appeared in Lisa's life just when she needed him most – and for that, she knew she would remain forever grateful. Even now, she found herself missing him.

Pulling her phone from her bag she stared at it in frustration. If only she'd taken more care to charge it properly, she could be calling him right now, asking him if he missed her too… A loud car horn startled her.

Looking up, she saw a stretch Limousine cruising towards her. It glided slowly in front of her and came to a halt as a passenger window wound down to reveal a young blonde woman, chewing gum. Lisa's jaw dropped open at the sight of her. 'You didn't expect we'd be coming by bus, did you?' said Dee, with a smile.

A chauffeur stepped out of the vehicle and opened a passenger door to reveal two other familiar faces peering back at Lisa from the luxurious interior.

'What're you waiting for?' asked Patsy, a cheery redhead, slapping the leather seat beside her as she poured a flute of champagne from the limo's bar. Lisa took her seat and as the chauffeur closed the door after her, she stared around, stunned, taking in the fibre-optic mood lighting and video system.

'What d'you think?' said Sandra, leaning in towards Lisa as Patsy handed a glass of champagne to her.

Lisa shook her head. 'This is going to cost us a fortune…'

"Us?" said Dee. 'We thought *you* could pay for it seeing as you're *saving* a fortune by not coming away with us.'

'Yeah,' said Patsy, inspecting the bubbles in her champagne. 'Blowing us out just to get wed?'

'How could you *do* that?' asked Sandra.

'Breaking up the coven?' said Dee, with a mock tragic expression as she indicated the limousine's plush interior. 'We had to push the boat out, Lise,' she smiled and topped up her own glass.

Lisa stared at them. 'You… are joking.'

A pause followed before Patsy shrieked. 'Course we are! This belongs to Kevin.'

Lisa turned to Sandra. 'Your *cousin*, Kevin?'

Sandra nodded proudly and leaned closer to Lisa to whisper: 'It's on its way to an airport pick up, but the customers'll be none the wiser after it's dropped us off,' she gave a wink.

Lisa noted their slow smiles and sighed with relief. 'I've missed you.'

'Snap,' said Dee – sincerely this time – as she leaned in to embrace her. 'But the night's young so…'

All three leaned closer to slip their arms around Lisa, raising their glasses as they began to chant. 'Hubble bubble…'

As their glasses met, they cried out in unison. 'Let's cause trouble!' And downed the rest of their champagne.

CHAPTER NINE

A heavy bass line reverberated across the dance floor.

The crowd at Crazy Henry's had been going for a while. From the bar Lisa observed a mass of ultra-violet smiles and gyrating bodies. There seemed to be more students than she'd ever remembered before – a new generation from a different class; girls with ballet-straight backs hiding their privilege behind tattoos and piercings.

Beside her, Patsy and Sandra were nodding along to the music while Dee at a distance was trying to get a barman's attention. The club had once been the focal point of Lisa's week but now the style of the place seemed cheap and uninspiring compared to the nightlife she had grown used to in Tenerife.

She raised a smile for Sandra and Patsy in the hope they wouldn't guess what she was thinking, then she glanced up at the industrial lighting rigs hanging from exposed gantries – a contrast to her favourite beachfront clubs with their spectacular sea views and laser displays lighting up the night skies.

Suddenly Dee was back, indicating a row of shot glasses being set up on the bar. 'Ready for your Snake Bites?' She wore a grin but Lisa stared ruefully at the drinks as Sandra and Patsy quickly downed their own.

Straight afterwards Patsy asked: 'Come on, Lise, what's up wi'yer?'

'Nothing,' she replied quickly. 'I… just thought we were going for a meal. I should have had something to line my stomach.'

Dee paid the barman. 'And some pork scratchings.' She winked at the barman as he tossed the packet across but Lisa still stared at the shot glass on the bar.

'What's wrong?' asked Dee, 'not becoming a lightweight, are we?'

Lisa gave a guilty look. 'I promised Bruce I'd go easy.'

'Hear that, girls?' said Dee. 'This is what happens when you get engaged.'

Patsy smiled. 'Yeah, next up you'll be wearing jogging bottoms under your egg-stained dressing gown.'

'Little tartan slippers with them buttons on?' said Sandra.

'Leave it out!' ordered Lisa.

'Don't worry,' said Dee. 'We're just jealous that's all.'

Patsy came closer. 'So you might as well own up.'

'To what?' asked Lisa.

Sandra leaned forward. 'He's a minger, right? That's why you haven't shown us a photo?'

At their looks, Lisa reached into her bag for her keys and proudly held up the plastic fob which showed a photo of Bruce at the Miramar pool bar, sporting a suntan and a pair of Raybans.

'Well?' she said proudly, waiting for their response.

Patsy gave a wolf whistle.

'Looks like someone's been having handsome lessons,' said Dee.

'So, what's the catch?' asked Sandra.

Lisa turned to face her but Patsy piped up. 'Aye. You can't tell us a fella that fit hasn't got owt wrong with him.'

'He snores,' said Sandra.

'Farts,' said Patsy.

'Got little hairs hanging out of his nose?' said Dee.

'Or on his back,' said Sandra.

'Gross!' said Patsy, wincing.

Dee nudged her. 'He could always get a wax.'

'He doesn't need one!' Lisa protested. 'He's perfect.'

The others looked on, silenced, as Lisa stared down at the photo.

'Course he is,' said Dee finally. 'Or you wouldn't be getting wed.'

In the background, the heavy number playing on the dancefloor segued into a lighter track.

Patsy nudged Sandra. 'Come on, what're we waiting for?'

Slapping their empty shot glasses on the bar, the two moved off while Dee looked sidelong at Lisa as she gave her attention to the crowd on the dancefloor. 'Thank God it's Friday...'

Lisa turned to see Dee smile as she went on: 'That's how it always was, right? Go out. Get steaming. Feel the vibe. Recognise we're free? For the weekend, at least,' she gave a wink and signaled to the barman for a refill.

'Yeah,' Lisa said. 'I was thinking about that earlier.'

'Good,' said Dee. 'That means you haven't forgotten us.'

Lisa glanced back at her. 'How could I ever do that?'

Dee noted Lisa was still toying with the key fob. 'You're trading us in for a fella. That's not such a bad thing now I've seen what he looks like. So, why're you looking so worried?'

Lisa looked at her. Dee moved in closer and smiled: 'Having second thoughts about blowing us out for the States? It's the big trip, Lise. The one we always said we'd take as soon as we'd saved enough. San Francisco... Vegas... the Grand Canyon and Los Angeles – *and* that includes Hollywood. It's not going to be the same without you.'

Lisa met Dee's gaze. 'You'll have a great time.'

'Yeah,' said Dee, before nodding towards Patsy and Sandra on the dance floor. 'Wait till La La Land meets those two,' she smiled again as Patsy and Sandra waved back at her. Distracted, Lisa slipped her keys back into her bag as Dee observed her. 'You know I'm only teasing you because I'm jealous.'

'Jealous?' said Lisa. 'You're off on this trip – and I've got a fortnight in Madeira.'

'You'll have a honeymoon,' said Dee, 'and a new life to look forward to,' she handed Lisa's shot glass to her.

Lisa stared at it. 'Yeah,' she said finally, trying to return Dee's smile before finally glancing away.

'So what is it?' asked Dee, serious now. 'I know you, Lise, and I know something's wrong. Not getting cold feet, are you?'

Meeting Dee's gaze, Lisa finally set down her shot glass. 'If you must know,' she began. 'It's Mum. She's... not happy about things. The wedding, I mean.'

'Don't tell me. She wants the full works... Westminster Abbey... a choir of angels?' She paused then: 'Actually, I thought you'd want the same.'

'Maybe I did,' Lisa admitted. 'It wasn't easy putting her off but…' she broke off for a moment and re-organised her thoughts. 'You know what Mum's like; nothing… and no-one is good enough for her girls?'

'That's Maggie all right.'

Lisa braced herself. 'But if you get wed in church it's… meetings with the vicar and…' she trailed off for a moment.

'And?'

'And… I just didn't want her to know.'

'Know what?' asked Dee, confused.

Lisa hesitated, then said: 'Bruce has been married before.' A pause settled before Dee took this in. She gave a shrug. 'So what?'

'So you know what Mum would say: "used goods"? She'd have to know all the details and to be honest… none of that really matters. It was all over a long time ago.'

Dee took a moment to consider this. 'But… you're the one who has to give up on your fairytale wedding?'

'I'd give up anything,' said Lisa softly, 'as long as we're wed.'

Dee took this in.

'He really *is* the one?'

Lisa slowly nodded.

Dee moved closer. 'So… how d'you know? I mean, how can you be so sure? *I* thought I was sure about Darren and look what happened—'

Lisa spoke quickly. 'Darren was never right for you. He didn't deserve you. He was a player.'

'Yeah,' Dee sighed, 'and I found out the hard way,' she looked directly at Lisa, 'I don't want you doing the same.'

'I won't,' said Lisa, confirmed. 'Bruce is different. I know it.'

Dee looked back at her unsure. 'How?'

'Because he's not like any other fella I've been with. He's really...' she broke off as she searched for the right words, '...into me,' she gave a slow smile. 'And he knows how to show it.'

'That good, eh?'

'Better.'

Dee considered this. 'Lucky you. Hope he knows how to make you laugh as well,' she leaned closer. 'Not at the same time, of course,' she winked then turned to pick up the shot glasses from the bar. 'I'm going to miss you, but I'm really happy for you.'

Lisa smiled. 'You... won't say anything, will you? About the divorce?'

Dee handed the shot glass to her. Lisa stared at it, accepting it for what it was – a form of communion – an old ritual but one that would also cement a new promise. 'Course I won't,' said Dee. They finally knocked back their shots.

An hour later, Patsy and Sandra tumbled out of Crazy Henry's, propping one another up – unsuccessfully. Dee and Lisa followed. A bouncer steadied a stumbling Patsy.

'Ooooh, you're not gonna frisk me, are you?' she cried. '*Pleeease*?' As she laughed and hiccupped at the same time, a young guy leaned in to her and whispered: 'Your place or mine?'

Sandra responded in a loud whisper: 'You go to your place – she'll come to mine.'

The guy looked back at Sandra, leaning in to her as he asked: 'Was I talking to you?'

'Hope not,' said Sandra.' Cos I haven't got the energy to fake it tonight.' As she winked at him, the young man's mates whistled at his expense before the men all staggered off together into the night.

'Right,' said Dee, taking control. 'Time for something to eat.'

'Now?' asked Lisa.

'It's never too late for a kebab,' said Patsy.

'And there's a new Turkish place opened up on King Street,' said Dee. 'We can have the full sit-down.'

'Plus there's a waiter after Patsy. Always gives her a bit on the side?' She nudged Patsy.

Lisa shook her head. 'I'm sorry, girls, but I've got to get back.'

'Oh come on,' grumbled Patsy, 'we haven't seen you for months—'

'I know,' said Lisa, pained, 'but… I promised Bruce I wouldn't be late.'

Patsy and Sandra groaned in disappointment but Dee plucked her phone from her pocket and said, 'All right Missus, let's get you an Uber.'

Lisa shook her head. 'S'okay. At this time of night it'll be quicker if I get a taxi at the rank.'

'Sure?' asked Dee.

Lisa surveyed her girls, knowing full well they were set on a late-night adventure – one in which she would have happily joined them if she had only downed more Snake Bites and thought less about Bruce. Instead, she felt only relief at being let off the hook. 'Go on. The lot of you,' she said. 'Don't make that waiter have to wait, Patsy,' she leaned in to kiss them all goodnight.

Patsy pointed a drunken finger at her. 'And you tell that fella of yours to bring some mates for us to the wedding.'

Lisa smiled. 'I will.'

Patsy and Sandra began to move off unsteadily. Lisa's smile faded as she turned to Dee.

'About what I told you…'

'Don't worry,' said Dee with a tipsy smile. 'My lips are sealed,' she raised a hand, locked her lips with an imaginary key and tossed it away. Before either could say another word to each other, a tidal wave of customers swept out of Crazy Henry's, creating a gulf between the two women. In the next instant, Lisa's friends were waving back at her, heading further into the dark night as Lisa was left staring after them.

A moment later, she moved on herself, setting off at a pace along a side road that led to Marston station.

Spots of light rain were falling on pavements that were still wet from an earlier shower.

Milling on the opposite side of the street, the group of drunken young guys from Crazy Henry's offered wolf whistles to Lisa and a few unintelligible comments before they finally staggered on and away from her. Their voices retreated into the distance as a taxi suddenly approached. Lisa put out her hand – then noticed the For Hire sign wasn't lit. As the vehicle passed by, she dug deep into her bag for her phone – before remembering that the battery was down.

Staring around, she saw that she was now alone. It wasn't the first time she had found herself walking the streets of Marston in the early hours of the morning, in search of a lift home, but on any other night out with the girls she would have felt buoyed by alcohol – Dutch courage.

Nevertheless, she was still in the town centre – her own *home* town – on streets she knew so well. But tonight felt different, perhaps because she had been away for so long or perhaps because a memory was still sharp in her mind about a girl in Tenerife – a girl who had chosen to take a lift from a stranger.

Bruce was right to have reminded her about that. Being alone, and out of control from the effects of drink or drugs, would put any young woman at risk, especially away from her own country and unable to speak the language.

Lisa hadn't told her mother what had happened. It would only have worried her, jarred Maggie's vision of her daughter's life abroad.

She found herself thinking about Maggie's reaction to Lisa giving up her job. Maggie had long been convinced that working in a holiday resort in Tenerife, or anywhere else, was a liberating thing for a young woman to do – but only because it was something she would also have wanted to do at Lisa's age.

In fact, reality was quite different from Maggie's dream. 'Brits Abroad' had gained a poor reputation in the resorts in which Lisa had worked. The under-thirties used their '*todo incluido*' package holidays to enjoy plenty of free 'pre-drinking' in the hotel bars before heading off to local clubs and returning next morning off their faces, or heads, throwing up in the streets or over themselves.

Girls far younger than Lisa came away for a week or a fortnight's holiday, looking for what? Romance, adventure, and experience – or perhaps simply a brief escape from their lives. In doing so, they risked STI's and teenage pregnancies and invited the disrespect of the local Tenerife community. *Putas,* 'young whores', was the label the girls attracted – their wild *despedidas*, farewell celebrations, resulting in many of them missing their return flights home next day, after having been arrested or suffering from hangovers so severe they required a visit from the hotel doctor to administer an anti-nausea injection.

Lisa had never told her mother the real story.

Why would she want to destroy Maggie's dream with tales of young mums on holiday abandoning kids in pushchairs in the main plaza because they were too drunk to remember where they left them? Nor had she shared the news of what had happened to the young seventeen-year old who had been found, close to Playa de la Tejita, half naked and out of her head on ketamine.

The beach was close to the laid back haven of El Medano where a group of surfers had found the teenager, bruised, cut and still hallucinating as she had struggled her way on to a dirt track leading up to the road.

Days later, she had emerged from the trauma with only jagged shards of memories; stumbling out of a local club, after having become separated from her friends, taking a lift from a stranger but remembering little about him after he had offered her some Coke to sober her up. Nothing for the police to go on in spite of appeals for information that had circulated across the island. The girl had been flown home but the memory of the incident remained with all the British workers – including Lisa and Bruce.

Lisa quickened her pace, reminding herself that this was Marston, not Playa de la Tejita, but as she did so she stumbled clumsily on her high heels.

Recovering, she saw that one of her ankle straps was undone

and reached down to fasten it, failing to notice the car that was turning the corner into the street behind her. It slowed and came to a quiet stop. Lisa became aware of it only on hearing the engine start up again. Glancing back she saw the vehicle's headlights were shining so brightly on to the wet road they obscured the driver.

She walked on, quickening her pace but the car now followed at a slow steady speed while keeping its distance. Something was wrong. She could hear blood pumping in her ears in time with her footsteps as she finally began to break into a run, eyes fixed on the light of a street lamp at the junction ahead. Beyond it lay the main road and the taxi rank. Could she reach both before the car reached her?

Headlights began to flood the pavement ahead of her. Lisa's heart began to pound as the car suddenly accelerated, its horn sounding loudly, assaulting the silence. A door swung open, straight into her path. A man's voice spoke. 'Looks like you could do with a lift.' From the driver's seat, Bruce offered her a smile.

Moments later, Lisa was sitting beside her fiancé, fastening her seatbelt as Bruce asked: 'Had a good time?'

Lisa smiled. 'Better for seeing you. What're you doing here?'

'I drove over to the house,' he explained. 'Took a few things with me – some files to do with work. When I finished, I thought I'd cruise past that pub you mentioned.'

Lisa looked at him, confused. 'The George?' She shook her head. 'We didn't go there.'

'No?'

'We ended up at Crazy Henry's instead. The club on the High Street?'

Bruce's smile snapped into place. 'Then it's lucky I found you. I told you to be careful.'

She nodded. 'I know.' Leaning closer, she kissed him. 'You rescued me. It could've been a while till I got a cab,' she smiled again. 'I thought you were a kerb crawler.'

'Lucky I wasn't,' he said softly.

Feeling safe at last, Lisa heaved a sigh and leaned her head against Bruce's shoulder. Watching one of his strong hands clutch the steering wheel, while the other turned the key in the ignition, she remained unaware of his cold expression as he drove into the night, staring flatly at the slick greasy road ahead.

CHAPTER TEN

A leaden sky was overtaking a dying day as a dog's bark resounded, bouncing off the high stone walls of Jeff's garden.

'Give it a rest, Bella, will you!' On Jeff's order, the terrier skulked away while continuing to eye the visitor he had just welcomed through the garden gate. Jeff shepherded the dog towards the house and shooed her inside before closing the door. 'Sorry about that,' he said to Bruce standing behind him, 'I don't know what's got into her. She's usually good as gold.'

Bruce managed a cool smile. 'Women, eh?'

Jeff rolled his eyes. 'You can say that again.' He slapped his palm on Bruce's shoulder. 'It's good of you to pop round, son, considering everything on your plate right now – or… is there something you need?'

'Nothing,' said Bruce. 'Only… well, I've been thinking about that rockery you mentioned.' He cast an eye around Jeff's garden. 'And I reckon we could get another one up for you here. If you wanted, that is? And it wouldn't take much.' He nodded towards the shed. 'I could break up that old path and re-use the concrete. I'm no expert on rockeries but I built a good few walls in the Army.'

Jeff looked sidelong at him. 'They teach you bricklaying as well now, do they?'

Bruce shrugged. 'I did a bit before I joined up. In fact, if it wasn't for the Guards I might still be slapping mortar for a living, but they got me on comms and then computers... and I'm grateful for that.'

Jeff took a moment to process this, reflecting on the fact that working in a colliery had left him with little more than a sense of camaraderie with his former miners and an inadequate pension.

'D'you miss it?' Jeff asked. 'Army life?'

Bruce considered the question then shrugged. 'Not now, but if I'd stayed, who knows? I might be Sergeant Major by now.'

Jeff winked. 'And I'd still be waiting for my rockery.' He smiled and slapped his hands together. 'Well, if you're up for it, then so am I!'

Bruce focused on Jeff's smile – so trusting – just like Lisa's. 'That's great,' he replied finally. 'It'll have to be after me and Lise come back from honeymoon though. But you decide what you want – *and* where – and I'll provide the muscle.'

'Thank you,' said Jeff sincerely before he took off his cap and wiped his brow with it. 'I don't know how I'm going to repay you.' He nodded towards the shed. 'Fancy a tipple?'

Bruce shook his head. 'I'm fine, Jeff. And no repayment needed. It'll be good to keep my hand in.' As he started to move off, Jeff trailed quickly after him. 'Well, how about a quick bevvy down the club? There's a darts match on tonight and I could introduce you to the boys?'

Bruce turned back to him. 'I... should get back to Lise.'

'And let me drink on my own?'

'You'll have 'the boys' and…' he smiled then leaned forward to whisper in Jeff's ear. 'I wouldn't want Maggie thinking I was leading you astray.'

Jeff tapped his nose. 'I'll say nowt if you don't. Besides, she'll be none the wiser. She rang to say she'll be back a bit late tonight. Got a plumber coming in at the factory.' He slapped Bruce again on the shoulder. 'So, what d'you say?'

Bruce hesitated before making his decision. 'Nice idea but… another time, Jeff.'

At exactly the same time, a plumber was crouched under a sink in the ladies' toilets of Masters & Son. Maggie looked on, watching carefully as he pulled out the trap and allowed a torrent of filthy water to flood into a bucket.

'Well?' she asked, stepping forward.

The plumber continued to sift through the waste water. After a few tense moments, he looked up at Maggie and finally shook his head. 'Nothing.'

Disappointed, Maggie nodded her thanks then stared dismally down into the bucket of water before moving off into the hallway.

Closing the door after herself, Maggie stood stock still and considered all she had heard from Naila.

Suspicion could splinter the solidarity she had generated in her workforce over the last two decades – especially since the union had gone. Samira had reminded her that while her British Pakistani workers might have much in common with each another, especially within their own communities, there was also plenty to differentiate them. Young women of Naila's age identified as much, if not more, with Marston's broader community than with their own senior family members, and Samira had also pointed out to Maggie that Naila might have reason to view Rona as an intruder into her world – *if* she felt the woman wasn't to be trusted.

Maggie had struggled with this, priding herself on being a good judge of character but now questioning whether her defence of Rona had been influenced by the fact that the woman was a good worker – someone Maggie could rely on to help meet Jason's new orders. But there was something else, something Maggie had yet to fully identify, which caused her to feel defensive of her new worker. Reflecting on this, she was just about to return to her office when a voice called out.

'Maggie?'

Turning, she saw someone hurrying along the corridor towards her. 'Tracey—' Maggie broke off as the young woman reached her, catching her breath as she did so. 'I found it, Mags,' she began, 'just now at home?' Extending her left hand Tracey Tyler revealed the diamond engagement ring on her finger. 'It was down the side of Caden's cot, would you believe it? Must've come off when I changed the mattress.' In the next instant, she took on a guilty expression as she continued in staccato sentences. 'I… don't know what to say except… I'm sorry. I never meant to cause any fuss, but I told Naila… and the next thing she was blaming the refugee, saying she was going to talk to you? I shouldn't have let her.'

Maggie took a moment to process this then stared down at the ring on Tracey's finger. 'It's all right,' she said gently, 'no harm done.'

Tracey looked placated. 'Thanks, Mags.' As she turned to go, Maggie stared after her – then closed her eyes in relief.

Half an hour later, Jeff arrived at Marston Social Club to be met with the familiar smell of beer, pipe tobacco – and meat pasties warming in the bar's microwave. For decades the club had been the heart of Marston's mining community and despite the colliery's closure, the same heart continued to beat.

Jeff headed slowly through the club's lobby, its walls plastered with framed photographs; a testament to the social bonds that had survived the death of the local industry. The old colliery buses that had once transferred miners to the pit were now used as transport for beanos and other social events.

An annual miners' gala still took place featuring a fancy dress parade and a colliery brass band which continued to play and recruit members. Diverse clubs had sprung up out of the miners' traditional leisure activities; bowls, boxing, angling – and a gardening association, to which Jeff belonged and through which he had been provided with much-needed work after he had taken early retirement – until new health problems had put an end to it.

Jeff reached the bar just as a dart landed firmly in a board. A man's gruff voice announced: 'Treble twenty scored. Fifty to finish!'

Glancing towards the area where the match was taking place, Jeff took out his wallet and turned to face the barman who was drying glasses. 'Give us a pint, Ted, will you?'

Another dart whistled its way into the board as a fresh shout went up. 'Ten scored! Double twenty to finish!'

Ted the barman handed Jeff his pint and both men gave their

attention to the match where a young man stood positioned at the oche, licking dry lips before taking aim once more. A third dart landed in the board.

'He's only done it,' said Ted.

The scorer called out to confirm the result: 'Double Twenty! Hawks win!'

The Hawks team quickly gathered around to congratulate their young hero, slapping him on the back before he was handed a drink. Jeff nodded towards the player as he asked: 'Who's that then – William Tell?'

Ted leaned on the bar and took Jeff's payment: 'Tommy Wicks's grandson.'

'Never,' said Jeff, looking back to finally recognise the young man as the relative of the Marston pit's old foreman. He called out to him. 'Hey! Shane lad.' As the young man looked up, Jeff beckoned him over.

Shane Wicks came across and held out his hand. 'Mr Sheild. Long time – no see.'

Jeff shook the young man's hand, noting its strength and registering Shane's well-built frame.

'I hardly recognised you. What've they been feeding you?'

'Army rations,' said Shane. 'I signed up nearly a year ago.'

Jeff shook his head slowly as he made a realisation. 'Of course you did. I remember now… your grandad told me before he passed away. He were right proud of you—' He suddenly broke off, snapping his fingers as he remembered: 'Welsh Guards, right?'

Shane nodded proudly. 'That's right.'

'Our Lisa's just back from Tenerife. Getting wed to a fella who used to be in the Royal Welsh.'

'No way.'

'I left him not half hour ago. Big fella. Bruce Carter?'

Shane shook his head. 'I wouldn't know him. Probably before my time.'

'Aye,' said Jeff. 'Well… we'll have to get the pair of you together soon. What d'you say?'

Shane shrugged and gave a smile. 'I'd be up for that.' A call went up from the darts team for Shane to rejoin them.

'Go on,' said Jeff. 'I don't want to keep you.'

Shane started to move off then turned back to Jeff to add: 'I hope the wedding goes okay.'

'So do I, son,' said Jeff. Lifting his pint, he repeated once more, this time to himself: 'So do I.'

CHAPTER ELEVEN

Jeff raised a hipflask to his lips and noticed his hand was trembling.

He knew he shouldn't drink so much but alcohol had become the crutch that enabled him to move forward from one day to the next – the friend that could be relied upon whether congratulations or commiserations were in order. Some of the former miners used pills prescribed from the local GP – an SSRI called Sirtraline – dubbed locally as Certitude – in order to try and accept futures devoid of any certainty other than the fact that they were framed by redundancy.

The drug seemed to help take the edge off that truth, keeping other members of the local community on an even keel – so while escaping the depths of depression they seemed also deprived of the heights of euphoria.

It was something Jeff had witnessed at the social club during the odd football match when a few would be observing, rather than experiencing the excitement of a game half-won. Jeff preferred to self-medicate with alcohol, as and when required, and bear the brunt of Maggie's censure. Now, staring at his trembling hands, he wished he had something else to steady his nerves.

It had been years since he had felt such anxiety, not since the morning he had found himself pacing in a doctor's waiting room, waiting for a diagnosis – not for himself but for Natalie. In his heart, he had known what the consultant was going to say.

After the first few sentences he had tuned out and stopped listening, having heard all he needed or wanted to hear. Trying to escape from the grim prognosis, he had left it instead to Maggie to respond for them both, pragmatic as ever, asking questions about care and timescales.

Jeff had sat beside her; a deaf mute, watching lips mouth responses until he had glanced down to see his hands trembling – just as they were now. The sudden noise of a car pulling up outside the house severed the link with the past.

Brought back to the present, Jeff quickly pocketed his hipflask and headed across to the window to see an ivory Austin Princess parking up on the cobbled driveway, its bonnet decorated with white ribbon. The tight collar of a starched white shirt suddenly felt suffocating. Jeff ran a finger under it and loosened his silk tie before heading to the door to shout up the stairs.

'Car's here!'

A moment later, Maggie appeared at the top of the stairs, dressed in a cream trouser suit from Jessop's.

'We should be going,' Jeff told her, nodding his head towards the front door as he tapped his watch. Remaining calm, Maggie replied only: 'We'll go when we're ready.'

With that, Maggie stepped back into her daughter's old bedroom to find her Lisa looking down uncertainly at the wedding dress she wore, her fingers poised nervously above its low neckline as she asked: 'Are you... sure I look okay?'

Maggie nodded. 'You look more than that. You're—' She broke off as she suddenly remembered something. 'Pearls!' she cried. 'You haven't got 'em on.'

Lisa shook her head. 'I don't want them,' she said starkly. 'I'm wearing this.'

Taking something from the dressing table, Lisa held up the present Maggie had given her on her return from Tenerife. The silver locket was open, revealing two photos; Jeff and Maggie on one side. Natalie on the other.

'Always a family,' said Lisa, almost questioningly.

Maggie nodded in response. 'Always.'

A moment passed before Maggie took the locket from Lisa and placed it carefully around her daughter's neck before securing its clasp. Then she leaned closer and planted a kiss on her temple, closing her eyes for a moment as she tried to summon the sweet smell of her child, almost lost beneath the overwhelming citrus notes of a designer perfume. Opening her eyes, she smiled at their reflection in the dressing room mirror. 'Always a family,' she whispered.

Half an hour later, the gentle strains of Fauré sailed on the air as Maggie climbed the staircase of Marston Register Office together with Lisa and Jeff.

'That music's our signal,' said Jeff, primed for action, about to surge forward when Maggie laid a hand firmly on his arm.

'Hold on,' she ordered. 'It's a wedding not a ruddy battle,' she turned to Lisa. 'Take your time, love, they can't start without you.'

Moving on, they finally entered the ceremony room where Maggie took a seat as Jeff escorted Lisa on towards Bruce, who was seated in the front row, facing the registrar – an efficient looking woman with cropped red hair who signaled Lisa's arrival to him with a sharp nod. Bruce rose to his feet, smiling at Lisa as he held her look while Jeff took his place beside Maggie.

'Welcome,' said the registrar. 'As you all know, we're gathered here today for the wedding of Lisa and Bruce…'

All eyes were trained upon the couple but as the registrar continued. Maggie allowed herself to glance around the room, counting fewer than twenty guests. They included Dee, Patsy and Sandra, some fidgety kids with their young parents and a few older couples.

The scene was far removed from how she had always imagined her daughters' weddings might be. Throughout the years, she had dreamed only of impressive church ceremonies and receptions that would attest to her love, but now she realised there had been other emotions at play.

Apart from a desire to make up for her own Spartan wedding, Maggie now knew she had needed to invest in one daughter's future in order to compensate for the loss of another. In the next instant, as though aware of Maggie's train of thought, Jeff's hand moved closer to her, his fingers searching for hers, providing comfort or perhaps seeking it. She turned to him and raised a smile then looked back again at Lisa who was staring up into Bruce's eyes as though there was no-one else in the room.

The registrar went on. '…So if you repeat after me: I do solemnly declare.'

Jeff's eyes remained trained on Lisa as she made her wedding vows but Maggie eyes still scanned the room – acutely aware that something was wrong.

An hour later, after photographs had been taken and confetti thrown, Maggie found herself staring up at a banner strung across the function room of Marston's Social Club. It spelled out the message: '*CONGRATULATIONS LISA AND BRUCE*'. Bella the dog, wearing a silver bow around her collar, jumped up and down in an effort to steal wedding cake from the hands of young children, while a sudden burst of laughter went up from the bar where Dee, Patsy and Sandra were having their glasses filled by Ted the barman in order to toast Lisa.

'Cheers!' said Dee before the women sipped their champagne. 'It was a smashing ceremony, Lise.'

'Yeah,' said Patsy, 'not a dry seat in the house,' she giggled as Sandra leaned in closer to confide: 'Having clapped eyes on your Bruce I can see why you've blown us out for the States,' she winked. 'Better things to do?'

Lisa returned her smile. 'You'll have a great trip.'

'But it won't be the same without you,' said Patsy. 'End of an era,' she sighed and drained her champagne flute.

Dee held Lisa's look. 'Start of a new one for you though.'

'Aye,' said Lisa.

As Sandra and Patsy moved off to the buffet, Dee watched them go then moved closer to Lisa to broach something. 'So, it all went okay in the end – with your mum?'

'So far.' Lisa looked across the room to where her mother was still chatting to a group of women.

Dee picked up on her tone. 'What's that supposed to mean?'

'It means,' said Lisa, 'she still doesn't know – about what I told you?' Dee read her look. Lisa whispered. 'So, you won't say anything?'

'Course not,' said Dee softly. 'I told you, your secret's safe with me, but… you and Bruce are married now so it's a done deal. All in the past?' She offered a reassuring smile and Lisa returned it – relieved. 'Yeah. Yeah, you're right.'

'Then be happy, Lise,' she moved closer and kissed her friend before joining Patsy and Sandra at the buffet. Lisa glanced around to see Bruce standing at the end of the bar, staring across at her. She moved quickly to him and explained. 'Just been talking to the girls.'

'I saw you. Old school friends, right?' Lisa nodded and Bruce observed her as she continued to watch the girls tucking in to the buffet. 'Guess we all have to move on,' he added.

Lisa looked back at him but he smiled and threw a glance towards the dance floor. 'Have you seen your Dad?' He indicated Jeff, a drink in one hand and a cigar in the other.

'Oh God,' said Lisa. 'Mum'll kill him if she catches him smoking—'

'Don't worry,' said Bruce. 'If he can't enjoy himself on your wedding day—'

'You don't understand,' said Lisa, concerned. 'I need to keep an eye on him.'

Bruce leaned back on the bar. 'You're beginning to sound like your mum. He's not a child.' Bruce sipped his drink but Lisa remained silent, staring away as if to escape scrutiny. 'What is it?' asked Bruce.

Lisa took a deep breath. 'Dad doesn't like people knowing and he wouldn't want anyone thinking he's an invalid either but…' she trailed off.

'But what?' asked Bruce. 'If you're talking about his heart attack, he told me all about it, but that's not the end of the world these days—'

'It's more than that,' said Lisa breaking in. 'Dad's got a heart condition. It's the reason he had to give up his allotment. He should be taking things easy, watching what he eats – *and* drinks. It's the reason Mum nags him. She has to.'

Bruce glanced back at Jeff on the dance floor then at Maggie still talking to the same group of women beyond the bar.

'Then he should know better,' said Bruce. 'He needs to take more care of himself.'

'I know,' said Lisa, impatient, 'and I don't know why he doesn't. It's like he's… playing Russian Roulette – waiting for the bullet to come around?' She went on. 'He's on medication. And the doctor said he's doing okay – as *long* as he behaves himself.'

Bruce turned back to her and she read the look on his face. 'I know what you're thinking, but it's not what Natalie had. That was something called cardiomyopathy. It can run in families, but… I haven't got it. I had tests done and I'm okay,' she held his gaze and managed a smile.

Bruce pulled her close. 'Thank God for that.' he whispered, holding her tightly in his arms. As they broke apart, he leaned in to kiss her but before he could say another word a voice shattered the moment.

'Great party!' A sharp-suited young man now stood before them.

Lisa instantly recognised him. 'Kevin…'

'Didn't mean to gatecrash,' he began, 'but I had to come and wish you all the best, didn't I?' Reaching into his breast pocket

Kevin pulled out a business card and offered it to Bruce. 'If you ever need a stretch limo, mate, just call that number. I could've given you a special rate for today if I'd had some notice. Lisa'll tell you – no rubbish.' He grinned proudly while Bruce looked to Lisa for an explanation.

'Kev is Sandra's cousin. We've known each other for ages.'

Before Bruce could respond, Kevin turned quickly to Lisa. 'Up for a dance?'

On the spot, Lisa looked back at Bruce. 'Well I…'

'Go on,' said Bruce smoothly. 'You heard what Kevin said; he's come down specially.'

The young man winked at Bruce. 'That's right,' he said. Tipping a thumb in Bruce's direction, he now went on to Lisa. 'You should listen to your man here. He talks sense.' With that, he plucked the glass from Lisa's hand and dumped it on Bruce before grabbing Lisa's arm and moving off with her to the dance floor.

Bruce stared after them, then set Lisa's glass on the bar and caught sight of Jeff approaching, panting for breath. 'You all right there, Jeff?'

Allowing himself a moment to recover, Jeff finally replied: 'Surviving.' He offered a mischievous smile and leaned in close to Bruce as he confided: 'Actually I feel bloody marvelous, but that'll be the brandy. Or rather… cognac.' Looking around for signs of Maggie, he produced the hip flask from his inside jacket pocket and offered it to Bruce – who refused it. 'Not for me, thanks, Jeff. 'Got a flight to catch tonight, remember?'

'Course you have. Honeymoon in Madeira? Me and Mags had a week in Skegness. Still,' he went on, 'at least I finally got you here – to the club, I mean.' He took a furtive sip from his flask, slapped Bruce on the shoulder and surveyed the function room. 'I know it's not grand but the bar's subsidised and there's a lot to be said for a cheap pint.' He slipped his flask back into his pocket while Bruce's gaze returned to Lisa dancing with Kevin. Jeff went on: 'Shame you didn't make it down here with me last time.'

'Sorry?' asked Bruce, watching Kevin leaning in to whisper something to Lisa.

'I ran into Shane,' said Jeff. 'That's Tommy Wicks's grandson. Wizard at the ol' darts.' Jeff mimed a throw but Bruce failed to see it as he continued to observe Lisa, laughing, as she danced with Kevin.

'I'd forgotten all about it till that night,' said Jeff. 'But Shane's the one that's in the Royal Welsh.'

Bruce's eyes flickered. Looking away from the dance floor he now gave Jeff his full attention.

'The Guards.' Jeff went on. 'Same regiment as you. I said how we should all get together for a pint. Nice idea, right?'

Bruce raised a smile but his tone was hesitant. 'Well I—'

'Of course, it's too ruddy late now,' said Jeff breaking in as he explained: 'I just heard he's been sent overseas. NATO exercise. Not sure when he'll be back.'

Bruce took a moment to absorb this. 'Shame.' he said finally.

'Yeah,' Jeff agreed, 'sorry about that, son.' He sighed wistfully and a moment passed before the music came to an end. The DJ waved to Bruce – and gave a nod.

'Would you excuse me, Jeff?' Setting down his glass, Bruce moved off quickly while Maggie, at a distance, stared beyond the group of women she had been talking to, to see Bruce approaching Lisa. She quickly joined Jeff at the bar but before she could speak, her words were drowned out by the DJ's loud announcement as he introduced a special request for a very special couple. The opening bars of a familiar song began to play and Jeff turned to Maggie. 'Hear that?' he said. 'That's *Love Me Tender*. Our Lisa must've asked for it special. It's what we danced to at our wedding.'

Maggie stared away to the dance floor – to Lisa and Bruce – as the club lighting dimmed and a single spotlight followed the pair in a close dance. She swallowed hard. Jeff took her hand in his. 'Now don't get upset, love. It's a happy occasion.' He gave her a wink and began singing along, slightly out of tune, before glancing back at Bruce and Lisa slow-dancing together – their eyes fixed on one another as though every other guest had dissolved into the background. Maggie noted the reactions of the guests as they remained focused on the couple – Bruce's hands on Lisa's trim waist as he pulled her closer. For a moment, Maggie was sure she saw him glance across to Maggie herself, a tight smile playing on his lips, before he leaned ever closer to his bride and kissed her. Applause rang out followed by whistles of appreciation from the guests. Jeff continued singing but after a moment, he turned again to his wife – only to see that Maggie was no longer there. Looking around, he caught sight of her heading out of the room.

Jeff followed after Maggie to find her hurrying along the corridor in the direction of the club's kitchen. He called out loudly and she looked back only to register the bemused look on his face before she moved on and entered the kitchen. Moments later, Jeff did the same, confused to see his wife standing by the sink, staring unfocused at the window before her. 'What're you doing here?' he asked.

'Nothing,' said Maggie, 'I just needed a minute to myself.'

Jeff closed the door after himself and moved to her. ''You... not feeling well?' Glancing back at him, she failed to reply. Puzzled by her silence, Jeff asked: 'Well, what is it?' He pointed back towards the door as music from the function room echoed in the empty kitchen. 'They're doing the wedding dance. Don't you want to—?'

'No,' said Maggie firmly. 'I *don't* want to watch. I've seen enough for today,' she looked away again. Jeff shook his head, confounded by her mood. 'I... don't understand.'

'Don't you?' Maggie said challengingly. 'Think,' she went on. 'What is it you just saw in there?'

Jeff shrugged. 'Same as you,' he said simply. 'Our Lisa. In love. Just wed. What else am I meant to see?'

Maggie paused as though working something out for herself. 'Nothing,' she said dully. 'No-one. Just like in that register office this morning.'

Jeff heaved a long sigh, wishing he could reach for the flask of cognac in his pocket.

Maggie explained. 'There's not a soul here for him,' she said. 'On his wedding day? No family. But no friends either – even from the Army,' she paused, then: 'Don't you see?'

'See what?' asked Jeff, increasingly confused.

'He's got no-one. *No-one* in the world but our Lisa,' she stared at Jeff. 'Why?'

Uncomfortable beneath her searching look, Jeff shrugged once more. 'I... don't know. But what does it matter as long as our Lisa loves him?'

'Is that really all you care about?'

'Aye,' said Jeff, cognac still coursing through his veins. 'She's our daughter. And that lad might not be *your* choice – and maybe he's not mine – but he's our Lisa's and if you don't get used to that—' He suddenly stopped himself, fearful of saying too much.

Maggie turned back to him. 'Well?'

Jeff saw the fire in her eyes but took a deep breath before he explained. 'It's her life, Maggie. Not yours. And if you can't learn to accept that and start getting used to Bruce – you'll go the right way about losing her.'

Seeing Maggie recoil from this, Jeff felt instantly conflicted; part of him wanting to comfort her while the greater part of him needed to explain his own truth. Having tried to do so, he now gave up and walked to the door where he looked back once before leaving. As he did so, Maggie heard the music from the function room coming to an end – to be replaced by loud applause and whistles.

A dripping tap drew Maggie's attention back to the sink. Wedding flowers lay on the draining board, alongside abandoned wrapping paper decorated with a mass of tiny silver hearts. Instinctively, she began to tidy it all away. A gift tag dropped into the sink. Tap water began to drip slowly onto a handwritten message:

To Lisa and Bruce. Wishing you the very best for a happy future.

Maggie's eyes fixed on these words, watching as they slowly began to disappear, ink dissolving in the water, spiraling down the drain.

CHAPTER TWELVE

A few hours later, Maggie found herself staring down at a brief text message.

Flight on time. See you in a couple of weeks.
Love you! Lisa and Bruce xx

She focused on her daughter's name but once more it was coupled with another. Lisa and Bruce. Man and wife. A digital clock clicked forward to show the time as 1.32 a.m., reminding Maggie that she was, in fact, in Lisa's old bedroom and meant to be tidying away clothes. Jeff entered, still tipsy but with a dull ache in his head which he knew would only get worse.

He observed his wife as she busied herself, efficiently stuffing Lisa's wedding dress into a zipped bag on a hanger – then he hiccupped. Maggie continued fastening the bag. Uncomfortable, Jeff whispered: 'Look, why don't you leave all this?'

Maggie responded briskly. 'Best done sooner than later.'

'But she'll be none the wiser,' said Jeff. 'They're thousands of feet up in the air and not back for a fortnight.'

Maggie's fingers tightened on the dress clutched in her hand.

'Mags?'

Reacting to his concerned tone, Maggie glanced from the dress to Lisa's satin shoes, stacked neatly in a yin and yang position in a box on the bed.

'I did the same for our Natalie…' she said softly, almost to herself: 'Every last thing of hers… all packed away.'

Jeff came forward and gently laid his hand on hers. 'It's not the same, love.' He tried to ease her grip on the dress. 'Lisa's coming back. So you're worrying about nothing.' He managed to take the dress from her and hung it on the wardrobe door. Empty-handed now, Maggie looked at him – lost.

'Am I?' she asked.

'Aye,' said Jeff firmly. 'Lisa's got her head screwed on. She knows what she's doing. I told you that from the start…'

'He's a nice enough fella,' said Maggie. 'That's what you said.'

'Aye,' said Jeff, confirmed. 'And I meant it.' He held out his arms to her and Maggie took a step towards him. Framed by moonlight streaming in through the window, he held her tightly as he whispered: 'I promise you, you're worrying about nothing.'

A little over an hour later, Lisa set down her bag and did a 360-degree turn, taking in every feature of an elegant hotel room.

'Oh… will you look at this?' She gestured as she went on: 'Sheets turned down, flowers everywhere. They've even sent up champagne.' As she plucked the bottle from its bucket, iced water dripped on to the pretty pink shift dress she wore – but her tipsy smile showed she didn't care. 'And it's not just cheap bubbles either,' she added, noting the label. Peeling off the wire *muselet* from the cork, she prepared to open the bottle.

Bruce stepped forward. 'Here, give it to me.' He reached out to take it but Lisa was insistent.

'I can do it,' she smiled. 'I've had plenty of practice.' With a flourish, she opened the bottle – perfectly – then noted Bruce's cold look. 'What's wrong?' she asked. 'You got a mood on or something? You hardly said a word on the flight.'

He watched her pouring two flutes of champagne. 'I don't want any.'

Lisa shrugged. 'Why not? I've opened it now and it's on the house,' she offered him a glass. Bruce eyed it, and the bottle in her hand, as though he was staring straight through them both. He spoke softly. 'Don't you think you've had enough?'

Lisa gave a small choking sound. "Enough'? Excuse me, but if you've forgotten, it's our wedding day—'

'Yeah,' said Bruce. 'Not a night out with the girls.' He turned away from her and loosened the collar of his shirt. Lisa noted the way he tugged at it in irritation.

'And what's that supposed to mean?'

He turned back to her with a challenging look. Despite feeling pressured she managed a defensive shrug and sipped her champagne before she considered the glass in her hand. 'All right,' she conceded. 'So maybe I have had a few. And maybe my girls are a bit full on sometimes, but there's no harm in them. They're off to America soon and I won't see them for weeks. They just like a laugh, that's all.'

'So was it them who chose your dress?'

Lisa looked back at him. 'My wedding dress?'

He gave a nod.

She frowned. 'I… thought you liked it?'

He looked away and she took a step towards him. '*Everyone* liked it.'

'Yeah,' Bruce agreed. 'Especially that guy on the dance floor.'

As he looked back at her, Lisa scoffed. 'You… don't mean Kevin? Oh come on, you can't think—' She broke off before explaining: 'I've known Kev half my life,' she gave a relieved smile, realising she felt flattered by Bruce's jealousy.

She took another step towards him. 'As for my dress sense… if you really don't like it, then…' She took another sip of champagne then set her glass down and reached behind her back for the zip of her dress. Pulling on it she allowed the straps of her dress to fall from her shoulders.

As Bruce turned slowly to face her, his gaze shifted to her slender body, pert breasts and skin still tanned against the white lace of her skimpy panties. Snaking her arms around his neck, she pressed her body against his as she craned her pretty face to kiss him. As their lips met she made a soft moaning sound, anticipating his body, until, in the next instant she felt his strong hands on her forearm before he suddenly wrenched her away from him. 'I need some air.' Turning smartly from her, he headed for the door.

'Bruce? Where are you—'

The door slammed behind him, silencing her. Stunned, Lisa hesitated for a moment, about to go after him when she was halted by the sight of her half-naked reflection in the mirror. She looked small, diminished, abandoned. She curled her arms around her body, half for comfort – but the greater part of her in shame.

*

The air was refreshingly cool as Bruce took the marble staircase. He moved quickly in case Lisa dared to come after him, but she failed to follow. Once he was out of the empty hotel foyer, he took a few deep breaths allowing the sea breeze blowing in across the marina to calm him.

The scene straight ahead looked just like a postcard: yachts bobbing in the distance, navigation lights shining in the reflection of oil-dark water... He felt the vibration of a call coming in on his phone. Taking it from his pocket he saw it was from Lisa and allowed it to ring a little longer before it went to voicemail.

He paused, then held the phone up to his face, viewing the port from the phone's camera lens before pressing the video button. As soon he began filming, he began to feel calmer as though he was creating some manageable distance from reality. He always felt more in control as a spectator than a participant and now he lost himself in the scene before him. Restaurants lined the marina but at this late hour the waiters were beginning to clear tables. Music was still playing at a gaudy bar where some younger people were milling outside.

He took stock, then decided to stop filming and moved on towards them. Finding a seat at a quayside table, he picked up a menu and considered the name – Tiki Bar. There was nothing Hawaiian about the place, apart from the tacky cocktails on offer served in coconut shells. His attention was drawn to English voices at the bar.

'Oh, come on,' said a girl behind him. 'Let's go back to the hotel and you can have another one there.'

'With the Saga Louts for company?' her friend sneered. 'Maybe you fancy a game of dominoes as well?'

Bruce took his phone from his jacket pocket and held it up again, this time to observe through its lens the two girls behind him, perched on stools at the bar.

'But they'll all be in bed by now,' said a tall brunette.

'I prefer it here,' said a feisty blonde.

'Fine,' said her friend. 'Then stay. But I'm going back,' she slid from her stool as her companion protested. 'Nicky?'

The girl looked back at her. 'I mean it, Cheryl. I'm going.'

'Go on, then,' said Cheryl, sulkily. 'See if I care,' she offered an insolent look and sipped her drink. A moment later, her friend grabbed her bag and headed off, passing close to Bruce's table. He stared after her then saw a waiter had appeared, standing ready to take his order.

'A beer,' Bruce said sparely.

The waiter nodded and as he wiped down the table to set a coaster on it, Bruce glanced across his shoulder to note the blonde, sitting alone, looking lost for a moment until he caught her gaze. He offered a smile. The waiter began to walk off but Bruce caught him in time.

'Make that two.'

The waiter nodded and headed to the bar. Cheryl returned Bruce's smile.

Some time later in a dark room, the warm night air lifted voile curtains at a window. Moonlight streamed across a rumpled bed. Bruce's strong hand stroked the sinuous lines of a young woman's thigh. She turned quickly, reacting to his touch, her breaths coming fast, not from passion but a desperate need for consolation. Lisa's tear-stained face looked up at him as she went to speak but he pressed a finger to her lips. Another moment passed before he finally said what he knew she was desperate to hear.

'It's okay, little girl.' he said softly. 'I'm here now.'

The words were like honey to a wound. Lisa closed her eyes, allowing him to move gently on top of her. She clung tightly to him.

'What do you want to say?' he asked softly, kissing her neck until his fingers replaced his lips at her throat. He paused before turning her head towards him, his grip tightening around her neck, just the way he knew she liked it.

'Well?'

'I've… been a bad girl.'

'And what do bad girls do?'

Lisa's breaths came sharper now as she waited for his grip to tighten further.

'They… say sorry.'

Bruce's face moved closer to hers as he whispered. 'They say what?'

Lisa took a moment to find her breath. He moved a hand to her breast, his fingers tightly squeezing her nipple.

'Sorry,' she repeated.

Bruce waited for her eyes to lock with his own before he told her: 'I can't hear you.'

She could feel his strength – the pressure of his other hand against her throat, the tight pain in her nipple, his weight bearing down on her – but the real pressure was her own need to give in to him – to surrender. At this moment in time, it would be all too easy but if she could only hold out for a few more moments the relief would be all the greater – it would transform into pleasure – the kind of pleasure he had introduced her to.

'Well?'

The breeze blew wide the voile curtain and Lisa let out a gasp. 'Sorry…' She waited for the rush of relief but his hand was still at her throat. Surely he could see that her eyes were now shining with a new fear. This wasn't part of the game. They had never played it this way. Something had shifted. His face moved closer as he whispered: 'I didn't hear you.'

She was struggling to breathe, hands clawing at his – her manicured nails digging deep into his flesh. 'I'm… sorry…' Somehow the words escaped – garbled but finally acknowledged. His fingers released their hold on her throat and began to gently caress her cheek. He waited until she had finally caught her breath, until her neck craned up towards him again, her mouth open waiting for his lips to finally cover hers. He knew she had learned her lesson.

CHAPTER THIRTEEN

The postcard photo in Maggie's hand showed a pretty marina with holidaymakers seated at harbour bars.

'Spain?'

At Rona's question, Maggie shook her head. 'Funchal,' she said. 'Capital of Madeira. An island in the Atlantic. Warm winters,' she paused and gave a sigh. 'I've always wanted to go there,' she turned the card and pointed to the stamps on the back. 'Must've put the 'snail' in snail mail because it's taken almost a fortnight to get here. They're due back tonight but this is the first I've heard since the wedding. No calls. No FaceTime. Just this,' she showed the short message to Rona:-

Having a wonderful time. You'd love it here.
All our love,
Lisa and Bruce xx

There again – two names instead of one. Maggie glanced at the old photograph of Lisa sitting at the poolside bar in Tenerife and leaned forward, using the same pin to affix the new postcard to her wall. Rona watched her and commented: 'She's on her honeymoon.'

Looking back, Maggie saw Rona's knowing smile. 'Aye, she's got better things to do?' She gave a nod. 'You're right.' Then she eyed the collection of cards on her noticeboard and spoke softly, almost to herself. 'She's someone's wife now.'

'But whatever she does,' said Rona, 'and wherever she goes, she'll always be your daughter.'

'True,' Maggie looked back at her, 'and in the words of the old fridge magnet: 'a daughter's a little girl who grows up to be your best friend." Reassured by this, she left a pause and considered the young woman beside her. 'You got family?'

Rona's smile began to falter. 'Sorry,' said Maggie quickly. 'I should mind my own business.'

'I have a daughter too,' said Rona quickly. 'Yara. It means… little butterfly.'

'In Kurdish?'

'Arabic. My language is Kurmanji.'

Maggie considered this, then: 'How old is she?'

'Nearly three. She lives with my mother until…' She trailed off.

'Until?'

'Until we can be together again.'

Maggie watched the young woman's gaze drift back to the postcards pinned to the wall, then she asked tentatively: 'And… what about her Dad?'

Rona looked troubled and lowered her gaze.

'There I go again,' said Maggie. 'Just ignore me. I'm too ruddy nosy for my own good. You don't have to tell me anything you don't want to, all right? Besides,' she added, 'that's not the reason I wanted to talk to you,' she moved to the window facing the factory floor. 'I... just need to know,' she went on, 'how things are – down there?'

For a moment, Rona said nothing then gave a quick nod of her head. 'Okay,' she said finally, with a tight smile that failed to conceal her anxiety. It was a look that took Maggie back to another time, when Natalie had moved up to the local grammar school.

She had never revealed the bullying, her inability to fit in and her desperate need to escape – not until the day she had left with her excellent grades – the scholastic success that Maggie had enjoyed by proxy. Perhaps, thought Maggie now, having her own eyes set on an academic prize for her daughter had blinded her to what Natalie had been going through. If only she had seen beyond her daughter's stoic façade – but it was too late to make amends. Or was it?

'Are you sure everything's okay?' she asked Rona.

Her new worker gave a quick nod. Maggie sat down and stared again at Lisa's postcard.

'Little butterfly... Shame we haven't got a name for that in English,' she paused, then admitted: 'I'm... ashamed to say I haven't got a clue where you come from. Kurdistan, is it?'

Rona shook her head. 'Kurdistan is a dream,' she explained, 'for all Kurds. We no longer have a homeland. We are...' she searched for a word. 'Scattered. Iraq, Iran, Turkey...' She frowned. 'I'm from Syria but half of our people have already fled from there.'

Maggie gave a nod, remembering that she had gleaned very little from television news bulletins. A civil war. Another violent conflict to add to all the others. Rona lowered her eyes and remained silent. Maggie filled the space, speaking softly. 'One day you and your family will be together again.'

At this, Rona looked away, perhaps, thought Maggie, in an effort to avoid any further intrusive questions, until she noticed Rona's gaze was actually fixed on something lying on Maggie's desk. 'Somewhere... important?' Rona asked.

Maggie picked up a leaflet bearing an image of an historic building on its front. 'It's no stately home, if that's what you mean. The Grand Hotel in Bradford,' she explained, eyeing the image herself before she opened the leaflet and read aloud the first line. "Where Victorian grandeur meets contemporary luxury..." Five star, of course,' she showed the leaflet to Rona and confided: 'Jason... Mr Masters... stays there on business. Sometimes I have to track him down.'

She took the leaflet back and tossed it on to her desk. 'Best get back to work now, or those pyjamas'll never make themselves.'

Rona got up obediently and moved to the door. Maggie watched her then suddenly called out. 'I'll try and get some overtime agreed soon. As soon as Mr Masters comes back from Bradford.'

She gave a wink and Rona nodded. 'Thank you, Maggie,' she replied with a warm smile.

Once Rona had left, Maggie tossed the hotel leaflet on to her desk and stared again at Lisa's postcards, unnerved for a moment as she considered how much had taken place during the period of time between receiving them. It had passed all too quickly for her to take stock – let alone any control. She breathed deeply and consoled herself with one fact – of which Rona had just reminded her: Lisa would always be her daughter – whatever she did and wherever she went – and she would be back very soon. With this in mind, Maggie picked up her phone and dialed the landline number for Lisa and Bruce's new home, Woodside. After a few rings she left a voicemail message. 'It's only me,' she began. 'I know you're not back yet but I just wanted to say…' She smiled to herself. 'Welcome home.'

That evening, Bruce entered the living room of his new home and tossed a handful of flyers and junk mail on to a coffee table before hitting the play button on the answering machine. Maggie's voice instantly greeted him.

'It's only me, and I know you're not back yet, but I just wanted to say… welcome home. If your flight happens to get in on time, give us a call. I'll cook supper for you if you've nothing in.'

The message clicked off and Bruce turned to Lisa behind him in the hall. She quickly set down some bags and slipped out of her coat before stepping forward. 'I'll call her,' she said, making a move towards the phone, but Bruce was quicker and picked up the receiver. 'I'll do it,' he said firmly. 'Why don't you go and make some coffee?'

Lisa's eyes met his. Without another word, she gave a nod and left the room.

Maggie and Jeff were watching the television news when the phone rang. Checking the caller ID on the handset, Maggie waved a hand in Jeff's direction and mouthed: 'Turn that thing down.'

Jeff quickly complied and Maggie smiled expectantly as she answered the call.

'Welcome home, love. How was it?'

Bruce's voice sounded unexpectedly on the line. 'Couldn't have been better.'

Jeff saw Maggie's smile fade as she replied. 'Sorry, I... thought you were—'

'She's not feeling too well, Maggie.'

'What?'

'Lisa. But it's nothing to worry about. Upset stomach. Holiday bug.'

Maggie shot a look to Jeff as she continued to Bruce on the phone: 'She never gets 'bugs'. Our Lisa's got a stomach like a Sherman tank.'

At this, Jeff looked across, whispering. 'What is it?'

Maggie said nothing, waiting for Bruce's reply.

'First time for everything,' said Bruce smoothly.

'Let me talk to her,' said Maggie.

'Too late,' said Bruce. 'She's taken herself off to bed. And I know it's only early but... it's been a long day – for both of us,' he added.

Maggie made a decision. 'All right,' she said. 'But if she's no better in the morning, I'll come over with whatever she needs.'

'That's good of you, Maggie,' said Bruce. 'But I think she's got everything she needs.'

A click sounded on the line. Maggie glanced across at Jeff who asked: ''She all right?'

'Tummy bug.'

Jeff frowned at this and finally offered an opinion. ''Sounds like an excuse to me.' Maggie looked up sharply but saw Jeff leaning back in his Lazy Boy as he went on: 'They probably just want a bit more time to themselves.' He reached for the TV remote and brought up the sound on the evening news, while Maggie stared back at the phone.

*

At Woodside, Bruce looked away from the phone to see Lisa standing in the doorframe, a mug of coffee in her hand.

'Well?' she asked tentatively.

'It's okay,' he said gently. 'I explained. Told her you've not been well.'

Lisa bit her lip. 'I could've told her that myself?'

'And if you had, she'd only have started fussing... asking questions. You know what your mum's like.' He paused. 'She was fine.'

'Sure?'

Bruce smiled. 'Sure I'm sure.' He took the mug from her and set it down on the coffee table before turning back to her. He reached out, his hands gently framing her face. 'Why don't you go upstairs, have a nice bath and relax.' He paused. 'You'll feel better now we're home.'

'And... what about you?'

'I need to check on a few things in my office,' he said finally. 'I've been expecting some important e-mails. From clients.'

Lisa frowned. 'Can't you do that on your phone?'

'I need my files. They're all in the basement.' His look was unambiguous but Lisa was still standing there – even though he had asked her to leave. He picked up his coffee with one hand and steered her into the hallway with the other. She turned to him sharply. 'Are you... sure Mum was okay?'

'Good as gold.' He gave a stiff smile and glanced up towards the landing. Lisa hesitated then made a move to one of the bags in the hall and took something from it. She handed a gift to Bruce. 'What's this?'

'For you. I got it in Funchal. A present for your office.'

Bruce unwrapped tissue paper from the object to find a glass ball nestled in the palm of his hand – a blue wave trapped in time within it as it crashed against the interior. 'It's a paperweight,' Lisa explained, 'the man in the shop said they were all hand blown so no two pieces are the same.' She looked up at him, expectant.

'Thanks,' said Bruce, offering only another smile before he looked up again towards the landing. 'Go on now.'

His smile remained fixed as he watched her making her way slowly upstairs. On reaching the top, she turned to look down at him but he nodded again – his cue for her to move on. After she did so, he waited until he heard the sound of water running into the bath before he turned to face the basement door. Eyeing the security keypad he had installed, he quickly tapped a short code into it. The basement door opened and he stepped inside, glad of having some space to himself – at last.

CHAPTER FOURTEEN

At 5 p.m. the following afternoon, the factory bell was sounding as Maggie's workers left Masters & Son for the day. Getting into her coat, she hurried down the metal staircase to the factory floor where she noticed Rona at her locker.

From a distance, Maggie continued to observe her, noting that her new worker was actually a striking young woman. Her long blonde hair was clearly dyed, an inch of dark growth having grown at its roots, but as Rona shook it loose so that it fell beyond her shoulders, Maggie was suddenly struck by a memory from long ago – an image of two young girls, sitting by a sunny window plaiting their hair before school.

Maggie continued to watch her new worker as she took off her shapeless work coat. Rona had a good figure and if she chose to plaster her face with make up as most of the other factory girls did, she would probably match a celebrity for glamour.

Perhaps, Maggie now considered, Rona's beauty was yet another thing that set her apart from her fellow workers

– something else that jarred with young Naila Akhtar. No other incidents had occurred since Rona had been wrongly blamed for the theft of Tracey's ring, and Maggie liked to think that perhaps Naila had learned from her mistake. With that in mind, she sidled up to Rona as she fussed with something in her locker. 'What're you up to?'

Rona nodded to her locker. 'Tidying up,' she smiled. 'I like things tidy.'

'So do I,' said Maggie, remaining close. Rona tried to read her boss's mood. 'Something wrong?'

Maggie shook her head. 'No, I—' She broke off as she caught sight of something pinned to the inside of the locker door – a photo – two figures set against a rural backdrop; a dark-haired little girl in an older woman's arms. Rona read the question in her boss's eyes and answered it. 'Yara.'

'With your mum?'

Rona nodded.

Maggie studied the photo, noting the setting: orchard trees laden with fruit, small oranges or perhaps tangerines... She gave a small shrug as she admitted: 'I don't even know where Syria is.'

'Far away.'

'From your family... your friends.'

Rona glanced quickly away from the photo. 'My people have few friends.'

'Kurdish people, you mean?'

Rona gave a sharp nod. 'There's an old Kurdish saying, 'No friends but the mountains'. Every country uses us... feeds us to the wolves. America, Syria, Iran, Turkey—' She broke off suddenly, as though scared of having said too much.

Maggie remained silent and looked again at the photo – a smiling child in a grandmother's arms. 'And the mountains are far away,' she said, before turning back to Rona. She spoke softly. 'You have a friend in me.'

A moment passed before Rona gave a quick smile. Reaching to take out her anorak, she closed the locker door, her hand remaining on it, exposing a small tattoo on her wrist – a tiny butterfly. Aware that Maggie had noted this, she quickly turned the key in the lock and slipped into her anorak as she asked: 'And Lisa. How is she now? Happy to be home?'

Maggie shook her head. 'I'm not sure,' she said. 'I've not seen her yet. She's not been well. I left a couple of messages for her today but her phone's been off.'

A moment passed between the two women. Rona noted Maggie's concern. 'Then… maybe a visit from you will make her feel better?'

Maggie looked back and connected with Rona's smile.

Outside the factory gates at the same time, a bus began to move off from the nearby stop leaving someone in its wake. Naila lit a cigarette and was about to slip her lighter in her pocket when she caught sight of two women exiting the factory – Maggie and Rona chatting together like old friends. Naila's face set.

Whatever they were talking about it was clear to Naila that the refugee was playing Maggie like an old fiddle, sucking up to her for work, maybe even for some overtime, though no-one else seemed to have been offered any yet.

Since Tracey's ring had been found, the others were now turning a deaf ear to Naila's warnings that Rona Abdi was as phony as her dyed blonde hair. Naila exhaled a plume of grey smoke into the air, observing coldly as Maggie laid a hand on Rona's arm – a gesture of friendship or perhaps comfort. Judging by the expression on Maggie's face, the refugee was no doubt spinning Maggie a yarn to gain sympathy.

Naila continued to watch from distance until the two women parted company at the factory gates – each heading off in opposite directions; Maggie was taking the canal towpath while the new worker headed on towards town. Drawing deep on the cigarette between her cold fingers, Naila pulled up the hood of her jacket – and began to follow Rona.

Twenty minutes later, Maggie's eyes fixed on the letters etched in glass on the stylish sign outside her daughter's new home – Woodside. The house was in an isolated position on an un-adopted road. Woods backed on to the property and as a breeze stiffened through tall trees, Maggie's hand suddenly hesitated at the doorbell. She wondered whether Lisa might resent her turning up like this out of the blue, then she reconsidered what Rona had told her: *'maybe a visit from you will make her feel better…'*

She rang the doorbell and waited. Silence. Then she rang again, this time more insistently. Nothing. Maggie pulled up her collar and headed to the rear of the house. Trying the back door she found it was locked. Looking up in frustration, she could see no sign of life at the upper windows. About to take her phone from her bag she suddenly stopped on hearing something. A voice was sounding faintly on the other side of the door.

'Who's there?'

Maggie shoved her phone back into her bag and turned back to the door.

'Lisa, love, it's me.'

A long pause followed before Maggie heard the sound of slide bolts being drawn. A key finally turned in a lock and the back door opened gingerly, revealing Lisa's pale face peering around the edge of the door, eyes blinking against the light before she opened the door wider.

'Mum?'

Moments later, Maggie followed Lisa into the kitchen and watched her carefully re-lock the back door. Lisa tried to manage a smile while her hand pulled her dressing gown tightly across her waist.

'You've lost weight,' said Maggie.

'I've… had a tummy bug.'

Maggie pulled her phone from her pocket. 'I'll call the doctor.'

'There's no need,' said Lisa, snatching Maggie's phone from her hand and slipping it back into her mother's coat pocket. 'I'm fine now.'

Maggie saw the dark circles slung beneath her daughter's pale blue eyes. 'You don't look it. In fact, you look terrible—'

'Thanks a lot,' said Lisa, turning away.

'Well, how much weight have you lost?'

Lisa glanced down at the dressing gown. 'Does it matter?' She slumped on to a stool. 'I had some to lose.'

'Says who?'

'Says no-one,' Clearly irritated, Lisa pushed a hand through her uncombed hair and tried to make amends. 'Look… I'm a lot better, I… just don't have much appetite yet.'

'All the same,' said Maggie, 'you have to eat to get your strength back,' she moved smartly to the fridge and opened it.

Lisa moved quickly to close it. 'Will you stop fussing!'

Maggie pointed to the fridge door. 'There's no food in there. Why didn't you tell me? I could've brought something over—'

'I don't need anything,' Lisa insisted, 'Bruce is picking up shopping on his way home. He's meeting a client in Bradford then he'll—'

'Bradford?' echoed Maggie, shocked. 'He's there while you're—'

'I just told you,' argued Lisa, breaking in. 'I'm fine. And if I'd needed anything I would've called, but I don't. I'm just tired, so… if you don't mind, I'd like to go back to bed,' she picked up Maggie's phone and handed it back to her.

Maggie stared at it for a moment then took it. 'All right,' she said, calmly. 'But… can I have a hug first?'

Lisa paused then moved forward, allowing herself to be enveloped in her mother's embrace. Straight after, Maggie pushed back Lisa's hair from her face before giving her a kiss and offering her arm. 'Let me see you upstairs?'

Lisa hesitated then took her mother's arm, but as they stepped into the hallway, Maggie stopped in her tracks as she noted the basement door and its keypad for the alarm system. She pointed to it. 'What's all this?'

'The old cellar,' said Lisa wearily. 'The previous owner converted the basement – everyone's got one these days. Bruce has taken it over for his office. He needs the alarm because he's got important data on his computers. Sophisticated equipment – expensive – so we have to be careful… what with the woods out the back?'

Maggie glanced back towards the kitchen as the branches of tall oaks beyond the window bowed in the wind. She found herself whispering her thoughts. 'Why ever did you move so far out?'

Lisa shrugged and shook her head. 'I don't know,' she admitted. 'If it was down to me I'd rather have stayed in town but—'

'Then move,' said Maggie. 'There's a new place for rent on the High Street…'

Lisa shook her head. 'We'd be breaking the lease.'

'So, break it. Don't put up with anything you don't want.' At this, they shared a quick look – a silent agreement – before Maggie suddenly entreated her. 'Come home with me and I'll take care of you – until you feel properly better?'

Lisa appeared torn. Maggie willed her to agree, and for a moment convinced herself that Lisa was about to do so – when the front door abruptly opened.

Bruce stood at the threshold, shopping bags in his hands. He paused, trying to make sense of what he saw, then finally spoke. 'Hello Maggie.' he said smoothly. He offered a charming smile and closed the door behind him before stepping forward to kiss Lisa – who explained.

'Mum just popped round to see how I was.'

Bruce took this in and nodded. 'That's good of you, Maggie, but I thought I told you; Lisa's been poorly,' he glanced back at her, 'but she'll be right as rain soon, won't you, love?'

Lisa nodded quickly. Bruce indicated the shopping bags. 'I got everything you wanted.' As he moved quickly into the kitchen, Maggie and Lisa followed after him. 'And I also managed to get your locket fixed.' He dumped the shopping bags on to the kitchen counter.

'Your… locket?' asked Maggie. She turned to Lisa. 'What's wrong with it?'

'Nothing,' said Lisa quickly. 'It's just I—'

'She broke the clasp,' said Bruce, speaking over her. 'Bit clumsy, eh, Lise? But it's good as new.' Reaching into his pocket, he produced a jeweller's envelope from which he spilled the locket into his palm. As he held it up, Maggie saw that the two photos inside now showed Lisa and Bruce on one side – and only Bruce on the other. Lisa quickly stepped forward and closed it.

'Here,' said Bruce as he gently lifted her hair to place the silver chain around her neck. Securing the clasp, his palms remained close to her throat as he gave a satisfied look while Lisa remained motionless. Silent. 'That's better.' he said. Looking back at Maggie, he smiled brightly. 'Thanks for coming, Maggie.' He leaned in and kissed her cheek. 'But as you can see,' he held her gaze as he added: 'we're just fine, aren't we, Lise?'

Maggie turned to her daughter for a response but found she was still staring at Bruce. 'Aye,' Lisa said finally. 'We're fine.'

Maggie surveyed the pair, standing close together, offering a united front. Feeling excluded, she turned on her heels and headed smartly for the door when Bruce called to her. 'Oh and Maggie?' At the front door, Maggie looked back while Bruce continued. 'Tell Jeff I'll try and pop round this week. I may be able to help him in the garden with something.' He gave another warm smile – his arm tightly encircling Lisa's shoulder – as Maggie turned and left.

Once outside, Maggie paused for a moment to consider what she had just heard, then she put a hand to her cheek and shivered, not from the cold, but from the touch of Bruce's cold lips on her face.

*

On the other side of Marston at exactly the same time, Naila was following Rona at a distance, careful to hang back so she couldn't be seen. She wasn't sure what she was seeking, convinced only that she needed to know more about her workmate – the refugee who was being shown so much attention and loyalty by their boss.

It smarted that she had been proved wrong about the theft of Tracey's ring but nothing could shake Naila's conviction that she was right about the stranger who had insinuated herself into Maggie's trust. Naila couldn't be sure exactly how Rona had woven her spell, but she was sure Rona Abdi was not to be trusted and the fact that she had defended herself so well on the factory floor, in front of everyone, only rankled further.

If things were allowed to continue, it wouldn't be long before the others began to accept Rona and take her word against Naila's – especially if Maggie encouraged them to do so. Samira was already dropping hints about giving the new worker a chance, arguing that they were all on the same side, but Samira had long crossed over to the other side herself; to Maggie's side – management. Maybe Samira couldn't be trusted these days either.

At this thought, Naila suddenly stopped in her tracks, just as Rona began crossing the main road ahead. A lorry appeared, blocking Naila's vision for a moment, but once it had passed she could see Rona again, approaching a rundown housing estate, her pace slowing as though she was coming to the end of a walk home.

A group of teenagers, milling at the entrance to the estate, acknowledged Rona as she neared them, then continued to talk amongst themselves, as the woman walked on, passing a few scruffy kids kicking a football in defiance of a sign marked *No Ball Games*.

Naila's face set as Rona headed towards the entrance to a block of flats. The light had now long faded so there was nothing more to see – or do – except perhaps turn back and head home – when a man's voice suddenly called out.

'Hey!'

Alarmed, Naila looked back, fearing she had been caught out, before she realised the man wasn't calling to her, but to Rona, who had failed to respond. He yelled again – louder this time.

'Leyla!'

At this, Rona instantly turned, responding to the name. Naila frowned, holding back, pressing herself close to a dank wall when she observed the look of recognition on Rona's face as the man smiled and crossed the road to her.

Naila took note as the two embraced before exchanging some conversation and walking on together towards the dingy estate. As they disappeared into the darkness, Naila gave a deep exhalation and leaned back against the wall behind her. A street lamp above her suddenly flashed on and she allowed herself to smile – knowing this had all been worthwhile.

CHAPTER FIFTEEN

'What were you talking about?' Bruce closed the fridge door, satisfied that he had stored his shopping items neatly inside, then he carefully wiped his hands on a dish cloth before staring across at Lisa who was sitting at the kitchen island.

'Nothing, really,' she said idly. 'She wasn't here long.'

'So, why did she come round?' He set the dish cloth down on the island and stood close to Lisa so that she was forced to stare up at him.

She gave a casual shrug. 'Just to see how I am.'

Bruce held her gaze. 'I told her how you are, remember? I explained as soon as we got back. You've not been well.'

Lisa frowned. 'I know.'

Bruce took a deep breath and looked away to the window. 'But she didn't believe me.'

'Of course she did.' Lisa said quickly.

'Then why did she come round? To check up? To see for herself I'm not lying?'

'No one said you were lying,' Lisa argued. 'You told her the truth; I've not been well, but…I'm feeling better.'

Bruce looked back at her. 'Of course you are.' He gave an unexpected smile which Lisa returned, and for a moment the chill between them thawed, until the wind strengthened outside sending a gust of dry leaves up to scratch at the window.

Lisa flinched at the sound then looked back at him. 'She… did mention there's a new place to rent in town?'

Bruce eyed her flatly before tipping his head in confusion. 'And why would she mention that?'

Lisa gave a small shrug. 'She just asked why we wanted to live so far out of the way here?'

'When you could be closer to your mum and dad?'

Lisa gave a small nod.

'*And* your friends?'

Lisa nodded again.

'So that's what you were talking about.'

'We weren't really talking.'

'No?'

'She just mentioned it.'

'And now you think it's a good idea?'

Lisa hesitated before replying, unable to read the look in his eyes. 'I… don't know.'

'Well you must have some idea or you wouldn't have brought it up.'

'You just asked me what we were talking about.'

'And *you* said she happened to 'mention' it.'

'She did.' Frustration mounting, Lisa pushed a hand through her matted hair before getting up.

'Forget it,' she said, 'like you say, we're settled here now – and that's what I told her,' she began to move to the door.

'Except you don't feel settled,' said Bruce, 'you're only here because I signed the lease.'

Lisa looked back at him, knowing this was true. She said nothing, but it was clear he wasn't going to let this drop. 'You still haven't forgiven me for that, have you?' he said. 'Is that why you want to move back into town?'

'No, I...' Lisa broke off and began again. 'Look, you're twisting everything I say. I didn't mean it like that.'

'Then what did you mean?'

'Can we talk about something else?'

Bruce held her look – then his face broke into an unexpected smile. 'Sure.' he said. Reaching out, he placed the palm of his hand against one of her cheeks and leaned in to plant a kiss on the other, remaining close as he whispered: 'You know I only asked because I love you?'

Lisa nodded slowly, feeling the warmth of his hand against her cheek, reassuring but seemingly directing her attention to focus fully on what he was saying. His voice lowered further. 'I've been taking good care of you, haven't I?'

She nodded again before whispering: 'Yes.'

'What did you say?'

She took a deep breath, then repeated: 'You've been taking good care of me.'

'That's right,' he said, holding her gaze. 'Because I'm your husband.' He whispered to her now. 'And I love you.'

He watched her mouth begin to fall slightly open as his right hand moved up beneath her dressing gown. Tracing the soft flesh of her inner thigh, his touch then slowed before he reached higher, his eyes remaining fixed on hers as his fingers separated her lips and pushed their way inside her. He saw her eyelids flicker and finally close then he breathed deeper, waiting for her next response.

Her own breaths quickened before she suddenly frowned. 'No,' she said urgently.

Bruce stopped and Lisa's eyes opened. 'What did you say?' he asked, watching her tongue slide across dry lips.

She swallowed hard. 'I said… no… not now.'

Bruce felt his breath steadying as he took full control of himself. He nodded slowly and in the next instant, Lisa found herself relaxing as he took a step away from her, giving her the space she needed to explain. 'It's not that I don't want to,' she began. 'It's just—' She broke off, aware only that he had turned so quickly she had failed to realise he was twisting her body around so she was now facing the kitchen island – its sharp counter edge shoved hard against her diaphragm.

One of his hands was pressing on the back of her neck, forcing her down so she found herself staring at tiny crystals of brown sugar sprinkled on the granite counter top. She heard herself cry out.

'What're you doing!'

Bruce's body was pressed tightly against her back, one hand tugging at her dressing gown, roughly this time, before his clammy hand clamped tight over her groin. 'Bruce…?'

He spoke over her, leaning forward to whisper close into her ear. 'I keep telling you – they'll never understand.' His tone was as firm as his grip. 'You know that now, don't you?' His fingers were pressing hard to find entry inside her.

She closed her eyes, knowing she had to do whatever she could to make him stop; to lash out somehow and cause him to free her, so she could be allowed the right to choose. But she also knew the greater part of her wanted him to continue, to grant him total control so her only choice would be to submit.

Having no choice at all meant having no chance of making a mistake. He felt the fight go out of her. His fingers met her moist consent. His breaths came deeper as he reached for the dish cloth and slipped it around the front of her neck using both hands to yank her head back towards his face. 'They'll never understand,' he repeated, 'about you and me.' Then he suddenly tore deep inside her from behind, and in that instant she knew he was right – just as she knew that some pain brings an exquisite form of pleasure – like the pain she was feeling now.

With that realisation, she finally opened her eyes and saw herself in the reflection of the glass cooker door across the room, her head pulled back towards Bruce like a horse on tight reins. He pushed mercilessly, harder and harder, allowing only small moans to escape with her every breath, while a fierce cold gale continued to blow outside.

CHAPTER SIXTEEN

Later that same evening, Maggie paced back and forth in front of the television as Jeff tried to watch the news. 'I'm telling you,' she said. 'She's all alone in that house.'

'I thought you said Bruce was with her.' He tossed a peanut to the dog.

'He was when I left,' said Maggie, 'but he'd been in Bradford all day.'

Jeff considered this. 'A fella's got to work, Mags. And in case you've forgotten, right now he's the only one bringing in a wage.'

'And whose fault's that?' Maggie turned and eyed him. 'Our Lisa had a good job.'

'Aye,' said Jeff. 'Abroad.'

'She said she'd find something for herself back here.'

'Well, give her a chance. They're only just back from honeymoon.' He paused for a moment and tried again. 'Look,' he went on, 'she told you she's all right and she knows where we are if she needs us. *If* she does – she'll call us.'

'*If* he lets her,' said Maggie darkly.

Jeff looked up. 'So we're back to this again?'

'I don't trust him.'

'You don't like him'.

'And neither does Bella – or did you not notice?'

Jeff glanced at the dog sitting beside him. He knew Maggie was right; the animal had never warmed to Bruce but he sighed. 'Going on the dog's say-so now, are we?'

Maggie's eyes narrowed. 'Why d'you always have to go against me?'

Jeff frowned. 'I don't.'

'You do where he's concerned.'

'*He's* got a name – Bruce – and have you ever considered it's *you* who's gone against *him*? Right from the start, you hardly gave the bloke a chance. Typical mother in law—'

Maggie broke in sharply. 'Don't you dare turn this into some bar-room joke. I'm talking about our daughter's future.'

'And she's told you she wants to spend her future with Bruce. But where you're concerned he can't do owt right, can he?

'And just what *has* he done?' asked Maggie. "Got her to give up work?'

'You don't know that.'

'Moved her away from everyone she knows?'

'She's got a say in what she does and where she lives.'

'Has she? You've not seen that new place of theirs. He's got a basement all to himself – a locked door to keep her out!'

Jeff fixed her with his gaze, noting his wife's lips pressed tight with resentment. 'Then if you ask me,' he began, 'he's got his head screwed on.' Maggie gaped at this, incredulous, but Jeff went on. '*I* told him he could do with a space of his own – and you know why? To get away from all this.' He got up and moved to the door.

Maggie called after him. 'I should've known! All boys together? It's a ruddy wonder you don't take him down the club with you!'

'It wasn't for want of trying,' said Jeff, 'but he said he had to get back for Lisa.' On his knowing look, Maggie turned angrily away. Jeff tried to calm himself then moved to her again.

'Look,' he said, gently this time, 'you've got to get over this, Maggie. If you don't, you'll go the right way about losing her.'

'Is that right?' She said bitterly.

'I mean it.'

'And so do I,' said Maggie, defiantly. 'She doesn't know what she's got herself into.'

'Or maybe she knows exactly,' said Jeff. 'Maybe she wants a fella with a mind of his own instead of a 'yes' man like me.' Looking back at him, Maggie saw that Jeff meant this. Without another word she turned for the door.

'Oh come on, Maggie. Don't run away. You think you're losing another daughter but you're not – Lisa's just trying to move on. And *you* have to do the same.'

A moment passed before Maggie stopped in her tracks, and considered Jeff's words. Shocked by his perspective, she stared back at him, confused and defeated. 'What else can I do?' she said. 'Our Natalie's gone.'

'Aye,' said Jeff, trying hard not to soften. 'But she's not our Lisa.' He took a deep breath – then a step towards her. 'Though you want her to be,' he said softly. 'That's why you pushed her to go to college when she told you all along she didn't want to go.'

'I didn't push her,' Maggie argued. 'Lisa wanted it too – she just needed a bit of persuading.'

'She did it for you,' said Jeff. 'The same reason Nat went to that posh school and why Lisa took a job at the resort.' He paused again. 'To make you happy.'

Maggie stared back at her husband, her lips set tight in defiance, but Jeff remained calm as he faced her down. Maggie turned again for the door, this time moving into the hallway to grab her coat. Jeff called out after her. 'All right, *don't* listen! Keep hearing what you want to hear.'

At this, Maggie's hand faltered at the front door but she summoned resolve and walked straight out, slamming the door behind her.

Once outside, Maggie took a deep breath, part of her wanting to go back and find a better way to put her case to Jeff while the greater part of her knew it was no use. It was clear whose side Jeff was on. He was championing Bruce and closing his mind to everything she had to say. If that wasn't the case, he would surely have come after her by now, but the front door behind her remained closed. Looking up at the sky, she saw it was about to rain, but she steeled herself and pulled on her coat to move quickly down the street.

Jeff knew he needed to go after Maggie – but something had stopped him in his tracks. He put his hand to his chest – halted by what felt like a knife through his heart. He tried to calm himself, to regulate his breathing, telling himself this would pass. He was upset, frustrated, but in a moment the pain would ease and he would be able to breathe again without the elephant lying on his chest.

He knew he should listen to Maggie when she warned him to be careful about his health, but she was always nagging about his drinking or his diet. As Bruce had said, giving up booze couldn't guarantee a long life but it would certainly seem longer without it. Besides, the pills always worked when Jeff needed them and in the next moment, he caught sight of his jacket hanging on the bannister and took hold of it as he fumbled in its pockets for them. Car keys... door keys... loose change... pocket litter... no pills.

Jeff tried to remain calm as he moved slowly back along the hallway towards the kitchen, pressing his palms against the walls to keep himself upright. The tightness in his chest was getting worse but it always passed after one of his pills. He usually kept them on him at all times but he couldn't remember now where he had left them. Maybe it was the pain that was making it difficult to think...

As soon as Jeff reached the kitchen, he lurched forward towards a dresser drawer and tried to wrench it open. Inside, he found packets of over-the-counter remedies and bottles of cough mixture. His breathing was coming quicker as he tossed them onto the kitchen table, searching for one precious plastic tub.

The bottles rolled across the table's surface before finally hitting the floor. Glass smashed on the ceramic floor tiles, pills bounced and syrupy medicine spread out in pools. Maggie wouldn't be pleased when she saw the mess he was making... Clutching his chest, Jeff stared towards the rain-splattered window and out across the garden to his shed as he made a bitter realisation.

*

Jeff staggered to the back door as Bella trailed after him, following obediently up the garden path before sitting on her haunches and watching carefully as Jeff tried the shed door – only to find it was locked.

His hand moved to his face, feeling beads of sweat mingling with cold rain. The pain was excruciating – a great weight bearing down on him – but as the dog began whimpering Jeff struggled to take a breath and used it to whisper to her:

'S'all right, Bella, love. S'all right.' He lurched his way to a window sill, lined with terracotta pots, all carefully planted with pretty winter pansies.

Tipping one up, he fumbled beneath it, aware that he was now gasping, and grasping for life. His fingers met with a small key but the effort of grabbing it proved too much and he sank to his knees, taking with him the pots which smashed into small pieces on the paving stones.

As Jeff fell backwards, lying on the cold stone path, Bella licked his hand – then began to bark.

At Woodside, Lisa was lying on the bed as an American sit-com played on the TV. Bored with it, Lisa flicked the remote and found a shopping channel. She sighed to herself, wondering how much longer it would be before Bruce finished in his office for the evening. It had been some time since he had left her to do some work – or was it that he simply wanted to be apart from her? She imagined him in his special work space, his den, his retreat from her – his mantuary – just like her dad's shed. Funny that they were both so alike that way…

*

Downstairs in his basement, Bruce was studying a spreadsheet on a large computer screen fixed to the wall above his desk.

He reached up and stretched his aching arms then closed the programme and shut down the computer before staring around the room. In the few weeks before the wedding, he had done a good job of kitting it all out.

A sleek steel shelving system housed files and a single framed photograph of Lisa and Bruce on their wedding day. A day to remember… then his gaze moved to the paperweight she had given him – a souvenir of an even more memorable honeymoon. A hi-tech music system was in place alongside some classic vinyl albums. Everything was neat and orderly.

Nothing out of place. In fact, he was sure this space would easily pass an Army inspection. A black computer case lay propped upright on the floor beside him. He reached down, unzipped it and took a silver laptop from it before setting it down on his tidy desk. Opening the lid, he switched it on and closed his eyes before typing a password.

Out in the street, drenched in the falling rain, Maggie walked towards the bus shelter at the end of the street. Sitting down on a narrow bench, she closed her eyes and tried hard to imagine that she was somewhere else while failing to block out the soundtrack of a flood-lit construction site across the road.

A cement mixer was turning while a trio of pneumatic drills was breaking up concrete. A lorry went past, creating a small tsunami from rainwater gathered in the gutter and for a moment, Jeff's words continued to echo:

'You've got to get over this. If you don't, you'll go the right way about losing her… You think you're losing another daughter – but

you're not – our Lisa's just trying to move on. And you have to do the same.'

Maggie tried to shake the truth from her mind but as the din of the construction site drills suddenly stopped she turned her head and focused on another sound. Somewhere in the distance, a dog was barking. Maggie looked back in the direction she had come. She wasn't mistaken. It was Bella.

In his basement office, Bruce tapped an icon and opened a desktop file. A moment later, a familiar panorama appeared on the screen on his wall – a pretty marina, yacht masts swaying in the night breeze, neon lettering spelling out the words Tiki Bar.

The view suddenly vanished but Bruce's gaze remained fixed on the screen, on which a new image now appeared. A young girl, childlike, blonde hair falling to her shoulders, was dancing on an empty, moonlit beach while facing away from the camera. Bruce's hand reached to fondle the paperweight on his desk – a blue wave still trapped in time within it – but his eyes remained fixed on the young girl on the screen as she knocked back the drink in her hand before turning towards the lens. Her eyes looked strangely unfocused as she played up to the camera, dancing flirtatiously, teasingly – until a hand came into view and plucked the spaghetti-strap of her top from her shoulder. She stared back, confused and offended as she asked: 'What're you're doing?'

Maggie's front door burst open and she entered to find Jeff's jacket lying on the floor in the hallway. She called out his name. Silence – but for a dog still barking in the garden. Moving quickly into the kitchen, Maggie stopped in her tracks at the sight of the dresser drawer open, broken glass scattered amongst pools of medicine on the floor. The dog continued to bark in the garden. Maggie hurried outside to see Bella sitting on guard beside something near the shed…

On Bruce's screen, the blonde girl on the beach was scowling – swaying unsteadily on her bare feet. A man's hand moved forward into the frame.

The girl tried to push it away but it proved stronger than her own as it wrenched the skimpy top from her body. She backed away, trying to cover her bare breasts but the camera moved in tighter on her face. Still staring into the lens, the girl pleaded as tears began to fall, before she let out a scream as a hand pushed her roughly back on to the sand. The camera closed in.

'Please…' the girl begged, 'you're scaring me… Mike?'

Maggie had just reached the garden shed. At the sight of her, Bella whimpered and continued to lick Jeff's hand. Maggie crouched down to her husband, her face contorted by a terrible fear. 'Oh please God, no…'

On the screen in Bruce's basement office, the blonde girl was whimpering – like a dog. Her face came into sharp focus and Bruce leaned forward towards the screen on his office wall, moving ever closer, his features impassive, but his dark eyes reflecting the image of a terrified young girl still pleading pitifully for mercy.

CHAPTER SEVENTEEN

Extract 2 from the transcript of a recorded interview with
Mrs Margaret Sheild
Date: 3rd April 2024
Conducted by: Officers of Marston Police
Location: Marston Police Station, West Yorkshire

As soon as I found Jeff, I dialed 999 but when he opened his eyes and looked towards the shed, I knew what he was trying to tell me. I went inside and tore the place apart, tossing everything to the floor: pots, tools, old newspapers until I finally found that little tub of pills on the window ledge. My fingers curled around it – a lifeline.

When I stepped back outside I could see Jeff was worse – his skin was pale and clammy and his lips were turning blue.

He was struggling hard for breath but I managed to lift his head in my hands and I forced that tiny pill under his tongue. It had always worked before when we needed it and I prayed it would again. The rain was beating down as I cradled his head against my chest but his eyes were closing. "You'll be all right now,' I kept saying. 'You'll be fine, y'hear?' I rocked him in my arms and planted kisses on his forehead.

Then I felt a terrible fear come over me as I looked down at him. What would I do without him? There and then, I realised it was down to me to shake the life back into him. 'I know you can hear me,' I said. 'So come back, you bloody bastard!' I waited, the dog still staring up at me, and after a lifetime Jeff finally opened his eyes – and took a proper breath. I pulled him towards me and I held him, close to my heart – while the rain beat down…

An hour after the paramedics left, everything had gone quiet. Jeff was sleeping peacefully, tucked up in bed with Bella at his side. I uncurled my fingers and looked down at that little tub of pills in my hand – Jeff's lifeline – and mine.

I put the pills down on the bedside table then I turned around towards the display of photos I keep on our chest of drawers.

There are snaps of me and Jeff with our Lisa and Natalie as teenagers, and some of the girls when they were much younger, with Jeff in the garden during school summer holidays. I thought back to that summer, and realised I would have been at work then, like I was most of the time the girls were growing up, so Jeff had taken my place and filled the space in that photo and in their childhood.

I would never get back that time with them, the time I'd spent meeting deadlines for orders and sorting out spats like the one between Naila and Rona. I leaned forward towards those photos and I studied the girls' faces.

Our Natalie was gone so it pained me to look at her and I found myself staring instead at our Lisa. For some reason it felt as if she was a million miles away but the phone was right there and I knew it would be so easy to pick it up and call her, explain what had happened to Jeff, to say sorry and agree that life's too short for all this heartache. But then I thought to myself: what if Jeff got upset all over again – or Lisa's condition worsened from being worried about her dad?

Whose fault was it that any of this had happened at all? I turned away from the photos, and I looked back at my husband lying there in bed, ashen, exhausted, and I knew that it was all my fault. Jeff's chest still rose with every breath he took. But one day it wouldn't. I had to be careful – very careful – never to upset him like this again.

I crept across the room and went out into the hallway, closing the door behind me. Then I took something from my pocket – my mobile phone. I found a number on it and I dialed – then I waited for someone to answer.

As soon as they did, I said: 'Hello?' I left a long pause and then found the confidence to go on. 'Denise, love, it's me – Lisa's mum, Maggie.' I inched further away from the bedroom door. 'Yeah, it was a grand 'do',' I said, 'and it was nice to see you too.' Then I braced myself to find the words I needed to say. 'Look, I... know you're getting ready to go away but I wondered if you've time to meet up?' I shook my head at her question. 'No,' I said. 'Just you and me. You see... I need to ask you something. Something important.'

CHAPTER EIGHTEEN

Bruce was in the bedroom, slipping into a heavy navy blue work shirt when he suddenly heard Lisa's voice calling to him from the hallway.

'How long will you be?'

Bruce found himself tracing the raised anchor design on the metal shirt button beneath his finger, before he fastened it and called back: 'Couple of hours should do it.' He ran his hands through his dark hair.

Lisa asked: 'And is that helping Dad in the garden or sinking a few pints?'

He turned to see she was now leaning on the doorframe, a wry smile on her face, and an open bag of crisps in her hand.

'Why?' he asked.

'Because I was thinking… maybe I could come with you?' She stepped forward, the question still written on her face. Bruce hesitated – long enough to prompt her to explain further. 'I won't get in the way, I promise. I could go and do something with Mum. I haven't seen either of them properly since we got back.'

'You've not been well,' Bruce reminded her as he moved past her into the hallway.

'I know. But I feel better now. I've even got my appetite back,' she offered a casual smile before popping a crisp into her mouth.

'I can see that.' he said. He moved quickly downstairs while Lisa frowned and went after him.

'And what's that supposed to mean?'

'Nothing,' he said brightly, grabbing his jacket and brushing it down with his hand. 'You've put on a few pounds lately, haven't you?'

'Have I?'

He slipped into his jacket and nodded to the jeans she was wearing. 'They used to be a nice fit.'

Lisa glanced down at them. 'They still are.'

Bruce eyed her and smiled. 'If you say so.' He moved to the door and opened it.

'Well… aren't they?' she asked, now unsure. Looking back at her, he said nothing. 'Bruce, are you saying I'm—'

'You're perfect.' he said quickly, putting a finger to her lips.

She gave a slow smile. 'That's more like it'. Leaning in close she kissed him. As they broke apart her eyes scanned his face before she asked: 'Why don't we go back to bed?'

'Lisa…'

'Well why not? It's Sunday – meant to be a day of rest.'

He looked at her unmoved. She ran her fingers through his hair and went on. 'Carry on like this and I'll think you don't fancy me anymore,' she eyed him, unsure, waiting for a response.

'I've been working hard,' he said finally. 'And… I made a promise to your Dad, remember?'

'I know you did,' she suddenly softened. 'And I do understand, so... give him my love?'

Bruce smiled. 'I will.' He had just started to move away – when he remembered to add: 'And don't worry about missing your mum.' As Lisa looked at him, he explained. 'Your Dad said she was meeting someone in town.'

'Oh? Who?'

Bruce shrugged. 'See you later.' He smiled and left the house. Once the door had closed after him, Lisa stared down at the bag of crisps in her hand then made a decision and headed to the kitchen – and dumped them in the bin.

In the George and Dragon pub, Maggie took a crisp from a bowl on the bar. Before it had reached her mouth, a familiar voice sounded. 'You know what they say? A minute at the lips – an inch on the hips.'

Maggie turned to see Dee, smiling, behind her and replied: 'Bit ruddy late for that.'

Dee leaned forward and gave her a peck on the cheek. 'Y'all right, Mags?' She sat down beside her.

'All the better for seeing you.' Maggie took her purse from her bag. 'What'll you have?'

As the barman came across to serve, Dee smiled. 'A latte. No, make that a glass of Pinot,' she turned to Maggie and smiled. 'I know it's early, but they don't call me the 'great white wino' for nothing.' Her smile faltered as she saw Maggie seemed preoccupied. 'Everything okay?'

Maggie paused. 'Jeff had a bad turn.'

'I'm sorry to hear that—'

'It's okay,' said Maggie quickly. 'He's all right now. And I haven't told our Lisa. I… don't want to worry her. They've only just got back from honeymoon.'

'I know,' said Dee. 'Got to give newly-weds a bit of space, right?' She smiled again as the barman brought her wine. 'Cheers,' she sipped her wine and saw Maggie was staring thoughtfully down at the bar. 'So what's this all about, Mags?'

At Marston Social Club, a football match was showing on a giant plasma TV screen. A player made a bid towards the goal before attempting a strike – and missing. A series of groans followed from the members settled around the screen. Mainly men, they watched the game intently, pints and bar snacks before them as Jeff entered. Ted, the barman, got to his feet.

'All right, Jeff?' Returning to the bar Ted picked up an empty pint glass to serve.

Jeff nodded and said, quickly. 'Just a half today.'

Ted swapped glasses and began to pour. 'You okay?'

Jeff nodded stoically, reluctant to explain about his attack. That was something women did, chatting for hours about various complaints; about who was suffering from what, and who might be next in line for the cemetery. Glancing around at the men in the bar, their attention fixed on the football match, Jeff was sure they must feel as he did; that if something wasn't talked about, it might never happen.

'If you want to sit down, I'll bring it over?' said Ted, noting Jeff was staring towards the TV screen.

'No, I… can't stop,' Jeff explained. 'I got my son-in-law coming round. Helping out with the garden.'

More groans sounded from the football crowd as Ted nodded towards the game. 'Looks like you won't be missing much.' he said ruefully before taking Jeff's money and moving to the till. He suddenly remembered something. Taking a letter from a shelf above the till, he explained: 'I almost forgot… this came for you yesterday.'

'Me?'

Ted nodded and handed the envelope to Jeff, who began searching his pockets for his glasses. Ted rejoined the football fans. Slipping on his glasses Jeff stared down at the envelope – and his name below a strange stamp.

The George and Dragon was quickly filling up with office workers as Maggie reflected on something Dee had just told her. 'So… you haven't seen her at all since she got back?'

Dee shook her head. 'I've called a few times. Bruce said she wasn't well. Nothing serious though. Holiday bug?' She sipped her drink.

Maggie looked thoughtful. 'You didn't actually get to talk to her?'

Dee shook her head. 'I didn't expect to if she's not well. Bruce said she'd give me a call once she felt a bit better. That was only a couple of days ago.'

As Maggie considered this, Dee picked up her drink, then hesitated before asking: 'She's all right, isn't she?'

Bruce stood at Maggie and Jeff's front door and rang the bell. No reply. He rang again. Still no reply. Peering through the letterbox, he glimpsed only an empty hallway. He called into it.

'Anyone home?'

Silence.

Checking his watch, he moved to the garden gate. It pushed

open beneath his hand. He glanced around the empty garden – then moved on towards Jeff's shed.

At the George and Dragon pub, Maggie unburdened herself to Dee. 'I don't trust him,' she said flatly. 'Jeff'll tell you I don't like him but it amounts to the same thing.'

'Does it?' asked Dee, unconvinced. 'Look, Lisa's your daughter and you're bound to want the best for her but—'

Maggie spoke over her. 'She didn't ruddy get it, did she?' Heads turned among the office workers at the bar. Maggie lowered her voice. 'Look at the wedding,' she went on. 'Half-baked register office affair? It was all over in ten minutes. And if we hadn't booked the club she wouldn't even have had a party'.

Dee gave a shrug. 'Maybe she wasn't too fussed about having one.'

Maggie remained firm. 'She always said she'd have a grand 'do".

'Well,' said Dee, 'you know what they say about us women changing our minds?' She offered a smile but Maggie remained unmoved. 'Or having them changed for us,' she said darkly.

Dee looked away and tried again. 'I think you're on the wrong track. Maybe Lisa wanted things that way.'

Maggie looked up. 'She told you that?'

Dee shrugged, feeling under pressure. 'Sort of,' she quickly finished her wine as Maggie looked on. Dee checked her watch – knowing it was time to leave – before she said something she might regret.

'And what's that s'posed to mean?' Maggie asked, with some suspicion.

Looking around, Dee felt increasingly uncomfortable, but Maggie pressed on. 'Tell me?'

After a pause, Dee slowly shook her head. 'I can't, Maggie,' she said, conflicted. 'But I swear it was Lisa's decision – not his.'

Bruce was still in the garden, close to Jeff's shed, using a long stick to prod the bonfire he had just started in an old brazier stacked with wood. He watched the flames begin to rise. He liked starting fires – it made him to feel in control – the way he always liked to be. Someone had once said there was something primeval about fire lighting – and maybe they were right; maybe something had been passed down in genetic memory about a fire at a cave entrance keeping predators at bay.

He liked the idea of that cave. Most men did.

The safe space – away from all the dangers of the world – away from everyone. The man cave. The 'mantuary', as Lisa had once called his own private den, a fancy word to describe something very simple; a space in which he could escape from everything – and everyone – including Lisa.

He glanced across at Jeff's shed and allowed himself to smile. It wasn't much but it, too, served its purpose; an escape from Maggie – the mother-in-law from hell – the woman he had failed to charm, though he still felt he would do so. It was just a matter of time. Until then, he had vowed not to let her get too deep under his skin.

Instead, he would view her as a challenge – and continue to bond with Jeff. It was a good plan, one that might take time – but it would work. Staring away from the shed, Bruce was suddenly taken aback to catch sight of a shadow falling on the paving stones before him. Turning, he saw Jeff almost silhouetted by the winter sunlight behind him.

'There you are,' said Bruce. 'I knew you couldn't have gone

far. The back gate was open so I thought I'd make a start by clearing the area. We can use this for more rubbish?' He nodded towards the brazier, crackling and spitting.

'I was down the club,' said Jeff sparely.

Bruce smiled and gave a wink. 'I promise I won't tell Maggie.'

'Aye,' said Jeff. 'You're good at keeping secrets, aren't you?'

As the pale sun dipped behind a cloud Bruce looked back again and saw Jeff's cold expression.

At the George and Dragon, Maggie leaned forward and pleaded urgently with Dee. 'Just tell me what she said?'

Dee shook her head. 'I can't, Maggie. I shouldn't even be here, talking behind her back like this?'

Maggie leaned closer to her. 'D'you think I would have asked if I could do this any another way?' She broke off then continued – softly this time. 'Look, if you know something… *anything*… just tell me?'

Trapped in Maggie's gaze, Dee looked away, then finally replied. 'I know this is just what she didn't want.'

Maggie sat back on her stool, brought up short by this. Dee gave a heavy sigh. 'All she ever wanted was for you to like him. But if she thought, for one minute, that you were talking about him like this, to me, then…' She trailed off.

'Then' what?'

Dee shook her head, defeated. 'Then maybe she'd have gone along with a big church wedding.'

Maggie frowned. 'I don't understand.'

'She didn't want you worrying.'

'Worrying about *what*?'

Dee looked away again, this time as if searching for an

escape. Finding none, she finally admitted. 'Bruce has been married before.'

A stiff breeze blew parched leaves across Jeff's garden. Bruce shook his head. 'I'm... not sure what you're talking about.'

'Tommy Wicks's grandson,' said Jeff. 'I told you about him, remember?'

Bruce stared down at the stick in his hand and used it to stoke the fire. 'Can't say I do, Jeff,' he said casually. 'Sure you haven't had one too many?'

Jeff came forward and carefully studied Bruce – as if for the very first time. 'I had an idea you two would have something in common,' he explained. 'Turns out I was wrong.' He slipped his hand into his pocket. 'Shane's in Poland. NATO exercise. But he still found time to write to me. It's come by military mail.'

Bruce turned and eyed the letter in Jeff's hand. Jeff offered it to him. 'It's all about you.'

In the bar at the George and Dragon, Maggie tried hard to process Denise's news. 'Why didn't she tell me?'

'Why d'you think?' said Dee. 'Look, Maggie, you're no fan of his as it is, but if she'd told you Bruce had already got one failed marriage behind him...' she trailed off.

Maggie shook her head. 'She *should've* told me.'

'And if she had,' said Dee, 'you'd have had one more reason to find fault with him,' she gave a long exhalation before leaning closer. 'Look, me and the girls are going away tomorrow. Chances are I won't get to talk to Lisa... but she swore me to keep this a secret. Promise me you'll do the same?'

Maggie looked back at Dee, feeling as though the busy bar was suddenly closing in on her. She found herself nodding slowly. 'All right,' she said, defeated. 'I promise.'

Standing motionless in his garden, Jeff slapped the letter in his hand. 'A.T.A. Reservist, that's what you were. So why did you lie?' Bruce continued to prod the burning wood in the brazier. 'Well?' said Jeff, louder this time.

'Looks like you're the one with all the answers, Jeff,' said Bruce. He gave a shrug, still calm under pressure and finally turned away.

Jeff frowned. 'But... I'm giving you a chance to explain yourself.' His eyes narrowed as he slapped the letter in his hand. 'It says here you made quite a name for yourself. Insubordinate ... unfit for service? Spent most of your time banged up in the glasshouse...' At this, Bruce tossed the stick to the ground and picked up his jacket. As he began to move off, Jeff blocked his path. 'I'm *talking* to you.'

'No, Jeff,' said Bruce abruptly. 'You're yelling. Throwing your weight around. Just like *they* did.'

Jeff looked confused – then made a bitter realisation: 'So... it's true,' he said softly. 'You lied to us. To my Lisa,' seeing Bruce still impassive, Jeff went on. 'And Maggie knew. She saw through you from the start. She had your number—'

Bruce cut in. 'But you didn't listen, did you, Jeff?'

Jeff was stunned into silence. Bruce began to walk off.

'And what about the rest?' Jeff suddenly demanded. 'The girls. Near your barracks?'

At this, Bruce stopped in his tracks. His head snapped back. Unnerved by the cold look in his eyes, Jeff braced himself. 'I...

want to know what happened.' His breath seemed caught in his throat as he waited for a response.

Bruce considered him and left a long pause before he finally replied. 'What d'you think happened?' he asked calmly. He offered a curious smile then turned once more to leave.

This time Jeff went after him, putting himself between Bruce and the garden gate. 'You're going nowhere near my daughter, you hear? Not until I've talked to her.'

'And said what?' asked Bruce calmly. 'You're going to put her straight about me, are you, Jeff?' He paused. 'I don't think so.' He gave an incongruous smile. 'You see, at the end of the day, it's all about trust. You should've trusted Maggie – but you didn't. And now it's too late – because Lisa trusts me.'

He paused again, then: 'She trusts me more than anyone.'

Unable to bear the triumph in Bruce's smile, Jeff turned away, but this time it was Bruce who blocked his path. 'You won't turn her against me,' he said. 'Even those little squaddies with the pips on their shoulders… They all had to admit – I've got a way with women.' His smile was still in place. Jeff raised his hand, pointing to him with a trembling finger.

'You leave my girl alone.'

Bruce registered Jeff's breathlessness. 'Take it easy,' he said casually, placing his hand gently on Jeff's shoulder. Jeff stared at it, suddenly feeling chilled. He took his mobile from his pocket and switched it on.

'What are you doing, Jeff?'

'What do you *think* I'm doing?' Jeff began to dial. 'I'm calling the police—' He broke off, his fingers still fumbling for the keypad as the phone was lifted from his hand.

'To say what?' asked Bruce. 'That I told a little white lie

to impress my girlfriend? That's all you've got on me, Jeff. So why don't you calm down?' He slipped the phone into his own pocket.

Jeff began to shake his head. 'No...' he argued, trailing off as he tried to catch his breath.

'No?' echoed Bruce. 'Remember what Maggie always says? You mustn't overdo things. But look at you. You're all worked up – and about what?'

Struggling for breath, Jeff failed to answer and put a hand to his chest as Bruce went on: 'You never listen, do you? Secret brews in the shed? Hip flasks of cognac? Cigars?' Bruce shook his head slowly and leaned closer. 'It's a shame you don't take more care of yourself. Lisa said the same.'

Jeff frowned as he began to labour for breath. His hand slipped slowly inside his jacket – but Bruce saw and reacted quickly: 'Need a hand there?' He reached out but Jeff was faster, holding fast to a plastic tub of pills in his hand. Relieved, Jeff went to open it, but in the next moment it slipped through his trembling fingers and hit the ground.

'Allow me,' said Bruce as he bent down and picked them up. Jeff eyed him, grimacing in pain, clutching his chest. He swallowed his pride and begged: 'Please?'

For a moment, Bruce considered Jeff – then he gave a smile and held out the tub. Jeff went to take it but in one sudden move, Bruce withdrew his hand and held the pills high above his head. Keening in pain, Jeff struggled to reach for them but was left to claw at the fabric of Bruce's shirt.

His body tensed with each gasp, trying to cling on while feeling himself suffocating, sliding slowly down towards the ground, curling into a foetal position from which he found himself staring at the polished boots on Bruce's feet.

'Please…' Jeff murmured. '…for the love of…' As he broke off, Bruce slowly crouched down to him.

'Sorry, Jeff. I'm having a bit of trouble hearing what you're saying?' His tone was still cold and considered as he went on. 'And that's a real shame because if you can't explain, it looks like you won't get a chance to thank me properly for helping you to build a new rockery.' Bruce tilted his head to one side and glanced at the clearing near the shed. 'There again, perhaps there won't be any rockery – after all.'

Looking down, Bruce saw Jeff's eyes were now strangely unfocused, his fists clenched, though the rest of his body had become lifeless. Bruce reached to feel for a carotid pulse in Jeff's neck, then got to his feet and levered the toe of his boot into the small of Jeff's back, rolling him forward before allowing him to fall back again. A lifeless dummy. Then he stared down at the tub of pills still clutched in his own hand and in the next instant picked up the letter and envelope lying on the paving stones. He considered them both – then tossed them into the brazier. The fire continued to crackle and spit, devouring the letter, sent from so far away. As Bruce continued to watch, a strange sensation of exorcism came over him, black smoke rising, taken up on the cold breeze.

CHAPTER NINETEEN

In a corridor at Marston General Hospital, swing doors burst open beneath Maggie's hand. Visitors and orderlies ducked aside to make way as she tore along in search of a ward. Rounding a corner, she found it, confronted by the sight of Bruce comforting Lisa, her face buried in her husband's chest as he held her close.

'Lisa?'

On hearing her name, Lisa looked up, eyes raw with grief – confirming terrible news. Maggie shook her head. 'No,' she whispered. 'It's not true…'

Lisa turned away, unable to look at her. It was left to Bruce to fill the silence. 'I'm sorry, Maggie,' he began softly. 'I did my best but… Jeff was already gone when I got to him.'

For a moment, every sound in the busy hospital seemed to be sucked into a vacuum. All Maggie could hear was the beating of her own heart. She remained rooted to the spot as she tried to process this news, then she took a step towards Lisa – only to see the cold look in her daughter's eyes. 'He died on his own,' said Lisa. 'And all because of you.'

Maggie opened her mouth to speak but found her own voice silenced – all that emerged was a shocked whisper, barely audible: 'No.'

Lisa braced herself and came forward, her body language accusing, her face so close to her mother's that Maggie felt the physical force of the accusation to come.

'You should've been there with him.' Lisa went on. 'But you weren't.'

Maggie stared at her. Bruce laid a hand on Lisa's shoulder. 'You can't blame your mum. She couldn't have known what was going to happen.'

'No,' said Lisa, 'she couldn't know because she was out in the pub – with my mate!' She turned to Maggie, eyes blazing. 'You were seen,' she explained. 'So what were you doing with Dee? Prying?'

Maggie tried – and failed – to form a single word. Lisa turned back to Bruce. 'And all the time,' she went on, 'my dad was dying – alone.'

Maggie closed her eyes at the thought. Bruce chose another moment to intervene. 'Lisa...' he began softly.

'No,' she continued. 'She'll not deny it cos it's the truth!' Grabbing her coat and bag she moved to the door.

'Lisa, listen to me,' said Maggie, reaching out to her.

But on making contact, Lisa shrugged her mother off as though stung by her touch. 'So you can say what?' she asked, 'that it's all going to be all right?' She shook her head gravely. 'It's not. It's *never* going to be all right.' Her eyes narrowed. 'And you *dared* go on at me about giving up my job? *Yours* was to look after Dad – but you couldn't even do that,' she paused – for only a moment, before: 'I never want to see you again.' Lisa turned and ran off leaving Bruce staring back at Maggie. He shook his head, as if dumbstruck then followed after his wife.

Dazed, Maggie stood rooted to the spot until a nurse finally appeared and asked with concern: 'Would you… like some time with your husband?'

Some minutes later, Maggie entered a quiet room off the main ward – dimly lit by a single bedside lamp. The nurse spoke softly, letting Maggie know she could take all the time she needed.

Alone, Maggie moved to the bed and lowered her gaze to where Jeff lay before her. She felt her knees weaken and sank into a chair, fighting back a weight of emotion. Tentatively, she reached out towards Jeff's lifeless hand, then hesitated. His palm lay face down on the bed and the flesh on the back of his hand looked puckered and contoured with veins. A white hand. Too pallid.

A stranger's hand – unfamiliar but for the ring on his finger – the gold band that Maggie had placed on it almost thirty years ago. Thirty years. A 'pearl' anniversary. Maggie suddenly remembered that Lisa was to have worn pearls for her wedding – until she had changed her mind in favour of a silver locket. A locket containing photos of a family – Maggie, Jeff and Natalie – but now there was no family – only Maggie. Bruce had taken Lisa. And it was Bruce's image in the locket; Bruce who now occupied Lisa's heart.

Jeff's words echoed once more: *Our Lisa's just trying to move on. And you have to do the same…* Leaning forward, Maggie lowered her head and heard herself praying for forgiveness.

At Woodside, Lisa slumped on the sofa and sat motionless. Bruce moved to her and slipped his arm around her shoulder as they sat together in silence, watching cold rain beating down on the windows. She turned to him. 'You think I was too hard?'

He allowed her to simmer for a moment. 'You're upset. We all are.'

She nodded. 'But I was right. I *am* right,' she insisted, holding on to blame like a lifeline. 'If she'd *only* been there…' She trailed off and looked back at him, needing his approval – his absolution.

'Go down that route,' he began, 'and you might as well blame me too.' He looked pained then went on. 'If I'd only got there a few minutes earlier, maybe I could've—'

'You did everything you could,' she said quickly.

Looking back at her, Bruce recognised the expression on her pretty face; the frown she always wore when she was trying to organise her thoughts and make sense of the senseless.

'The only consolation I have,' she began, 'is that maybe… after Dad had taken his last breath… somehow he knew you were there?' She turned to him – heart breaking – her voice dropping to a whisper. 'He really liked you.'

Bruce nodded slowly. 'I liked him too,' he said gently. 'I just wish we'd had the chance… to get to know each other better.' He held her look for a moment before she pressed her cheek hard against his shoulder, confirming to him that he was now the only man in her life.

More than an hour later, Maggie entered her home. Closing the front door behind her – on the cold and the rain. She took off her coat and set down her handbag and a clear plastic bag that had been given to her by the hospital. It contained Jeff's effects.

She had been asked to check it at Marston General, but she'd done so only cursorily – unable to look at most of the items – the clothes Jeff had been wearing: his old gardening shoes, a pair of socks that had seen better days, a thermal vest, underpants, a yellow shirt she had bought him for Christmas, a green pullover and his favourite anorak.

A smaller bag contained Jeff's watch and his wedding ring, and some other items that had been recovered from his pockets: a beaten up old wallet, door keys on a ring with the initial 'J', some loose change, raffle tickets…

So many small things he had chosen to carry around with him – things Maggie had never seen before – lucky charms perhaps? Everything was placed back in the plastic bag: a small Swiss Army knife, a marble, a half-eaten pack of peppermints, something in Jeff's hand… an old button… Maggie couldn't keep track of it all, though she knew it would all need to be sorted. Not now – later – when she felt stronger.

In her own pocket was a manila envelope given to her by the hospital clerk – helpful information on registering a death and claiming a Widow's Pension. That's what she now was, no longer Jeff's wife, but his widow. She glanced upstairs – into a dark void – until Bella suddenly appeared on the top step, looking sleepy. Sleepy? Or could a dog's heart break too? As Maggie considered this, the phone rang.

She moved quickly into the living room to answer it, then realised there would have been other callers in her absence. She had left a message for Samira, explaining she was going to the hospital. News would be out.

Everyone would be calling. A fresh sense of panic mounted. What would she say? How could she explain the inexplicable? Her hand hovered above the receiver, fingers trembling, then the voicemail clicked on and a stranger's voice sounded. Familiar – yet foreign.

'I... just heard the news,' said Rona. 'I'm so sorry, Maggie. I'm thinking of you – and your daughter.' A sharp tone prefaced more silence. Maggie slumped down on to the sofa while Bella padded across and began licking her hand. In the still, silent room, Maggie stared towards Jeff's empty armchair.

CHAPTER TWENTY

Freshly dug soil framed the burial plot at Marston Cemetery. During the weeks since Jeff's funeral, weeds had grown up around the grave but Maggie had dealt with them and organised the engraving on the headstone – which now bore two names: Natalie Margaret Sheild and Jeffrey Arthur Sheild. A funeral prayer line had been in situ since Natalie's passing: '*A place is vacant in our hearts that never can be filled*'.

It was true then, but had felt truer for Maggie since Jeff's death, as the vacant space was even greater. She stared at the names, carved in Old English font which made it appear as though her daughter and husband might have passed many years ago, though a biting sense of grief told her otherwise. Her one consolation was that Jeff and Natalie were together at last – albeit in a cold grave.

She busied herself, pouring fresh water into a ceramic vase and arranging the pale hyacinths she had ordered from a local florist to mark the headstone's new engraving. As she did so, she breathed in the sweet scent of the blossoms on the cold air, trying to distract herself from the fact that she was alone, not only in the cemetery at this early hour – but in life. Closing her eyes, she said a silent prayer until a hand moved in and laid a single red rose on the grave in front of her. Turning slowly, she saw a figure towering above her.

Bruce spoke gently. 'I'm sorry, Maggie,' he began. 'Lisa got your card. But she didn't feel able to come.'

Maggie got to her feet. 'But you did?'

'To pay my respects.' Bruce took a deep breath and went on. 'You'll have to give her more time. All that anger has to go somewhere.'

Maggie glanced at him, but said nothing as she screwed florist's wrapping paper into a tight ball before shoving it into her bag.

Her silence was infuriating but Bruce knew he was doing well not to let it show. Instead he bit his lip and cursed Maggie's ability to ignore him. She had always managed to do so – even now – after everything that had happened.

'Look,' he began, calmly. 'Lisa doesn't understand what you were doing that day. Meeting up with her friend like that – behind her back?' Maggie kept her silence as she picked up the empty watering can. Bruce observed her, noting the implacable front she was putting on for his benefit. 'It's a crying shame,' he continued. 'The way things have turned out?'

He left that as a question, a chance for her to reply – but she rejected it. Taking a deep breath, he steadied himself as he prepared to strike a raw nerve. 'Maybe you should try and respect the fact that Lisa has her own relationships.' His words hit their mark.

Maggie turned quickly. 'Her relationship with *you*, you mean?' She eyed him up and down, cursorily, as though he was worthless, then her eyes narrowed as she asked: 'What were you doing there in our garden that day?'

'You know that,' said Bruce patiently. 'I was there to help Jeff. He wanted a rockery built.'

Maggie turned to view the headstone. 'Maybe if he hadn't,' she began, 'he'd still be here now.'

As she looked back again at Bruce, he barely managed to maintain his composure before asking: 'And what's that supposed to mean?'

'Jeff made a bonfire that day.'

'He... probably wanted to clear some rubbish.'

'Getting ready for you,' she said, 'overdoing things.'

Bruce paused as he registered her logic. 'I didn't ask him to do that, Maggie. I told you, I went there to help.'

'But you got there too late for that.'

'I called an ambulance—'

'And so did Jeff,' said Maggie, silencing him. She went on. 'The last number he dialed was for emergency services.'

Maggie waited for an answer but Bruce took his time, his mind travelling back to that last day with Jeff in the garden. He chose his words very carefully. 'Then he must have known he needed medical help. But it was too late. I called for an ambulance as soon as got there. He was already gone, Maggie.'

As she looked away, Bruce took a deep breath, aware that he has satisfied her curiosity. 'Don't you think I wish I'd got there sooner?' he asked. 'But I didn't.' His voice softened before he added: 'And I know you must feel the same—'

Maggie turned back to him, railing. 'You don't know how I feel!'

Bruce felt the fury in her words but carried on: 'That's true,' he said, holding her look. 'But I'm trying hard to understand.'

'Are you?' she asked, unconvinced. He saw the ghost of an incongruous smile beginning to form on her lips.

She stepped forward now and explained. 'Understand this,' she began, 'ever since you came into our lives, everything has gone rotten – like food left out in a thunderstorm. You're a black cloud hanging over me and my family. But you'll pass. I can promise you that,' she held his gaze, unflinching, and in that moment, as she stood beside Jeff's grave, Bruce recognised that she was stronger than he had ever imagined.

He took a step back then turned to go while Maggie watched him walking away, back along the cemetery path, growing ever smaller, until he finally disappeared.

On returning home, Maggie went upstairs and found Bella asleep on the bed. The dog looked up, pleased to have company, but Maggie's attention went directly to her wardrobe and a plastic bag lying inside it, marked Marston General Hospital.

It had been there since she had brought it home on the day of Jeff's death, but now, with the headstone complete and her exchange with Bruce having settled a score, she finally felt able to deal with it. She braced herself and lifted the bag on to the bed. Bella inched forward sniffing at it. Maggie stroked the dog then began to take out Jeff's clothes: anorak, pullover, shirt, underwear, socks and shoes. She stared at the items then took a laundry bag from under the bed and began to stuff the items inside before quickly zipping it up.

*

For the next half hour, Maggie emptied wardrobes and drawers, transferring the rest of Jeff's clothing into suitcases. Finally, she sat down on the bed and reached for a smaller hospital bag that contained Jeff's jewellery, keys and his mobile.

She studied the phone, then switched it on and found with surprise that it sprang into life. She scrolled through Jeff's contacts – not a great number of people – more a list of her husband's priorities: family, the club and a few old friends from the pits. Natalie's name was still there – the daughter whose presence could never be erased – but not Bruce.

Maggie then checked Dialed Numbers. The log showed the 999 call that had never connected. Call duration – only two seconds. No time at all. No time to save his life. Then she went through Jeff's wallet and all the pocket litter; the loose change and small items he had carried around… a glass marble, club raffle tickets, a Swiss Army knife, an old button…

It seemed so long ago that this had all been handed to her, but nothing compared to the years she now faced without him.

She thought back to the day at the hospital when she had signed for Jeff's effects without fully understanding what this signified. Now she realised that she was to be their custodian. She would do what she was sure Jeff would have wanted her to do: pass on his clothes to someone who needed them, but she would never give up the small items he had treasured enough to keep on his person – right to the end of his life.

When she was finished, she picked up Jeff's phone once more and checked the outgoing message. Jeff's voice suddenly filled the silent room: 'I'm not here right now, but leave a message and I'll get right back to you.' Maggie closed her eyes and allowed herself to pretend he was still there, before a loud beep signaled the pretence was over.

A few hours later, Maggie hesitated before entering the gates of Masters & Son.

After slipping into her work coat and punching in her card, she moved directly on to the factory floor where the loud clatter of sewing machine needles was suddenly silenced. Continuing on, she finally stood beneath the spiral staircase to her office.

The workers nudged one another, expectant, as Maggie turned to face them. Looking pale and drawn, she summoned all her resolve to address her girls.

'I just want to say…' she trailed off for a moment then forced herself to continue. 'Thank you. Thank you for the flowers, for all your cards and for all your…' She hesitated, finding it hard to say the word: 'sympathy.'

An awkward silence settled as she fought back tears. A voice filled it. 'Welcome home,' said Samira. She was standing at the top of the staircase, staring down, offering a sad but encouraging smile.

Maggie nodded to her, grateful for tempering the challenge she felt in this moment. 'Now,' she continued. 'Let's get on with some work, shall we?'

The girls resumed their machining while Maggie walked among them, halting in her tracks as she noted an empty space on the work line. Rona's space.

Before she could make sense of this, a voice sounded behind her – brittle, accusing. 'She lied.' Maggie turned to see Naila standing behind her, head held high – unrepentant. 'I was right,' the girl went on. 'She lied to us all.'

CHAPTER TWENTY-ONE

Maggie trailed a few steps behind a guard who led the way along a dimly lit corridor. She had waited almost an hour in the reception area of the short term holding facility in Leeds, unsure what she would say or do once the wait was over.

Now, as she reached the corridor's end, a door was opened to reveal a young woman sitting hunched over a table in a small cramped room. The guard departed, and Maggie waited for the sound of a key in the lock before she finally spoke.

'So,' she began, 'what am I meant to call you?'

Silence.

'Come on,' said Maggie, pointing back to the door. 'Have I been wasting my time trying to convince them your name's Rona Abid?'

Two words fell from the young woman's lips. 'It's Leyla.'

As though winded by this news, Maggie slumped down on to the hard chair behind her and stared across the table at the woman she thought she knew.

'So,' she began, 'Naila was right. You lied to me – you lied to us all. You're not from Syria – you're from—'

Leyla spoke over her. 'Does it matter where I'm from?

'Of course it does! You told me you were a refugee… that you had nowhere to go. You're no refugee. You're from bloody Turkey.'

'And *still* I have nowhere,' Leyla insisted. 'What I told you was true; I'm a Kurd. My people have nothing. No country of our own.' She paused, then: 'No friends but the mountains.'

'I… don't understand,' said Maggie, confused, 'tell me.'

Leyla held Maggie's look and took a deep breath before trying to explain. 'My family moved from the countryside to Istanbul when I was just one year old. They had been peasants without land of their own. They moved from their village to the city… for a better life, so we wouldn't live in poverty. But for me, growing up in the capital as a Kurd… was not something that I could be proud of. I was ashamed of who I was. I hated it when my mother came to my school, when she spoke to me in our language and let everyone know what we were,' she lowered her gaze and went on. 'I did not admit to anyone that I was a Kurd until I was in my 20s. When my close friends learned this, they were… speechless. I had managed my pretence very well. My lies. Then… one friend said 'But you don't look like a Kurd.' I asked what she meant. The others explained. 'Kurds aren't like us. They smell bad. They're stupid. But you… you could be one of us. So, perhaps you're not a real Kurd, after all.' After that, I… used to tell myself the same thing; I denied who I was; my culture, my people, my family…' until I met someone… a young man who understood why I did this. He told me it wasn't my fault, that we are pawns in other people's struggles. In Turkey we were never encouraged to be Kurds.

For years we weren't even allowed to speak our language... to sing our own songs. But this young man... he sang his songs. A musician. A poet. He wasn't afraid, like me, to be what I am.'

'The father of your daughter?'

Leyla nodded.

'And... what happened to him?'

'He loved too much. Loved being a Kurd. He joined others, to fight...'

'Fight?'

'For freedom. For the right of our daughter to speak her own tongue... to sing her own songs... learn her own language in school. He went to Syria. He never came back. And he never will.'

Maggie took a moment to process this. 'And you came here.'

Leyla nodded once more. 'Another man promised he would take care of me... and Yara,' she looked back at Maggie. 'She's the reason I'm here. To work,' she lowered her head. 'But I stayed too long... the man left and... the only way I could remain was to... pay someone.'

Maggie frowned at this. 'False papers, you mean?'

Leyla nodded slowly. 'Now I have to work to pay for them. *And* to send money for my daughter.' Her eyes moved to an image of a little girl – a photo Maggie had last seen hanging on the locker door – now pinned to a wall in the room of a detention centre. She looked back at Leyla, suddenly unsure. 'And... how do I know you're not lying about this too?' she asked. 'I took your side, against the others – against Naila.'

Leyla shook her head. 'She never trusted me from the start.'

'And she was right,' snapped Maggie. 'I should've listen to her,' she looked away, cursing her own stupidity as she went on. 'What was I thinking? *Why* would I take a stranger's word over hers?'

Leyla leaned closer, desperate for Maggie's understanding. 'Because we're *not* strangers. You *know* me. And I know *you*. Does it matter what country I come from? What name I use? I am the same as you – a woman trying to make things right for her family.' Maggie failed to look back at her. Leyla hesitated before calming herself to speak softly. 'I'm sorry. You've lost your husband too. You've taken time off work to come and see me—'

'No,' Maggie said flatly. 'I've been *given* time off. Compassionate leave they call it,' she shrugged. 'I can't say I wanted it but... everyone says I need it – including Jason,' she paused for a moment, then: 'Samira's in charge for now.'

As Maggie looked away, Leyla closed her eyes in an effort to erase the gulf which now lay between them and whispered: 'Life and death. They get in the way... they separate us. But always in my heart I feel for you, the only person who ever gave me... trust?' Opening her eyes now, she saw Maggie turning back to face her. 'We *are* the same, Maggie. The same woman,' she reached out and took Maggie's hand, holding it firmly against her chest, allowing Maggie feel the strong beat of her heart – a stranger's heart – though in that moment, she seemed family. Maggie's anger dissolved as she glanced at the photo on the wall. Freeing her hand she pointed to it. 'How the hell did it come to this?' she asked. 'Leaving your own kid behind?'

'I left because I don't want to just exist... I want us to live,' said Leyla. 'To *thrive*,' she paused and gave a dark look. 'And I've done worse things just to survive,' she went on: 'Without

Yara, that's all I do. But I always tell myself that one day I *will* start living again. And I began to believe that – when I was working with you. I let myself think… things *can* be different. *I* can be different…' she broke off for a moment and gave an ironic smile. 'Someone my daughter can be proud of.'

A moment passed between them before Leyla got to her feet. Maggie spoke quickly. 'They'll let you go, won't they?' she said urgently. 'I mean, it's not as though you're a criminal. You have to tell them what you've just told me. They know they can't keep you banged up forever. This is a short term facility. Seven days, they told me. Then they'll have to send you somewhere else.'

'A removal centre,' said Leyla, 'from there, they'll try to send me back.'

'Try?'

'I will stay,' Leyla said determinedly. '*And* work.'

'How?' Maggie asked, confused. 'You can't come back to the factory. They'll come looking for you.'

Leyla lowered her voice as she explained. 'I have a friend. He… says he can arrange something.'

Maggie read her guilty look. "He…" echoed Maggie. 'Another man,' she said, weighted. 'And just what do you have to do for him?'

Leyla turned away as she went on. 'I'll do whatever I need to,' she said, 'for my daughter – the same as *you* would – for Lisa.'

Maggie took a deep breath and lowered her head, defeated. 'I can't.' Leyla looked back at her and Maggie shook her head. 'She won't even see me. And it's all my fault. Jeff warned me. He said I'd lose her if I couldn't accept—' She broke off.

'What?' Leyla's eyes scanned Maggie's for an answer.

Finally Maggie gave it. 'That husband of hers,' she said. 'I'm scared. Scared of what he's doing to her?'

Leyla read the fear in her eyes. 'Then you have to *help* her.'

Maggie shook her head. 'You don't understand. She's not a child – she's a grown woman with her own mind…'

'*Listen* to your heart,' said Leyla. '*Trust it* – like you once trusted me,' she continued to hold Maggie's look as she went on. 'I *didn't* steal Naila's cigarettes. I'm no thief. You were right about that – *and* about me. ' She managed a sad smile while Maggie looked back at her questioningly, still suspicious, until Leyla nodded to confirm the truth. In the next moment Maggie returned her smile, but the connection between them was suddenly broken by the sound of a key turning in the door. Leyla leaned quickly forward and whispered: '*Trust* what you know – and use it.'

In the next instant, the door opened. The guard entered to signal the meeting was over, but as the two women broke away, Leyla kept her eyes fixed on Maggie with a look that would remain in her memory long after the door had closed.

'I don't know why you went to see her,' said Samira on the phone to Maggie that same evening.

Seated at her laptop in the kitchen with Bella at her feet, Maggie took off her reading glasses before replying. 'She's one of our workers.'

'*Was*,' said Samira pointedly. 'And you have Naila to thank for showing her up for what she really is.'

'And what's that?'

'A fraud.'

'Is she?' said Maggie, still feeling conflicted.

'You know yourself, she lied to us all—'

'Aye,' said Maggie quickly, 'she lied about her name and where she comes from. But what about everything else?'

Samira gave an audible sigh. 'You mean the way she took you in?'

Maggie paused, still unsure. 'I can't help thinking that if I was in her place I'd have done the same.'

Samira took her time before responding gently. 'And if I was you, Maggie, maybe I'd understand. But I don't.'

Maggie dwelt on this for a moment then chose to change the subject. 'How's it going with the orders?'

'Fine,' Samira replied, too briskly for Maggie's liking.

'You can tell me,' said Maggie.

'There's nowt for you to worry about.'

'You mean I'm dispensable?'

A pause followed. 'That's one thing you'll never be,' said Samira 'I'm just filling in, remember?'

'Aye,' said Maggie. 'So if it all goes tits up and we lose our jobs, I'll blame you.'

She smiled to herself but on the end of the line, Samira remained silent before framing her words very carefully. 'Take this time out for yourself, Maggie, and come back only when you're ready.'

Maggie remembered something. 'That's exactly what Jason said.'

'I know,' Samira replied.

Maggie noted Samira's guarded tone. 'Is there... something you're not telling me?' She braced herself now, knowing Samira would never lie to her.

For a moment, it appeared Samira had already left the line but then her voice sounded once more.

'Jason said he's going to write to you.'

'About what?' said Maggie. 'He's not sacking me, is he?'

Samira let the silence stretch – then: 'Not just you, Maggie.'

Maggie slumped back in her chair as though physically struck by the news. Samira went on. 'He's selling up... to a property developer. Says the business has been losing money—'

'Since *he* took over!'

'Mags—'

'No,' Maggie broke in fiercely. 'This is why he wanted me out of the way, isn't it? His father must be turning in his grave. I have to go and see him—'

'No, Mags,' said Samira. 'I... wasn't meant to tell you. But how could I not?'

Maggie took time to process this. 'Do the girls know?'

'No-one else. Just you and me. There'll be redundancy...'

'And no future.'

'It could all still fall through?' Samira was doing her best.

Maggie played along with her. 'Aye,' she said softly.

'Look, I know it's hard, Mags, but... promise you'll stay home and take it easy?'

Maggie closed her eyes. 'Do I have a choice?'

Once the call ended, Maggie sat stock still for a moment, hearing another voice in her head – reminding her of something. *'Trust what you know – and use it...'*

She opened her eyes and took in her surroundings once more. The laptop screen was still there in front of her, reminding her that it had taken some time to find the websites she had been looking for. As a distraction from Samira's news, Maggie picked up her glasses from the table and pinched the bridge of her nose before slipping them on again. She leaned forward and studied the screen. She had set herself the task of sifting through numerous dates and entries; cross referencing names which had led her precisely nowhere. But now she steeled herself – and tried again – typing in the same names into the new Search box before her. Beneath the table, Bella nuzzled Maggie's foot for attention. Without looking down at the dog, Maggie tried to calm her. 'In a minute, Bella, I promise—' Then she broke off abruptly as she stared at something on her screen; an online copy of an official document.

CERTIFIED COPY OF AN ENTRY OF MARRIAGE PURSUANT TO THE MARRIAGE ACT 1949

A name appeared in a column – Bruce Carter – followed by another – Christine Forrester. Maggie held her breath, taking a moment to absorb this before her fingers moved swiftly across the laptop's keypad. Following the screen's instructions, she tapped in a further command, and waited. A document appeared on the screen – an electoral roll entry for Ms Christine Forrester. The dog gave an impatient yap at her feet.

'Hold on, Bella!'

Maggie punched another command into her laptop then reached down and stroked the dog as she watched an address transform into an icon of the world, before the screen honed in on a single street. One house, amongst others, now came into sharp focus – 36 Parnell Road.

CHAPTER TWENTY-TWO

In a rundown area of Leeds, Maggie cruised slowly in her car while staring out of the windscreen at row after row of what she knew to be back-to-back houses.

Built two centuries ago, the 'back-to-backs' had become known as the worst type of slum. Associated with overcrowding, and poorly-lit with inadequate ventilation, many had been constructed over open sewers covered only by boards. Built by opportunists who had realised they could satisfy the needs of local mill-owners and maximise the number of workers dwelling in the smallest area while also saving on building roads and proper drainage, 'back-to-backs' had become a byword for the cramped conditions and inadequate sanitation that had enabled disease to spread among the workers of the great industrial cities of the north. Now, totally refurbished with all mod cons, 'back-to-backs' were finding new popularity – this time with buy-to-let investors; entrepreneurs who liked making a quick return, much like Jason Masters who was now selling his father's business.

Satellite dishes lined the pebble-dashed terrace that Maggie viewed from her car. One house in particular looked familiar – number 36. She braked, then steeled herself, taking a moment to settle her racing thoughts.

Reflecting on her recent meeting with Lisa's friend, Dee, Maggie couldn't help feeling guilty about going behind her daughter's back, but Dee was now halfway across the world, and the need to find out more about Bruce's former marriage had proved too overpowering. Born out of concern for her daughter, that same need had continued to feed a nagging suspicion that would only be satisfied with the truth.

Why had Lisa wanted to keep this earlier marriage a secret? Was she really trying to protect herself from Maggie's reaction – or from her husband's? There was only one way of finding out. Having come this far she knew she must go on. She would surely make things no worse than they were already.

Getting out of the car, she steeled herself to move on when a young boy glided towards her on a skateboard. Tumbling clumsily at Maggie's feet, he rubbed his knee and looked up at her as he forced back tears.

'Y'all right, son?'

The boy answered Maggie's question with a brave nod. Getting to his feet he allowed her to dust him down when a voice sounded at a distance.

'Ciaran? What're you doing there? Come inside!' A dark-haired woman in her late twenties was now standing at a front door, drying her hands on a tea towel. The boy called back to her.

'I'm okay!'

The woman eyed Maggie as she called to the boy again. '*Inside* – now!'

At this, the boy picked up his skateboard and reluctantly stomped his way to the house. As he entered, the young woman glanced cursorily back towards Maggie before turning to follow her son.

Maggie quickly re-focused on the door number – and called out: 'Christine?'

The woman turned back slowly. Maggie braced herself then asked: 'Could I have a word?'

A few moments later, Maggie entered a messy sitting room strewn with toys. A plasma screen TV was attached to the wall but the furniture had seen better days. Christine Forrester followed Maggie into the room, about to close the door after herself when Ciaran trailed in behind them. Flopping down on the sofa, the boy immediately reached for the TV remote.

His mother nodded to the door. 'Go upstairs and get yourself washed.'

Ciaran frowned sulkily before he began whining. 'But I wanna' watch—'

Christine seized the remote from him. 'Do what I say.'

The boy registered her stern expression then got to his feet and obeyed her. Christine tossed the remote on to the sofa and looked back at Maggie. 'All right,' she began. 'What's this about?'

Maggie managed a weak smile. 'I need to ask you a few questions.'

Christine wiped a weary hand through her long dark hair and heaved a sigh. 'Look, if it's about my rent arrears, I've already told the council that once my benefit's sorted I—'

'It's not,' said Maggie, breaking in. She paused then took a step forward: 'It's about your ex-husband. Bruce.'

Christine Forrester appeared to freeze, her eyes slowly narrowing with suspicion. 'Who are you?'

'I'm not from the council—'

'And you're not from Child Maintenance either. They were here the other day and they already know—' she broke off sharply.

'Know what?'

Christine took on a hunted look then stepped back to the door and opened it. 'Get out.'

Maggie held her ground. 'Look—'

'Didn't you hear me?'

Maggie braced herself and remained rooted to the spot. Christine pointed to her phone on the sofa. 'Whoever you are, you'd better go now or I'll call the police.'

'This won't take long,' said Maggie. Christine picked up the phone and Maggie continued. 'If you just let me explain...' she watched the woman dial. 'He's married my daughter.'

A moment passed before Christine Forrester looked back at Maggie. The phone slowly lowered in her hand.

In the bedroom at Woodside, Lisa looked on as Bruce closed a carefully packed suitcase.

'Seen my car keys anywhere?'

Lisa shook her head. Bruce nodded abruptly towards a chest of drawers. 'They were right there.'

Lisa picked up a newspaper from the chest and found the keys lying beneath it. Handing them to her husband she offered him an admonishing look.

Bruce apologised. 'Sorry, I... just don't want to be late for this meeting.' He slipped his suitcase to the floor then pulled Lisa to him and held her in his arms.

'Don't worry,' she said softly. 'It'll be okay.'

Pulling away from her, he asked: 'And what about you? 'Sure you'll be all right here on your own?'

'You'll only be away for one night?'

Bruce nodded. 'And I promise I'll call as soon as I get to the hotel.'

Lisa smiled. 'I'll be fine. In fact,' she paused for a moment then went on. 'I... thought I might get in touch with Mum. Ask her over?'

Bruce turned to look at her. Lisa explained. 'It's been a while now, and... well, the longer we leave things the harder it's going to be,' she paused.

Bruce considered this. Why was she choosing to suggest this now? It was frustrating but nevertheless he managed a smile. 'Of course.'

He saw Lisa looking grateful – but what was she about to say next?

'I've... been thinking about her a lot lately,' she began. 'I mean, I've got you, but Mum's all on her own. First Natalie... then Dad... now—'

'Lisa,' Bruce began, trying to interrupt this train of thought.

'I miss her,' said Lisa starkly.

Bruce took a deep breath and tried to calm himself. She certainly chose her moments; why did she have to bring this up now when he had so little time? Knowing he had to act fast, he pulled her to him again and held her close, managing to hide his resentment as he softly explained. 'Of course you do. And with me away you're bound to feel like this. But after all this time, don't you think you should do things properly?'

Lisa looked up at him. 'What d'you mean?'

'Plan things a bit more? At least, work out what you're going to say.'

She frowned. 'But... this is Mum we're talking about.'

'Of course. And we both know what she's like.' He held her gaze. 'I just wouldn't want either of you saying anything you might regret.'

'*Either* of us?' said Lisa picking up on the word. 'Are you... saying she's angry with me?'

Bruce failed to reply, convinced his silence would only serve to increase her suspicion.

She looked distressed now as she asked: 'What exactly did Mum say to you – at the cemetery?'

Bruce shook his head. 'It doesn't matter. She was upset and I'm sure she didn't mean anything.'

'Didn't mean what?'

'Look...'

'No!' said Lisa briskly. 'You don't have to make excuses for her, Bruce. She thinks I'm in the wrong, is that it?'

He left a suitable pause, then: 'Like I say, why don't you leave this until I'm home? We'll think of a way to get things back on track.' He could see she was torn. 'Promise me?' He held her gaze.

Finally, she folded. 'Okay,' she agreed. 'I promise.'

Satisfied, he kissed her – long and hard. When they finally broke apart, she gazed up at him, reaching up to stroke his face before she whispered: 'I'll miss you.'

'Me too.' Peeling her hand from his cheek, Bruce grabbed his suitcase and made his way into the hallway. Lisa followed, watching him as he headed downstairs where he grabbed his coat and glanced back at her.

'I'll call you later,' he said. Blowing a kiss, he waved from the door, and left.

At exactly the same time, Maggie was trying hard to explain to Christine Forrester. 'Her name is Lisa. They got married a few months ago.'

Christine shook her head. 'Why're you telling me this? Why should I care?'

Maggie could see she was putting up a good front but the young mother's tension was palpable as she flinched at the sound of her son calling down to her from upstairs. She moved to the door and shouted back to him. 'I'll be there in a minute!'

As she closed the door, Maggie asked: 'Does Ciaran ever see him?'

Christine looked back at Maggie but failed to reply.

'Well?' said Maggie, becoming impatient.

'No,' said Christine smartly.

'Why not? He's Bruce's son, isn't he?'

Christine chose her words carefully. 'Ciaran's *my* son. No more questions now. Just go.'

Silence fell – until the boy called down again. 'Mum!'

Torn, Christine went to respond to him but Maggie quickly asked: 'And does Bruce know where you are?'

Christine spun around. 'No,' she said firmly. 'And I don't want him to, d'you understand?' She held Maggie's look.

'Why not?' asked Maggie, moving closer. 'What did he do?'

Christine fell silent. Maggie frowned, her own tension mounting. 'Tell me.'

'Nothing,' said Christine quickly. 'He did *nothing*, all right?' She paused then continued in staccato phrases. 'We got married too young. But it's over. We're divorced. Now get out and leave me alone.'

Maggie took another step towards her and shook her head. 'It's not as easy as that, is it?' She looked around the room. 'You might not have been here long, Christine. But long enough to go on the electoral roll.'

Christine frowned. 'Is… that how you found me?'

Maggie nodded. 'A public records search. It didn't take long, Christine. And if *I* found you – *he* could too.'

At this, Christine suddenly put a fist to her mouth then moved to the window and looked out as though hunted. 'What d'you want?' she asked quickly. Maggie approached. 'Some answers, that's all. Then I'll go… and I promise, I'll never tell him. I swear.'

Christine looked back at Maggie, then finally nodded. 'All right,' she said, defeated. 'What is it you want to know?'

'What did he do?' Maggie asked softly. 'Was he… violent?'

Christine shook her head, seemingly confused, before she gave a bitter laugh. 'Violent? Of course he wasn't. He's Prince bloody Charming.'

It was Maggie's turn to look confused as Christine went on. 'At least he was when I met him,' she moved to the sofa and reached for a pack of cigarettes. With shaking hands, she lit one and took a deep drag before exhaling a long trail of smoke. 'I was 16, if you can imagine that?' She stared back at Maggie while picking chipped varnish from her fingernails. 'Little Miss

Innocent. Bunking in to a dance at the barracks,' she paused. 'Love at first sight. 'Believe in that, do you? Because that's what it was. One look and I was gone. All my mates were green with envy that I'd managed to cop off with the best of the bunch.' With trembling fingers she pressed the cigarette filter to her lips and took another deep drag of smoke. 'We got wed before I was even eighteen. There was no-one to argue. I'd been in care 'til then but now I was a pig in shit because I'd bagged myself the best looking fella in the regiment. To top it all – he loved me too,' she nodded to herself. 'Oh yeah, I was sure of that. He'd do anything for me. I was his… little girl.'

Maggie frowned at this but Christine went on. 'I'd never felt wanted before. Not like that. But as soon as the ring went on my finger, everything started to change. He never let me out of his sight. I belonged to him. Body and soul. Till death do us part. To honour and… obey?' She looked to the floor as though still reflecting on this, before stubbing out her cigarette, hard, into the ashtray. Getting to her feet she moved back to the window. 'Just before we got wed, I managed to get a place at college – hairdressing. I was looking forward to working but he soon had me giving that up. We… moved out to the sticks. I couldn't drive so I never got to see anyone. 'We don't need anyone else,' he used to say. 'From now on, it's just… you and me.'

She forced herself to go on. 'He made it all seem so… normal. But it wasn't. None of it. I had no mates, no money, no job? Just him,' she looked back at Maggie. 'So… no. He never hit me. Because he didn't need to. He just stripped everything away until there was nothing left – nothing but him. Sometimes I wish he *had* hit me – maybe I'd have come to my senses sooner.'

'But you did,' said Maggie. 'Come to your senses?'

Christine nodded slowly. 'I took off one night… me and Ciaran. We only had the clothes we stood up in. I knew he'd never forgive me,' she looked away.

'For taking his son?'

Christine looked back at Maggie with a curious expression – then she realised something. 'You don't know him at all, do you?' She came closer to Maggie as she went on. 'Bruce has no interest in kids. Even his own. He always said to me that if I ever got pregnant, he'd make me get rid of it. How could he possibly have a kid taking attention away from him?'

Maggie tried to make sense of this. 'But… you did get pregnant.'

Christine was about to answer when Ciaran's voice sounded once more. 'Mum!'

Christine looked conflicted but gave her reply to Maggie. 'You won't understand,' she said. 'But your daughter will.'

'Understand what?'

Christine made a move to the door but Maggie laid a hand on her arm to stop her. 'You *have* to talk to her,' she said urgently. 'She won't believe anything I say. He's got her wrapped around his little finger.'

Christine considered this, then said starkly: 'I've said all I'm saying. I've got my son to think of, and I'm not going to let his future be ruined by his dad's past.'

'What past?' said Maggie picking up on this.

Christine kept her silence.

Maggie stepped forward. 'There's something else, isn't there?' she said, 'something you're not telling me,' she hesitated, then: 'What is it? *What* won't I understand?'

In that moment, Maggie was sure Christine was about to divulge something very important – the answer to all her questions – but a child's voice broke the spell.

'Mum!' Ciaran was at the door, whining at his mother. 'You said you were coming!'

'I'm sorry, son,' said Christine. 'I had to talk to this lady but…' she broke off then turned to face Maggie as she said, 'she's leaving now.' Reaching out to her son, Christine pulled him close. Maggie recognised her time was up and picked up her bag. Moving into the hallway she was about to open the front door when Christine spoke once more – this time in an urgent whisper. 'Get your daughter away from him.'

Maggie turned and read the look on the young woman's face – fear masked by determination. Ciaran joined them in the hall, staring resentfully at Maggie before he clung to his mother, leaving Maggie unsure if it was Christine Forrester or her son who was gaining the most comfort in that moment.

Maggie left the house and moved quickly to her car. Getting into it, she then glanced back at the house and saw Christine Forrester standing with her son at the window, looking haunted – as if by an old ghost.

CHAPTER TWENTY-THREE

It was early evening and Lisa sat in front of an unwatched TV, her phone in hand. Bringing up the contact list, her finger hovered over the name, *Mum*. Remembering her promise, she scrolled back to find Bruce's number and dialed that instead.

The call came through to Bruce's hotel room. The TV was on but his shirt was off as he towel-dried his wet hair after a shower. Wrapping the towel around his neck he then reached to pick up his phone which was lying beside an empty room service tray. He saw Lisa's number, then heard her voice: 'I miss you.'

'Snap,' he replied, 'I was going to call you.'

'So why didn't you?'

'Because the meeting went on – longer than expected.' He lay back on the bed and picked up a high ball of Bourbon from the bedside table.

'But it went okay?'

Hearing the child-like curiosity in her voice, Bruce paused to prolong the suspense. He held up his glass to the light and considered the amber liquid inside. 'I got the contract.'

'I knew you would! When d'you start?'

'Couple of weeks' time. First job's in Leeds.'

'Leeds?' The joy had gone out of her voice. 'But… I thought you said it would be local?'

'I did. But things went better than I expected. I got the contract for a chain of three,' he explained, 'all prestige hotels – which means—'

'You'll be away,' said Lisa, deflated. 'But you could work from home, couldn't you?' she asked, suddenly hopeful. 'You've got your office here.'

Bruce paused then sipped his drink. 'There'll be lots of meetings so I'll need to be on the road for a while – just to set things up. But… you could come up at weekends.'

'I… won't get in the way?'

Bruce smiled. 'You think I'd leave you there all on your own?' He got up from the bed and moved to the wardrobe to select a clean white shirt. 'What've you been doing since I left?'

'Thinking about you.'

He paused, then: 'You didn't call your Mum?'

Lisa frowned. 'No.' Fighting some doubts, she went on. 'You're right.'

Bruce smiled. ''Course I am,' he said. 'Just leave things a bit longer – 'til you and I have had a chance to discuss it all properly.'

'I will,' she said. 'I miss you.'

'I miss you too, little girl. But I'll be back tomorrow, okay?'

'Okay.' Lisa echoed softly. 'Love you.'

'Love you too. Be good.' He ended the call, stared down at the mobile in his hand – and smiled to himself.

Lisa set her phone down and glanced around the living room as laughter blared from the TV. She heaved a sigh and got up from the sofa and was heading for the kitchen when she paused in the hallway – her gaze fixed on the door to Bruce's basement office – the physical barrier that at some point, every day and every evening, kept her separated from her husband. To Bruce this was his refuge, a man cave, a quiet place in which he could work.

That all seemed perfectly reasonable and she felt she might have accepted this if he had only taken time to explain this to her before. Instead, she had never been consulted about him having sole use of the basement – or even renting the house.

Bruce has executed a *fait accompli* and signed the lease himself, cutting her out of the process, and taking advantage of the fact that the renovated space in the cellar was there for him alone to occupy. He had moved a desk into it along with computer hardware, including a large screen and sound system – and then installed a special alarm system to which only he had access.

Whenever Lisa as much as hinted at how excluded this made her feel, Bruce dismissed her comments as over reactions and implied that she was viewing things from a faulty perspective. He would simply repeat that he had a responsibility to keep his clients' data secure and the basement office of his own home was the only place for this information to remain safe.

In effect, his rationale was that the door was no barrier at all but a drawbridge which could be opened any time he chose – although he wasn't prepared to do so just to satisfy his wife's curiosity.

Lisa dwelt on the word, knowing that 'curiosity' wasn't all that she felt. She reached out towards the tiny red light that constantly flashed on the alarm system's keypad. It went out only when a short code disabled the alarm and allowed the door to be opened. She had seen Bruce use the code scores of times – but still it remained unknown to her. Would it really be compromising his security to gain entry? Her fingers trembled before she finally made contact with the light – then flinched – as though having met with a sudden warning.

Ten minutes after his conversation with Lisa, Bruce stepped out of his Bradford hotel room. Once in the lift, he paused to check his appearance in the reflection of a smoked glass mirror, taking care to straighten the collar of his white shirt and rake fingers through his hair. Then he pressed the button for the ground floor and after the lift doors opened, he headed towards a dimly-lit bar at the threshold to the dining room.

As he entered, his eyes quickly scanned the room: a group of young office workers were laughing together; a middle-aged couple sitting in silence as they sipped cocktails; a family choosing food from the bar's snack menu.

Then his gaze fell on a young woman sitting alone at the bar. He moved on – then stopped in his tracks and took his mobile from his pocket. Turning towards the light of a chandelier, he checked his phone for messages – but used the opportunity to get a better look of the woman. She was attractive, with shoulder-length red hair, a short hemline and designer heels. Her manicured fingernails traced the rim of the glass in front of her. She looked lonely.

Bruce pocketed his phone and was about to join her at the

bar when a man entered. Looking around, his eyes fell on the redhead at the bar and he moved quickly to her.

Leaning forward, he kissed her, looking as though he might be apologising for being late before he sat down and called for the barman's attention. The redhead's smile showed her forgiveness.

Bruce's eyes narrowed as he glanced once more around the room, finding no-one of any interest before he moved on, sat down at a table and gave his full attention to a menu. He hadn't eaten much all day but the Bourbon had given him an appetite, though nothing much on offer took his fancy.

'Word of advice – the food here isn't too good.'

A woman was standing by his table. She was smiling, her long blonde hair parted on one side, falling low across half of her face – an attractive face – but spoiled by too much make-up. She was a stranger but there was still something familiar about her smile and the look she gave him. Bruce recognised it. She was working – looking for a punter. He set down his menu. 'Thanks for the advice. Maybe I'll just settle for a drink.' The woman was still there – her smile in place. Bruce was sure he was right about her, but a simple question would prove it. 'Care to join me?'

He indicated the seat beside him. The woman took it, sitting far too close to him, no doubt for the benefit of the hotel manager who was discussing something with the barman. The trick was always to give the impression you were a couple. 'Where are you from?' Bruce asked.

The woman was looking directly at him now – a hint of suspicion and maybe even a little fear in her eyes. 'Your accent,' Bruce went on. 'Italian?'

The woman gave another smile. 'Does it matter?'

He held her gaze and she slowly shook her head.

'Actually, I'm Kurdish,' she said finally. 'My name is Leyla.'

Bruce paused for a moment then smiled. 'I'm Mike.' He handed her the menu. 'What would you like?'

CHAPTER TWENTY-FOUR

It was almost ten when Bruce and Leyla reached his hotel room. At the door, they held a look, and a moment passed before he leaned in to kiss her.

As he did so, she suddenly froze, her eyes darting to a waiter passing in the corridor with a room service tray. Leyla waited for him to move on, then looked back at Bruce and whispered: 'I... have to be careful.'

Bruce gave a nod. 'Sure,' slipping the key card into the lock he allowed her to enter first.

Once inside, Leyla glanced quickly around the room, taking a mental screenshot of everything she saw. It was tidier than she was used to; businessmen could be slobs, too accustomed to having someone else to tidy up after them, but this room was immaculate. She took that as a good sign; if a man was careful with his own things, there was more chance he would be careful with a working girl.

'Make yourself comfortable,' said Bruce, moving to the mini-bar. 'What can I get you?'

Leyla shook her head.

'Oh come on,' he urged. 'All you've had so far is a Coke.'

'I told you,' she said. 'I don't like to drink.'

Bruce gave a tight smile as though accepting this but a tiny muscle continued to flex in his jaw as he picked up a high ball. 'You don't mind if I do?'

She shook her head. He turned to pour himself another Bourbon.

'We need to discuss what it is you want,' said Leyla, coming forward, still trying to look casual, inviting. It was always good to introduce a distraction when discussing money so she slipped a finger beneath the lapel of Bruce's jacket and ran a painted nail down slowly towards his waist – brand new nails acquired only that afternoon. Bruce knocked back his drink and replied. 'Maybe just some company,' he said gently.

Leyla looked wrong-footed. Dissatisfied, she moved to the bed and slipped out of her jacket before sitting down. 'Company comes at a price,' she said. Leaning back a little, she crossed her legs and bounced a foot up and down a few times.

Bruce stared down at the glass in his hand. 'Are you… sure you don't want a drink?'

She considered him again; he was being hospitable but she shook her head. Something was troubling her – something she couldn't quite put her manicured finger on.

He was an attractive man; smart and good company but there was something not quite right about him. Why did he need a working girl? Maybe his wife or partner was unable or unwilling to give him what he needed? Maybe his needs were more than even Leyla was prepared to give. The night was still early enough for her to find someone else. She made a decision.

Slipping back into her jacket, she picked up her bag and got up as if to leave. She would make an excuse. She had done it before with a punter. She could do so again now. She opened her mouth to speak, to find an excuse, but Bruce reached into his pocket and tossed his wallet on to the bed beside her. As it fell open, she saw it was full of notes. She looked back at him.

'Relax,' said Bruce. He was smiling now – exposing white polished teeth – like a film star. He moved towards her and slipped the silver chain of her bag from her shoulders, applying just the slightest pressure, enough for her to sit back down on the bed. She looked again at the wallet then returned his perfect smile. Still she felt some nagging unease. Nerves, perhaps.

'Maybe I *will* have a drink,' she said. 'Vodka. Large one. Straight.'

Turning back to the mini-bar, Bruce took two vodka miniatures from it and poured them into a glass. Still turned away from her, he asked: 'Ice?'

Leyla nodded and glanced around the room once more. She took a deep breath and tried to relax. She had been through a lot lately but she told herself now that there was no need to feel so uptight.

She had managed to escape the authorities and for the time being she was free again – and working – though back doing what she hated most. Nevertheless, doing it in this hotel seemed a step up. The Grand Hotel. Perfectly named, because she had seen, in Maggie's leaflet, just how grand it was – with a conference room that attracted businessmen who came to the city for meetings – like Maggie's boss and this man who was now standing in front of her offering her a drink. 'Must be Fate,' he was saying. 'Finding you tonight?'

Leyla gave a small shrug – and a curious look. 'Maybe I found *you*,' she said, feeling more in control. Her glass met his. She took a gulp of vodka and felt it sting the back of her throat before she leaned back on the bed and stared up at the ceiling – thoughtful now.

'You work here every night?' Bruce asked.

Leyla shook her head. 'First time.'

She turned on her side, still observing him as she took another gulp of her drink, feeling more relaxed by the second. Outside the window she could see the old bell tower on Bradford City Hall.

The clock face wasn't visible but she knew that the bells rang every fifteen minutes which would come in handy if she wasn't able to check her watch. She finished her drink and kept her eyes trained on the tower. Someone had recently told her it had been modelled on the Palazzo Vecchio in Florence. Italy.

That's where her new punter thought she might have come from. A coincidence – or maybe he was right and it really was Fate that she was here. Fate that she had seen the hotel leaflet in Maggie's office. Fate that she had met this man. If things continued to go well, one day she might even have enough money to visit Florence.

She could take Yara and together they could find other beautiful buildings and palaces. They might even make a better life for themselves in Italy rather than England. A better life… That's all she had ever been seeking.

She felt the vodka doing its job. She had almost forgotten her concerns about the punter but now she noticed he was reaching for something in his jacket pocket. That always unnerved her, especially after the creep who had pulled a knife on her – a decrepit old businessman who had needed to terrify her in order to generate enough excitement to get himself off. With relief she saw her new punter was pulling a phone from his pocket. Maybe he was going to turn it off so he wouldn't be disturbed – especially by a call from his wife. She knocked back the rest of her drink – and smiled playfully. 'Need to call someone?'

Bruce looked back at her but failed to reply. Instead he held the phone up and eyed her through the viewfinder…

A smile was still playing on her lips as she asked: 'What're you doing?'

Bruce said nothing but came a little closer, still eyeing her through the lens of his phone; focusing on her in close up: long legs, tight skirt, a tattoo on the back of her wrist – what looked like a little butterfly…

Leyla felt uncomfortable, embarrassed and exposed. 'Please,' she shook her head. 'I don't want you to do that.'

Ignoring her, Bruce continued filming, moving ever closer…

'Didn't you hear me?' she asked, becoming angry now. She couldn't be doing with film footage of herself in a hotel room. Perhaps this guy – this clean, meticulous customer was working for Immigration – and the whole thing was a trick. A sting. A set up. She knew she wouldn't be the first. 'Look, I don't like being—'

She had got up from the bed only to find the room was swaying. She blinked as she tried to make sense of what was happening. Too much to take in; a kaleidoscope of colours, emotions, fears. 'I… don't… feel…' she was trying hard to form words that wouldn't come – even in her own language.

Like a scream in a nightmare, she was silenced, unable to call out or to fight back.

The punter was standing directly above her now, the phone still in his hand, half concealing his face, just like her own new hairstyle was meant to do…

She tried to hide by looking away but the only thing she managed to focus on was her empty glass on the bedside table. 'You… did… something…'

She stretched a hand to the glass then saw the butterfly on her wrist – and beyond it – the door. A voice within her told her she could reach it if she summoned all her strength… She was strong… she had survived so far… and she could survive this…

She made a sudden lunge, propelling herself towards the door, Something stopped her. A strong hand was yanking her back, tugging on her newly-styled hair. Instantly, the pain took her back to a cat fight in a garment factory. Other voices cheering from the sidelines.

'Go Naila!'
'Watch her nails!'
'Take her down!'

Taunts from the merciless like those that had once sounded along the Via Dolorosa – the road along which Christ had been made to carry the heavy cross for his own crucifixion… the way of sorrow…

As the bells on the clock tower began to chime she knew, this time, there would be no-one coming to save her.

CHAPTER TWENTY-FIVE

Lisa was in her kitchen, making herself a coffee when she reached for the biscuit jar – then hesitated.

She had been doing so well lately, not allowing herself to be tempted too often by snacks and chocolates – though biscuits were another thing. Maybe just one? No. One would simply lead to another and then there would be several – too many – and Bruce would be bound to notice when he got back from his business trip. But she needed some comfort. She had so much on her mind. Too much. She wanted to explain something to him. Something important. But she couldn't think straight. She also needed someone to talk to. Her mum? If only Maggie hadn't been so interfering. If only Dee wasn't away with the girls in Florida. If only her dad was still alive…

Lisa had always been able to talk to Jeff. Just thinking of him caused her to look away sharply in an effort to stop herself from crying. She found herself staring around the empty room. Maggie had been right about the house; it was stylish and modern but cold and so far away from everything – and everyone – she knew.

The woods held no attraction for her; the tall trees swaying in the wind outside only made her feel hemmed in as though they were sentinels keeping watch on her. On moonlit nights their silhouettes rose up, blocking the light. On cloudy days they appeared to be marching closer…

Lisa had never been one for the countryside. She loved the bright lights of the city – and the seaside. Holidays in Blackpool and Skegness. 'Skeggie' had been Jeff's favourite destination, where he had been happy to sit on the beach for a week or more – never tiring of watching the tide come and go – a contrast to a life spent in a dark hole…a coal-black pit. Jeff used to say that walks in the country were for posh folk – and that he never knew a local person who walked just for the sake of it – only when they had somewhere to go and something to do.

Maybe he was right. Maggie certainly had no time for idle strolls. She was a grafter, but on her days off she would always head into town to go shopping. If her purse was empty – it was window shopping. Lisa stared again towards her own kitchen window. It wasn't yet light so all she could see was herself reflected back in the glass from the kitchen down-lights. It suddenly reminded her of seeing her reflection in the glass of the cooker door – her head jerked back by Bruce behind her…

She closed her eyes and allowed herself to revisit the emotions she had felt that afternoon; physical pain and fear but also a strange reassurance mingled with a sense of shame. Bruce was right.

How could anyone else understand the bond between them? It was a bond too private to share with anyone else – but Bruce. How would she ever explain to Dee, Patsy or Sandra that the thrill had crossed a line to become something she now feared.

The girls had shared secrets before but this was a secret too far. She imagined their reactions, their questions. Had any of this ever been about pleasure – or was it instead a need for punishment? She found herself biting down on her lower lip; pain reminding her that she was truly alive. Why wouldn't it? After all, she was the daughter who had survived, while Natalie now lay stripped of flesh by the years spent buried in the cold earth.

Soon Jeff would be the same; a pile of bones – unrecognisable even to those who remained – to those who had loved them both. Father and daughter. Was it true, she now wondered, that the dead are able to look on at those left behind? If so, what would Jeff and Natalie think of her relationship with Bruce – and what she had allowed him to do? It wasn't as though he had ever been truly violent. He didn't beat her. He cared for her, loved her, protected her – but he had also long recognised something within her – something that had set her apart from other women – a need in her that he alone satisfied. Was that the reason he had married her?

Lisa tried to make sense of this. He had been married before. A long time ago. Not a marriage like her own – but a mistake. He had told her all about it; explained that he had been too young to settle down, too immature – but the girl had tricked him by telling him that she was pregnant – knowing he would do the right thing. He had married her – only for her to "miscarry". A liar – and a bitch to have abused his trust like that. How could this woman have thought she could fool him into staying with her? Bruce had been too smart for that. He wouldn't make the same mistake again. In fact, he had been alone for several years until he finally recognised his soulmate

– a partner for life – Lisa. Why was it Maggie still felt that so hard to accept?

Lisa turned again to the window, aware that she could never be sure if anyone was there lurking among the trees, observing her. She quickly closed the blinds and vowed not to open them again until it was properly light. Heading back to the counter she picked up her mug. It was almost at her lips when the doorbell rang. She looked up sharply – and saw she had just spilled coffee. Who was it at the door? Not the postman – nor Bruce – maybe someone who had been watching her until she closed the blinds… She cleaned up her spilt coffee then made her way through the hallway, calling out. 'Who is it?'

Silence.

Moving on, she took a moment to calm herself and opened the front door. No-one there. But gazing down, she noticed a small dog sitting obediently on her doorstep. A moment passed before the animal jumped up excitedly. Lisa took the creature in her arms. 'Bella…'

A figure now stepped slowly into the doorframe. Tentative and unsure, Maggie summoned all her courage before explaining: 'She's been missing you.'

Lisa stared mutely at her mother, holding her look before finally admitting: 'I've missed her too.'

Minutes later, Lisa handed her mother a cup of tea in the kitchen.

'You were right,' said Maggie. 'What you said that day at the hospital?' She lowered her head, as she went on: 'I've blamed myself a million times for what happened. I should never have gone behind your back...'

'Mum—'

'No,' Maggie went on. 'You have to listen,' she arranged her thoughts before continuing. 'If I'd only stayed at home that day—'

Lisa broke in again. 'What's done is done—'

'But it's all my fault—'

'And it's in the past,' said Lisa. 'The thing to remember is,' she paused, then: 'we'll always be a family.'

At this, Maggie set down her cup and leaned forward to embrace her daughter. 'I've wanted to do this so much,' she admitted. 'I've missed the very smell of you.'

Amused, Lisa looked at her. 'What?'

'When you and Nat were little, I'd put you both to bed, kiss you good night and leave the room... with the smell of your hair still on my lips. Sugar and roses,' studying Lisa's face she saw the changes were unnerving; her daughter's cherub features had vanished, together with the mischief in her eyes.

Instead Lisa looked drained; conflicted as she whispered: 'I wanted to call you.'

'Why didn't you?' asked Maggie.

Lisa shook her head. 'I don't know. It was just... finding the right time. Like Bruce said...' she trailed off but Maggie pressed her to continue.

'*What* did he say?'

'It doesn't matter now,' said Lisa. 'All I know is – I don't want to fight anymore.'

'Neither do I,' said Maggie, allowing a silence to stretch before she summoned the nerve to go on. 'But I do want to ask a favour.'

*

Half an hour later, Bruce's car pulled up outside Woodside. Stepping out of the vehicle, he locked it, then took his suitcase from the boot and strode on towards his front door. Slipping his key into the lock, he suddenly heard a dog's bark.

Opening the door, he saw Bella in the hallway. The dog gave a low growl at the sight of him. Bruce took a moment to process this, his expression clouding before Lisa suddenly appeared in the hallway from the kitchen. She stopped at the sight of Bruce – then smiled and came forward to kiss him. Bruce pointed to the growling dog. 'What's going on?'

She picked up the dog and stopped its growling. 'You know Bella was Dad's dog,' she began, 'well, she's been missing him so much, I…' she trailed off for a moment then went on: 'I told Mum we'd keep her.'

Bruce stared at the dog cradled in his wife's arms, acting like a barrier between them, when a voice sounded from the top of the stairs. 'You don't mind, do you, Bruce?'

Looking up, he saw Maggie smiling down at him from the landing. Bruce glanced back at Lisa and regained his composure. 'Of course not,' he said casually. 'As long as Lisa's happy.'

'I am,' said Lisa, offering a relieved smile. 'I'm really happy,' she went on, nuzzling the dog. 'And like Mum said, she can keep me safe.'

'Safe?' Bruce frowned as Maggie joined them in the hallway.

'When you're working away,' said Maggie, 'with your new job?' She came closer. 'Lisa told me all about it,' she returned Lisa's smile then looked pointedly back at Bruce.

He took a moment to respond. 'Right,' he said. 'Good idea.'

Maggie continued to eye him. She could see he was putting up a good front – so good only she could appreciate it. 'Well,' she said finally. 'I'd best be going. I wouldn't want to outstay my welcome.'

Lisa set the dog down and helped Maggie into her coat. 'Thanks for coming, Mum.' Bruce looked on as Lisa embraced her mother. 'I'll see you soon?'

'Course you will, love,' said Maggie, turning back to Bruce to make sure he had heard. Then she opened the front door and stepped out, glancing back to see Lisa waving the dog's paw at her.

As the door closed, Lisa smiled at Bruce. He said nothing and simply moved into the living room as Lisa trailed after him. 'I didn't call her,' she said. 'She knew I'd been missing her,' she leaned forward to kiss him. 'It's so good to have you back.'

'Good to be back,' he said finally with a smile that failed to reach his eyes. His expression set as he glanced down at the dog. It was still staring up at him, watching his every move. Glancing towards the window, Bruce caught sight of Maggie's car still parked outside. He saw she was sitting in the driver's seat, looking back at him. The dog gave a sudden sharp bark that seemed to go straight through him and when he looked back again through the window it was to see Maggie giving a smile – one of triumph – before she put her foot on the accelerator and drove off.

Later that same night, Bruce watched Lisa sleeping peacefully beside him, her hand curled on the pillow beside her. She looked like a child – innocent, trusting, his little girl… He reached across her for his watch on the bedside table, all the while taking care not to wake her. It was almost 2.30. Getting up, he quickly grabbed a dressing gown and slipped into it as he headed downstairs.

He stopped in his tracks on noticing the kitchen door was open. He couldn't risk the dog barking – waking Lisa – that would ruin everything. A few moments later, he stepped silently into the kitchen and found Bella was asleep in her basket, settled beneath a fleece blanket that was covered in tiny paw prints.

For a moment, he watched the steady rise and fall of the terrier's back as it slept. Its fur was peppered with grey – a sign the animal was getting old and might not have many years left. As though startled by that thought, the dog suddenly woke, turning its head to see Bruce standing at the kitchen door.

Bruce knew the creature had good reason not to trust him – the feeling was mutual. Bruce had never understood why people chose to waste their affection on dumb animals. His own mother had done so to a host of cats, doting on them, talking to them, grooming them and grieving when they finally expired from a variety of conditions that had required a small fortune to be paid in vets' fees.

There had been only one time when Bruce had considered getting himself a proper animal – a German Shepherd or a Rottweiler – a guard dog that actually served a purpose. But the moment had passed quickly enough due to too many issues of care; having to walk the thing and pick up its shit as though the dog was the master and the owner its loyal servant. Now, staring down at the scrawny creature lying in a basket in his kitchen, Bruce failed to find a single redeeming feature. Bella was motionless though her gaze remained fixed on him – not scared at all – but fearless. Stupid animal…

Bruce moved slowly to the kitchen cupboards, reaching up to bring a biscuit tin down from a high shelf. Lisa had put it there – out of temptation's way. She was being good. A good girl. His good little girl. Opening the lid, he saw that she had been telling the truth; a selection of sweets and chocolate bars seemed largely untouched since the last time he had checked. He smiled to himself then looked back at the dog.

The animal had perked up. Perhaps it had even read his mind and recognised that food was now in the equation. Man's best friend? No loyalty where food was concerned. Dogs would go to anyone. Bruce grabbed a bar of milk chocolate from the tin, unwrapped a piece and broke off a square before putting it into his mouth. Bella sat at his feet, following every move.

Bruce whispered: 'Hungry?'

Bella cocked her head to one side as though straining to understand. Bruce broke off another piece of chocolate. The dog's gaze followed once more. Stupid – and too greedy for its own good…

Bruce thought to himself for a moment, realising that it was more than fifteen years since he had last seen the old sheep dog that had lived at the sweet shop near his old school – a shaggy, flea-ridden creature whose jaw never failed to drop open with excitement at the sight of a bunch of schoolkids, like Bruce, heading into the shop to spend pocket money.

The dog had always done well out of the kids but the shopkeeper had taken pains to warn his customers against giving any chocolate to his pet. 'Poisonous to dogs' read the handwritten poster on his wall showing a photo of the dog – and a bar of chocolate beside it – so there could be no mistake. But was it really true? After a few months, it had been time to find out.

An experiment had required the sacrifice of a whole bar but it had been worth it – because the following day, Bruce had his answer. The old dog was no longer there, and was never there again – wagging its tail when the school bell sounded…

Bruce stared down to see Bella was still looking up at him. Tossing a square of chocolate into the air, the dog leapt up and caught it – swallowing it whole in one eager greedy gulp. Checking the bar in his hand, Bruce gave a slow smile as he recognised there was more than enough to make this creature disappear for good.

CHAPTER TWENTY-SIX

Pale morning sunlight streamed across the bed. Bruce turned towards the window and saw Lisa wasn't there. He swallowed hard and checked the time on his watch. Almost 9.30. How could he have slept for so long? Had she gone downstairs yet – or was she still in the bathroom? He ran his hand through his dark hair, grabbed his dressing gown and put it on quickly, tying its cord around his waist. Then he took a few deep breaths to prepare himself – and called out.

'Lise?'

Silence.

Coming downstairs Bruce could hear music sounding from the radio in the kitchen. He stopped dead in his tracks at the sight that met him: the dog was in the hallway, its nose pressed tight against the foot of the basement door. Bruce hissed at the animal but Bella ignored him and began scratching furiously at the base of the door.

Bruce called again. 'Lisa?' As she appeared from the kitchen, Bruce pointed to the dog. 'Can't you stop her doing that?'

Lisa swept the dog up into her arms and sauntered back to the kitchen. 'Go easy on her,' she began, 'she can't help being inquisitive. That's a sign of intelligence. You're a very clever girl, aren't you, love?' She set the dog down before picking up a mop and placing it into a plastic bucket.

Bruce stared at her. 'What's going on?' He waited for an explanation.

Lisa finally gave it. 'You know that expression "sick as a dog"? Well, Bella wasn't too well last night,' she sighed ruefully. 'I reckon Mum must have let her near some chocolate yesterday,' she stroked Bella as she went on. 'It's happened before but… luckily it must have been the cheap kind. It's only the expensive stuff that's dangerous.'

'Expensive?'

'High cocoa content. It can poison dogs.'

'You don't say,' said Bruce dully.

'And she's also not used to locked doors,' Lisa added. She continued to pet the dog as Bruce looked on, resentful but impassive. 'And neither am I,' she added firmly before tipping her head towards the hall. 'The basement?'

At this, Bruce turned away and poured himself some coffee. Some morning this was turning out to be. It was as though the dog had given Lisa confidence – confidence to nag.

'Look, we've been through this,' he said. 'It's my office and I've got expensive equipment there.'

'Sure it's not a woman?'

Bruce looked back sharply and saw Lisa's smile before she stepped away breezily and set the mop and bucket in a cupboard.

'Why're you up so early?' he asked, keen to change the subject.

'Why else?' she said. 'I've got Bella to look after now, and that means walkies.'

The dog responded to the word with a sharp bark, the sound of which went straight through Bruce as he sipped his coffee.

Lisa noted her husband's flat expression. 'Well, maybe *you* should take her for a walk,' she suggested. 'It might help her to get used to you?' She offered a dog's lead to him – but Bruce stared down at Bella and shook his head.

'Haven't got time,' he said. 'I've got to meet one of the new clients.' He grabbed his jacket and moved to the door.

'Don't you want some breakfast?'

'No,' he said quickly. 'I'll catch some while I'm out. D'you want a lift into town?'

Lisa shook her head. 'We're going to take a walk through the woods,' she turned to stroke Bella. 'Aren't we?'

Bruce looked on – for as long as he could bear – observing Lisa fussing over the animal. 'I… thought you didn't like the woods?'

Lisa looked back at him. 'I don't. But with Bella with me, maybe things'll change,' she smiled brightly and flipped her hair from her jacket collar before clipping the dog's lead to its collar. The dog looked back at Bruce, its jaw open, panting, as though it might have been laughing at him.

'See you later,' said Bruce briskly, masking a weight of resentment as he headed out.

A few minutes later, Lisa left the house by the back door, heading towards the woods beyond the garden gate. Clouds had gathered and crows were circling in the tall oaks. She braced herself before picking up a stick and throwing it for the dog.

Bella ignored it and began barking at the crows instead. Unseen by Lisa, a car was lying in wait on the street. Birds scattered high up into the trees. Lisa walked on, then heard the sharp sound of a twig cracking behind her. Her heart beat fast as she turned quickly and saw that someone was standing behind her.

'Hello, love,' said Maggie. 'How about I take us out for lunch?

CHAPTER TWENTY-SEVEN

It seemed as though hours had passed since Lisa joined her mother on a mystery car journey. She stared though the passenger window as they sped through a dull high street, lined with boarded up stores interspersed with grimy pubs and a few charity shops. Bella whined on the back seat.

'She didn't get much of a walk this morning,' explained Lisa, 'I reckon she wants a wee,' she glanced at Maggie but saw her mother's eyes remained fixed on the road. 'And so do I.' Lisa added, pointedly.

'We're nearly there,' said Maggie.

'Good.' Lisa heaved a sigh and checked her watch. 'We could've taken Bella for a walk, eaten in town and been back home by now?'

Concentrating on her driving, Maggie failed to reply, aware she had said hardly a word throughout the journey.

'Well… can we stop soon?' said Lisa. 'Only the car's making me feel—' She broke off as Maggie finally braked – then she gave a long exhalation and sighed. 'Thank God for that.'

Grabbing the keys from the ignition, Maggie nodded to her daughter. 'Leave Bella in the car.'

Getting out, Maggie opened the door for Lisa who stared around at the shabby housing estate she had brought them to, before asking: 'What're we doing here?'

'There's someone I want you to meet.' Maggie explained. 'Come on.'

She moved purposefully on, passing a street sign for Parnell Road as Lisa hung back at the car, protesting. 'I thought you said we were going for lunch?'

Maggie called back to her. 'Afterwards.'

'After what?' Lisa asked tetchily. 'I haven't even had breakfast yet. Hold on, will you…?'

Maggie ignored her and continued to stride on up a messy path towards a familiar house – before she suddenly registered that the front door was boarded up. She checked the number again – 36. Hanging back at the car, Lisa called out: 'What are we doing here?'

Maggie glanced back at her, then again at the boarded up front door.

A voice sounded. 'She's been gone a couple of days now.' A woman was standing on the path of the next house.

'Gone where?' asked Maggie.

Setting down some shopping bags the woman shrugged. 'No-one knows for sure but… someone reckons she got behind with her rent and did a runner.' She pulled some keys from her pocket staring up at the house as she went on. 'Hope the council comes back soon and boards up those windows before the druggies get in.' Moving on to her own front door, she now opened it and disappeared inside.

Maggie stared once more at the door before her. This couldn't be happening. Not now. Not after she had brought Lisa all this way. She heard her daughter's voice calling from the pavement. 'Mum?'

Maggie ignored her, still trying to make sense of what she had just learned. Had Christine Forrester fled because of rent arrears – or due to Maggie's visit?

Lisa called again – louder this time. 'Mum!'

It took the sound of retching to bring Maggie back to the moment. She turned and saw her daughter still near the car, bent double as she vomited in the road. Maggie rushed to her.

'What is it, love? What's wrong?'

Lisa wiped her mouth before noticing two kids playing on the other side of the street, staring across at her.

'This… isn't the way I planned to tell you,' she began, trailing off before looking again at her mother. 'I'm pregnant.'

Half an hour later, Lisa and Maggie sat at a table in a café, mugs of tea and a round of toast before them.

'How long?' asked Maggie.

'Six weeks.' Lisa frowned. 'I… did the test yesterday morning.'

'And… you're sure?'

Lisa looked at her. 'I can read a pee stick'.

Maggie looked away, considering this, recognising how happy she should be at this news but knowing this was the last thing she expected or wanted to hear.

'Why didn't you tell me?'

'I just did. There's… been no time. I haven't even told Bruce yet.

'Why not?'

Uncomfortable under her mother's gaze, Lisa gave a small shrug. 'I... need time to get used to the idea.' On Maggie's knowing look, Lisa finally admitted: 'Look, it wasn't planned, all right?' She went on: 'We said we'd wait.'

'Wait for what?'

Lisa looked up sharply, but Maggie continued. 'You've got a house, Bruce earns good money and you said yourself you don't need to work...'

'I know.' Lisa agreed. 'But like Bruce always said, what's the rush? We... just wanted to enjoy a bit more time together.'

Maggie tried to hold her daughter's gaze but Lisa looked away. 'You're worried about telling him, aren't you?' Lisa continued to avoid her mother's gaze and stared abstractedly at the first drops of rain falling on the café window.

'Lisa?'

'He'll be fine,' she said, quickly reaching for her mug. 'Once he gets used to the idea, he'll be a perfect dad. I know he will. You've seen the way he dotes on me – can you imagine what he'll be like with his own kid?' She smiled at the thought. It was now Maggie's turn to look away.

Lisa went on. 'It'll be the making of us,' she insisted, taking a sip of tea.

Maggie turned to her. 'Parents make kids – not the other way around.'

The mug was still at Lisa's lips. 'I know that,' she said. 'But... you are happy for us?' Before Maggie could respond, Lisa spoke again. 'Well, don't you see? That's why I was so pleased to see you last night. It was like Fate.'

'Fate?' echoed Maggie, feeling increasingly torn. This couldn't go on – she would have to explain.

But it was Lisa who spoke next. 'I nearly told you then,' she explained, 'but I was worried. I mean, after everything that's happened, losing Dad,' she paused then looked searchingly at her mother. 'I don't think I could bear it if you weren't happy for us?' Maggie registered her daughter's broken smile but words failed to come. Lisa frowned, her suspicion growing. 'Who was it you wanted me to meet today?' Maggie said nothing and turned her head away. 'Mum?' She paused then went on: 'Who was it?'

Taking a deep breath, Maggie turned back to her daughter but in that moment she saw only the mother of a young son – Christine Forrester's words were echoing for her: *How could he possibly have a kid taking the attention away from him? Get your daughter out of there...*

Maggie tried to summon some happiness for Lisa but felt only the despair she had experienced on arriving at the empty house in Parnell Road to find its door boarded up. 'No-one important, love,' she said finally before manufacturing a smile and pushing a round of toast towards her daughter.

CHAPTER TWENTY-EIGHT

After dropping Lisa home, Maggie drove directly into town and parked outside Marston police station. Taking her phone from her pocket she checked it for messages then switched it off and got out of the car.

In the dingy police reception, Maggie found a belligerent middle aged man, reeking of alcohol, arguing with a desk sergeant. He pointed a finger at the police officer and swayed unsteadily on his feet. 'I know my rights,' the drunk slurred, trying unsuccessfully to slip an arm into his jacket as he went on, 'you had no right to keep me here. I demand to see my solicitor!'

The desk sergeant failed to raise his eyes from his paperwork as he asked, dully: 'Why don't you do yourself a favour and go home?'

The man shook his head: 'I'm going nowhere. Not until you—'

Having heard enough, Maggie stepped forward. 'Didn't you hear what he said?' she demanded. 'You've had your turn – now clear off!' The man tried to focus on her, staggering back on his heels for a moment while Maggie ignored him and turned her attention to the desk sergeant. 'I need to see someone.' The desk sergeant looked up from his paperwork. 'Now!' she said urgently.

Behind her, the drunk smiled and began a slow hand clap.

At exactly the same time, Lisa was in the kitchen at Woodside, filling the dog's bowl with food. Since returning home, she had rehearsed telling Bruce about the baby, but remained relieved that he still wasn't home. She felt half in mind to leave the news for another time – depending on his mood – but telling Maggie had complicated things.

She set Bella's food bowl down on the floor then heard the front door sound. Looking up, she saw Bruce enter, keys in hand. She smiled in an effort to cover her surprise but Bruce saw through it and asked: 'What's wrong?'

'Nothing I… didn't expect to see you back so soon.'

'Didn't you?' He tossed his keys on to the counter and looked back at her. 'I came home a while ago,' he said. 'You weren't here.' His tone made this seem like an accusation. 'Where d'you go?'

'Mum came over.'

'Mum?'

'To take me out,' she could see his gaze was still fixed on her so she went on. 'Just for a drive.'

'A drive,' said Bruce. 'Where to?'

Lisa shrugged and moved to the sink to wash her hands. 'I… don't know. Miles away. I wasn't really paying much attention. She said we could have some lunch together.'

'Where?'

Lisa shrugged. 'I don't know... A café.'

Bruce was still looking at her – coldly now. 'So, she drove you... miles away... just to eat in a café?'

Lisa gave a sudden nervous laugh. 'You're making it sound like I'm lying.'

'But you're not.' He was looking away from her now, checking his phone.

''Course I'm not. Why would I lie?'

'I don't know,' said Bruce. 'You tell me.'

Lisa fell silent and wiped a hand through her hair. None of this was going the way she had hoped; the way she had dared to imagine during the journey back from Leeds while Maggie had driven, her eyes fixed to the road. It had been easy not to say too much to her mother. Sickness had been a good excuse.

But something had got into Bruce, so, perhaps it was better to leave things until tomorrow – except for the fact that he would then surely ask why she hadn't explained straight away? After all, she had confided in Maggie about the unplanned pregnancy and if Bruce were to learn that she had been told first, it would only make things worse. She took a moment to compute this – too long for Bruce.

'All right,' he said. 'If you will have your little secrets.' He grabbed his door keys from the counter.

Lisa lurched quickly forward as she asked: 'Where're you going?' Ignoring her, Bruce continued on to the door. 'Please,' she said quickly, 'don't go,' she heard herself pleading with him. 'Don't walk out on me like this?'

Bruce stopped in his tracks and looked back at her. 'Like what?'

Lisa was silent for a moment, staring around at the stylish

kitchen in her new home that had become a prison. Her voice lowered to a whisper. 'Like you don't care?' She struggled to explain. 'I don't like being here on my own.'

His eyes were still trained on her. 'But you're not on your own,' he said calmly. 'You've got the dog now – thanks to Maggie.' He glanced down at Bella then back again at Lisa as his tone became brighter. 'Maybe you should spend a bit more time with your mum.' Lisa looked up at him in shock. He went on. 'You said you were missing her. Why don't you go home for a while – sort things out?'

Lisa shook her head, confounded. 'Sort what out? I... don't want to go home. *This* is my home.'

'But you just said you don't like it here.'

'Only when I'm alone but I want to be here with you.'

'Do you?' He spoke softly as he came closer. 'Then why did you rush off with your mum this morning when you told me you were walking the dog?'

Confused, Lisa began to back away. 'I... didn't rush off. I told you the truth. Mum turned up out of the blue... She said she wanted to take me for lunch. But we never got to the restaurant.'

'Why not?'

'Because I... didn't feel well.'

Bruce looked at her, studiously, then suddenly folded her in his arms, as he gently asked: 'Why didn't you tell me?' Feeling safe in his embrace, Lisa explained with relief: 'Because I was worried what you'd say.'

'Worried about what?'

She braced herself, summoning her courage, and confidence in the outcome, as she explained: 'About the baby.'

A moment passed before Bruce's hold began to loosen. She felt him letting go of her, allowing her to drift away. Looking up at him she saw his expression darken as he asked: 'What baby?'

At Marston Police Station, a young constable by the name of Sally Laker was sitting across a desk from Maggie, a pen in her hand as she took some notes. 'So, Lisa is your daughter?'

Maggie nodded. 'But like I explained, I'm here because of her husband.'

The PC looked up. Maggie observed her balancing the pen on her finger as if using it to weigh up what she had heard so far. Maggie went on: 'I think he may have a police record.'

'For?' The young officer was tapping the pen on her desk now, maybe with some impatience, aware she could be doing something else.

'I don't know,' said Maggie, 'that's why I'm here. You've got some kind of central computer, haven't you? You could look it up?'

Sally Laker looked up from her notes. 'I'd have to have reason to suspect—'

Maggie broke in: 'I'm *giving* you reason. I've just told you, I'm worried what he'll do to her.'

The constable put down her pen and sat back in her chair as she tried to take stock. 'You're telling me you believe your daughter's in some sort of danger?

'Aye', said Maggie, tersely. 'That exactly what I'm telling you.'

'And she's unable to contact us herself?'

'Well she wouldn't, would she? She doesn't even know it yet but... I've talked to his ex-wife and she's told me what he's like'.

'Then maybe we should speak to her.'

'You can't. I was there this afternoon. In Leeds.' Once more, Maggie thought of the boarded up house and felt a burden of guilt for having invaded Christine Forrester's safe life. 'She's moved away,' she explained. 'Maybe gone to a refuge. She must be scared witless that I found her. Don't you see?'

The young constable looked across at Maggie and witnessed the level of her concern. 'Would you like us to call on your daughter – check that she's okay?'

Maggie shook her head in frustration. 'No. That'll only make things worse. He'll know I've sent you,' she broke off for a moment and re-framed her thoughts. 'Look, I just want you to find out more about him; give me something I can show to her – something she'll *believe*.'

PC Laker put down her pen and pinched the bridge of her nose. 'I'm sorry, but I can't do that. There are rules governing the information we hold on police records.'

'But I'm telling you—'

'If your daughter needs help, Mrs Sheild, she can contact me,' she handed a card across the table. Maggie stared down at the details – a name and a number – then she stared across at officer before her. Her fair hair was tied back off her face. A young face with fresh skin and freckles. She was half Maggie's age and probably younger than Lisa. Maggie got up from her chair, tossed the card down on the table – and walked out.

At Woodside, Bruce was just sitting down on the sofa in the living room as he tried to assimilate Lisa's news. 'Why didn't you tell me?'

'I was going to,' Lisa began, 'but you've only just got back and…' she trailed off beneath his cold gaze.

'How did it happen?'

Lisa frowned. 'What d'you mean… how did it – '

He broke in impatiently: 'Did you stop taking your pills?'

Lisa shook her head. 'Of course not, but… maybe when I had that bug, and was sick…'

Bruce got up and crossed the room to the window. It was still raining but nonetheless he wished he was on the other side of the glass – outside – and not trapped in this room with Lisa and her news.

'I know it's a shock,' she said quickly. 'It was for me too but… it'll be all right.'

Looking back, he saw that she had managed a smile for him – a peace offering. Rejecting it, he walked straight out into the hallway where he suddenly paused, as though unsure where he was going.

Lisa went after him and found him standing at the foot of the stairs, looking lost. 'Bruce…?'

Without a word he began walking upstairs while Lisa quickly went after him, catching him up and tugging at his arm to prevent him walking away from her. 'Bruce, I swear I didn't do this on purpose. You do believe me, don't you?' Hearing those words, she suddenly realised how they must resonate for him; another woman had surely said the same; a wife he had left, whom he had resented and divorced. Lisa heard herself calling out to him again. 'Bruce?'

Having reached the top of the stairs, Bruce finally turned to face her. The dog began to growl but Bruce remained silent. Lisa reacted to his flat expression. 'What is it?' she asked, unnerved. 'What's wrong?'

The whining tone of her voice seemed to go straight through him – like fingernails scratching on a blackboard. In that moment it seemed like she was stuck to him, clinging tightly to his sleeve, like something he couldn't shake off. Her mouth was still moving and he closed his eyes so he wouldn't be able to see her any more, wouldn't feel her tugging on his sleeve, demanding his attention. He raised his arm high above his head. The dog gave a sudden loud bark.

CHAPTER TWENTY-NINE

Maggie drove back from the police station and parked outside her home. Staring out of the windscreen at the gloomy street, she allowed herself a few moments to consider all that had happened. She was going to become a grandmother, something she had always expected to happen when she and Jeff were finally retired – no work – just grandchildren and enough free time to enjoy them.

She had imagined the scenes that would then follow: Jeff entertaining the kids, planting seeds together in the back garden and watching them grow, as he had done when his own girls were young: mustard and cress, and lettuce, leaves of which they had fed to a docile pet tortoise called Trevor. During school summer holidays, and lunch breaks from the factory, Maggie had carefully observed her young daughters through the kitchen window, filling their junior watering cans, picking up crab apples from a small square of lawn. Maggie had always longed for more time with them but it had been Jeff who had actually made time. He wouldn't be here to enjoy Lisa's child, the child she was having with Bruce, and Maggie couldn't find it in her heart to be happy about any of it.

Getting out of the car, she threw another look down the empty street, its pavements slick with cold rain, and headed on to her front door to enter a cold unlit hallway. In the darkness, a voice sounded from the living room. Pushing open the door, Maggie saw the answerphone was blinking – a woman giving instructions. '… So if you could call Marston General Hospital…'

Maggie grabbed the phone receiver. 'Hello?'

Throughout the next moments, Maggie remained silent, straining to hear each word and every detail as the woman's voice explained something very important. Then she steeled herself. 'I'll be right there,' she said finally. Throwing down the phone, she left.

Half an hour later, Maggie's eyes scoped a hospital ward for signs of Lisa. She failed to find her among the patients – but registered a bed surrounded by curtains. Before she had time to take another step, the curtains slowly parted, exposing Lisa, fully dressed, lying on top of the bed. Maggie hurried across to her.

'Don't worry,' said Lisa quickly, 'I'm all right.'

Maggie saw that Lisa's features told a different story; tired eyes glazed with tears. A nurse returned to the bed and nodded to Maggie before explaining to Lisa: 'We're sorting out your discharge paperwork,' she turned to Maggie. 'Lisa can go home as soon as her husband's back.' The nurse gave a benign smile before moving off. Maggie sat down and reached for her daughter's hand. Lisa read the question in her mother's eyes – and answered it.

'It was an accident,' she said softly. 'I... lost my footing on the stairs,' she paused, rallying herself before insisting: 'I'm fine.'

Maggie paused. 'And the baby?' At this, Lisa slowly looked away to the wall. Maggie's words sounded as softly as a sigh. 'Oh Lisa...'

'It's okay,' said Lisa quickly. 'Bruce says we can try again. In time.'

Maggie took a moment to process this. 'You told him you were pregnant?'

Lisa nodded.

'And... what did he say?'

'He was fine about it'. Lisa summoned a faint smile.

Maggie tightened her grip on Lisa's hand, remaining calm as she said: 'Now tell me the truth?'

In the next moment, Lisa's lips slowly parted, about to betray a secret – until she hesitated, unable to explain the look in Bruce's eyes when she had told him about the baby. It was a look that still haunted her...

'Hello Maggie.'

Turning quickly, Maggie saw that Bruce was standing behind her, a clear plastic hospital bag in his hand. He turned to Lisa. 'I've got your things, love.'

Lisa nodded and got to her feet while Maggie moved quickly to help, but Lisa protested, impatient this time. 'I said I'm all right, Mum. Really I am.'

In the silence that followed, Bruce stepped forward and offered his arm. Lisa took it. Bruce explained to Maggie. 'I tried to call you but your phone was off.'

Maggie stammered. 'I know, I—' She broke off, unable to explain about the police.

'I have to get Lisa home,' he said calmly. 'And you don't need to worry because I'll take good care of her. You know that, don't you?' He held Maggie's look for a moment before he began to steer Lisa away.

Maggie felt a cry rising up from within her. 'Wait!'

Lisa turned quickly, alarmed as she glanced between her mother and her husband. In that moment Maggie knew that this was her opportunity – her chance to have her say and set the record straight once and for all – but she saw Lisa's desperate smile. 'Please Mum,' Lisa's eyes were imploring. 'I'll be fine,' she said, 'I promise. We can talk tomorrow.'

In the next instant, Maggie saw Lisa's grip tighten on Bruce's arm before she turned and moved off with him. Maggie watched them go, waiting until they had disappeared out of the ward before she found herself staring down at the hospital bed, noticing something had been left behind on the pillow – a tiny fabric ponytail holder. She picked it up and held it tightly in the palm of her hand before finally pressing it to her lips. In that moment, it seemed all that she had left.

An hour later, Maggie was driving home – paying little attention to the journey. Instead, she squinted against the rain falling hard on her windscreen while images flooded her mind: Lisa's face before her, glowing, suntanned…then her voice, sounding as clearly as if she was there with Maggie in the car. *I love him, Mum. He's a wonderful bloke. You'll see that for yourself in time.*

Maggie blinked. The image disappeared, to be replaced with a scene from Marston Register Office; Lisa and Bruce standing together in front of the registrar while Jeff turned to Maggie, smiling, holding her hand in an act of unity while they each experienced complex but conflicting emotions: Jeff's pride in his daughter and confidence about her future, while Maggie had been unable to relax and share her husband's faith in this marriage. Nevertheless, she had still returned Jeff's smile before staring, troubled, at all the empty seats... *Something was very wrong...* Then an Elvis song was playing, becoming background music in the club's kitchen as Maggie argued with Jeff. So much anger covering fear. *There's not a soul there for him. On his wedding day. Why?* No answers had come from Jeff – only a warning: *You've got to get over this... You'll go the right way about losing her.*

Losing Lisa? How could that possibly happen when even Maggie had been told: *She'll always be your daughter. Whatever she does, wherever she goes...* Rona had told her that and had then gone on to advise Maggie to *trust what you know... and use it.* This had led Maggie to use Dee's broken secret about Bruce's former marriage and so she had found Christine Forrester – only to lose her just when she needed her most; in order to explain to Lisa about Bruce Carter...

But then Rona was a fraud – she was really Leyla – no refugee – but an economic immigrant using false papers. She had probably lied about having a daughter herself so how could she possibly have known what Maggie was going through?

It was clear the woman had never really cared, because straight after Maggie's visit to the holding centre, Leyla had disappeared – gone to ground – maybe to take advantage of some other trusting fool...

Jeff had been right all along about losing Lisa – and Maggie should have listened but it was too late now. Jeff was no longer here. Maggie had lost him too and would soon lose her job

– everything she had lived for. In the next moment, she saw herself beside Jeff's bedside, his body before her, a cold lifeless hand gripped in her own…

As rain continued to fall on the car windscreen, that image slowly transformed into Lisa still insisting: *I'm all right, Mum.* But how could she be?

Maggie had just seen her in hospital, had felt her daughter's heartbreak then watched her walk away, unable to utter a single word to stop her, only to issue a silent scream at the sight of her with Bruce, a plastic bag in his hand containing her clothes. The bag had reminded Maggie of the one she had been given by the same hospital after Jeff's death – a bag filled with what they had called 'effects'; Jeff's clothes, shoes, so many small inconsequential things that he had carried around with him – that he had held on to – right to the end… Christine's voice sounded abruptly now. A warning to Maggie. *Get your daughter out of there… I should have come to my senses sooner…*

The traffic ahead ground to a sudden halt. Maggie stepped on the brake and switched on the windscreen wipers. They seemed to beat in time to those same words still echoing in Maggie's head: *I should have come to my senses sooner…*

As the glass cleared, Maggie stared straight ahead – not at the stalled traffic – but on recognising something important that had been there in front of her for a long time – unseen until that moment.

CHAPTER THIRTY

Lying on top of the bed with Bella at her side, Lisa scrolled through photos on her iPhone. They had arrived from Dee the night before but she had missed seeing them – until now. Holiday snaps, they showed the Witches of Ilkley thousands of miles away on the beach at Malibu; at least a dozen shots of the girls sipping cocktails; Dee waterskiing, Sandra windsurfing and Patsy being presented with a giant platter of seafood. A short message explained that they would be heading to Hollywood the next day. Today. An old cliché had been added: '*Wish you were here!*'

Lisa set down her phone, knowing it was more than distance that now separated her from her friends. They had each made their choices and were set on different paths. Lisa closed her eyes but saw an after-image of Dee, smiling on a sunlit beach; confident, fulfilled, happy. Surely Maggie would be happier with someone like Dee for a daughter – someone who had always seized life and everything it had to offer rather than settling down as Lisa had done. *Settling down.* Lisa considered the words. They summed up how her life had lost its direction, dissolving instead into the small particles of her day, drifting slowly downwards as if to the bottom of a bell jar – like sediment in water. She had *settled down* to life with Bruce in this house – so far away from everything she knew. Days spent waiting for him to return from meetings, waiting until he had finished in his private office – so private she wasn't even allowed near it. The mantuary…

Although her pregnancy had been unplanned she recognised now that she had been waiting for a baby, 'expecting' a child – to give her new purpose. After the positive test result it hadn't taken long for her to imagine herself as a mother, someone on whom another life depended, rather than the person she had become; the woman who relied so much on her partner – for everything.

How had this happened? How had she become so estranged not only from her friends and family but from the young woman she had once been? She picked up her phone again. She could call Dee – but to say what? To reproach her oldest friend for meeting with her mother behind her back? To share her grief at the loss of an unborn child?

Words did not exist to describe her desolation but even if she found them she knew she could never share them with the beaming sun-kissed faces in those photographs. She had always believed that friends were for life. Now she realised that her own life choices had separated her from those friends – had acted as a rejection of all they had once shared – and valued. She set the phone down again and failed to notice Bruce entering the room – a glass of water in his hand. He hesitated as he saw her looking so frail and broken.

'Sure you're okay?'

She nodded slowly.

'How about something to eat?'

She shook her head.

'I could order something in. Chinese?'

Lisa managed a weak smile for him. Her only appetite was a need to please him. 'Okay,' she said softly. 'Maybe some soup… chicken and sweetcorn?'

He smiled. 'It's yours.'

As he turned for the door, she called out to him. 'Bruce?'

He paused, wary and uncertain, before glancing back at her, knowing there was so much left unsaid between them – but not wanting to discuss it now.

'Could you run me a bath?'

He smiled, relieved. 'Sure.'

Once he left the room, Lisa's own brave smile faded as she pulled Bella close and stroked the dog for comfort.

In the bathroom, Bruce turned on the taps and watched the water flow, then he turned to check his appearance in the mirror. Smoothing a hand through his dark hair he considered his reflection coolly until steam built up, clouding the mirror's surface. He quickly wiped his hand across it until he saw himself reappear, reminding himself that he could negotiate this unexpected hitch and bring everything back on course – including Lisa. He braced himself before leaving the room.

At the same time, Maggie was rooting through a drawer in her bedroom, tossing scarves and jewellery on to her bed until she found what she was searching for – a small wooden box.

Opening it, her gaze lingered on a few precious items – Jeff's watch, his wedding ring, some glass marbles… She rummaged through his loose change, her fingers finally meeting – not a coin – but a distinctive metal shank button. Picking it up, she turned it in her hand, carefully tracing the anchor design with her finger. Then she turned to the phone.

Back at Woodside, Bruce was dialing the number on the menu in his hand for the Honeymoon Chinese Restaurant. His fingers drummed the kitchen counter as he waited impatiently for the call to connect. Finally it did so. 'Yeah,' he said. 'I'd like to order a takeaway.'

Upstairs, Lisa lay dozing with Bella beside her when her iPhone sounded. Staring at it on the bedside table beside her she tried to ignore the call. It continued to ring. She picked it up – and saw it was her mother who was calling. She fought a battle with herself – then answered.

'Mum?'

Maggie paused for a second. 'Are you on your own?'

Lisa raised herself. 'Sorry?'

'Can you talk?'

'Of course I can. Why?'

Maggie whispered urgently: 'Don't let Bruce hear this. *Any* of this.'

'Mum…?'

'I know what he did,' said Maggie, 'so you have to stop trying to protect him.'

Lisa closed her eyes as though trying to make her mother disappear. 'Please. Don't start this again.'

Lisa's voice sounded fragile. Maggie steeled herself to continue. Best to come straight out with it. Now or never. 'You think you love him,' she went on, 'but you can't, because you don't know him. You've been making excuses from the start. But now it's time for the truth.'

'Which is?' asked Lisa spikily.

'He's dangerous.'

'Stop it!'

'No,' said Maggie, defiant. 'I know he put you in hospital. And I know the reason why. He didn't want the baby. And I *knew* he wouldn't.'

Lisa found herself trembling as she held the phone in her hand. How could Maggie possibly know this? Her lips moved though no words emerged.

Maggie took advantage of her silence. 'He's never even tried to see his own son.'

Lisa breathed a shocked whisper. 'What?'

'In the car yesterday. I was taking you to see someone – his ex-wife, Christine. I know you didn't want me to find out that he'd been married – but I did. And I tracked her down because I needed to hear the truth.'

A moment's silence followed as Lisa became fully aware of Dee's betrayal at a meeting in the pub with her mother while her father lay dying at home. 'I'm putting this phone down—'

'No!' Maggie insisted. 'You're going to listen. If not for me – then for your dad.'

Lisa shook her head in confusion. 'Dad?'

'Bruce lied about the day he died.'

Lisa remained mute.

'He *lied*, Lisa,' Maggie repeated, 'and I can prove it.'

'No—'

Maggie broke in again. 'Remember what he said? That Jeff was already dead when Bruce found him? He wasn't. He couldn't have been,' she paused, then: 'I couldn't take in what they told me that day at the hospital. I had to sign for Jeff's things… and they said… your dad had something in his hand when the ambulance crew found him. It's been here all along… with everything else – everything I brought back – a metal button with an anchor on it, ripped off a shirt… or a jacket?' She looked down at the shank button in her hand, threads of cotton sprouting from the back of it. 'I should have taken more notice when they told me at the hospital, but I didn't, I couldn't. I was too upset. But now I know,' she went on: 'Your dad must have been holding it… to show us.'

Lisa's voice dropped to a whisper. 'Show us what?'

'That someone was with him *before* he died.' Maggie left a long pause, then: 'Bruce.'

The single word sounded to Lisa like a bell tolling. 'No,' she said, insistent. 'No, you've got this wrong. Bruce would never lie about something like that. Why would he?'

Maggie took a deep breath and found the words she needed: 'Find the jacket, Lisa. Find it and you'll *know*.'

Shaking with emotion Lisa ended the call, then switched off her phone and tossed it on to the bed as though she had been stung.

Maggie cried out to her: 'Lisa!' She quickly dialed again but this time heard only Lisa's voicemail message. Still reeling, Lisa continued to stare at her mobile when a voice suddenly sounded in the room.

'I've run your bath.'

Lisa saw Bruce was standing at the door. She gave a tight smile in an effort to regain control.

'Thanks,' she said weakly.

Bruce could see she was trembling and on the edge of tears. It was only to be expected, he thought, she'd just lost a baby – although it wasn't a baby, as such – little more than a tadpole – though it would have grown between them.

He had been through all that before and knew what to expect. He had sworn to himself that he would never put up with it again. Lisa would get over this – *if* he gave her enough attention.

Stepping forward, he leaned in to kiss her but the dog began a low growl, warning him off. He eyed Bella – the miserable creature was now daring to bare its teeth. The dog would have to go – sooner rather than later. For now, Bruce managed to ignore it as he explained to Lisa: 'I've ordered the meal but I can't get a delivery, so I'm going down to pick it up, okay?'

She gave a quick nod and he suddenly knew that she wanted to get rid of him. Why? He sat down beside her on the bed. Raising his hand towards her face, he saw her flinch. Hesitating, he gently pushed her fringe back from her face and held her gaze as he said: 'You know I'd never do anything to hurt you, don't you? Everything I do… everything I've done… is because I love you.'

Lisa nodded, slowly this time. Bruce kissed her tenderly. Straight after, she managed a brave smile for him and he returned it, feeling reassured.

'I won't be long, little girl.' Getting up, he headed to the door.

*

As soon as he left, Lisa stared down at her phone and checked that she had switched it off. She resolved not to accept another call from Maggie and took a deep breath before getting up. Moving to the wardrobe she caught sight of her reflection in the mirrored doors. For a moment she stood motionless, as if staring at a stranger, her features drawn, and eyes raw with grief.

Then she found some courage and slid open the doors. Before her, Bruce's clothes were hanging neatly on the left hand side – every single item facing the wall. She paused, hearing Maggie's words still echoing in her head – lies, all of it. Ignoring Bruce's shirts and jackets, she grabbed a red kimono dressing gown from her own section and slid the doors firmly shut before heading to the en-suite bathroom.

After taking only a few steps, she stopped in her tracks – the wardrobe was luring her back. Maggie was telling lies – but here was a chance to prove it. Emboldened, she moved back again and slid open the wardrobe doors – searching through Bruce's clothes, tentatively at first, then more purposefully, checking every single shirt and jacket hanging there. It took some time and proved fruitless.

Feeling vindicated, she picked up her dressing gown again and walked on to the bathroom, feeling her anger rising. Why couldn't Maggie leave things alone? Why had she not been able to trust her daughter's judgement, once and for all, instead of creating an even greater rift between them? Lisa loved Bruce. She *was* his 'little girl' – and grateful for it. He adored her. He had married her. Wasn't that proof enough?

In the bathroom, Lisa hung her kimono dressing gown on the back of the door then tested the temperature of the bath he had run for her. As she did so, she glimpsed her reflection again – this time in the mirror above the bath – and saw only rivulets of condensation streaming down its surface like tears.

Taking a deep breath she told herself there would be another baby – in time. But for now, she had to put it out of her mind. Move on. That's what she had been trying to do – ever since Nat's death. She had a life of her own but Maggie was always trying to drag her back, to how they once were, when Nat was alive and Maggie had control over everyone; her workers, her daughters and her husband. Maggie was always trying to manage things – including Lisa's life, but this new re-writing of history was the limit. Lisa told herself that what had happened on the stairs last night had been all her own fault – an accident caused because she had been so upset, so demanding of Bruce's attention. From now on, she had to rein in her emotions – become more in control – just like Bruce. He wouldn't want to live with an hysterical woman. A drama queen.

Perhaps that was another reason why his first marriage had failed. The former wife, Christine, his 'ex', the woman Maggie had gone to see, was clearly bitter about the way things had ended so she had made up stories for Maggie, who would have been a willing audience for them all. Maggie had never liked Bruce and now she was making up stories of her own, to justify her interference. She couldn't stop herself doing that because she had always wanted her daughters to live the life she had failed to live herself. Nat had gone along with it but after she had died, Maggie had looked to Lisa. All that pressure to go to college, to get a job, to travel. Lisa had done it all, just to please her mum, but nothing was ever enough. Bruce and Jeff had known each other for only a short while but still Lisa had been able to see how much her father had warmed to Bruce – and the feeling had been mutual. Jeff had welcomed Bruce into the family – for Lisa's sake – but Maggie hadn't liked that either. Maybe because she had always been jealous of him, wanting Lisa to remain her *own* little girl, never to share her with anyone…

Now it was time for Maggie to realise that Lisa belonged to Bruce – they were man and wife – till death us do part…

She slipped out of her nightdress and turned to lift the lid from the laundry basket, about to stuff the nightdress inside when she hesitated as her hand met with something else. Pulling it from the basket – she saw it was a heavy blue work shirt – one that Bruce seldom wore. It was usually washed with other blue colours, but for some time there hadn't been enough to make a full load. She slowly turned the shirt over in her hands – noticing the anchor pattern on a row of metal buttons before she felt a sudden dull ache in the pit of her stomach as she registered that one was missing.

CHAPTER THIRTY-ONE

On the outskirts of Marston, Bruce's car drew up outside the Honeymoon Chinese Restaurant. The place was always busy and today was no exception. The restaurant tables were full but the pretty young Chinese waitress who dealt with takeaways seemed unhurried. She instantly recognised her customer, her face breaking into a welcoming smile as she asked in her baby-sweet voice: 'How are you?'

'Fine, thanks, Mei.' Bruce nodded and returned Mei's smile but declined her offer of a menu.

'It's okay,' he went on. 'I know exactly what I want.'

At Woodside, Lisa hurried downstairs, clumsily pulling on a jumper over her jeans. As she entered the kitchen, she dropped her phone. The landline suddenly rang. Startled by the sound, she hesitated for a moment – then picked up the receiver.

Bruce was on the other end of the line. 'Sure you only want soup?' he asked. 'They've got won ton but no chicken and sweetcorn.' At that moment, he was looking directly across at

Mei – offering her another warm smile. She was cute, like a doll. Charmed, Mei smiled back.

At the end of the line, Lisa managed to find her voice. 'Whatever you think,' she said quickly.

Bruce picked up on her tone. 'Are you… okay?'

Lisa took a deep breath and tried to calm herself. She could hear blood pulsing in her ears as she stared towards the kitchen door. 'Yeah, I'm… just not that fussed,' she added. 'You choose.'

A moment passed before she put down the receiver.

As the line went dead, Bruce considered the brief exchange. He knew Lisa was upset but it wasn't like her to be so abrupt with him. He saw Mei looking on, her cute little face betraying concern. 'Won Ton it is.' he said decisively, slipping his mobile in his pocket.

Maggie sat in the driver's seat of her car, turning the engine over and over. It refused to start. She had flooded it – like Jeff had always warned her not to do. '*Too impatient*', he used to say, '*just let it sit*'. If only he were here now… She pounded her fists against the steering wheel then lay her forehead down on her hands for a moment, cursing the fact that everything was against her. Then she thought of Lisa – and looked up again.

Getting out of the car, she slammed the door behind her and took her mobile from her pocket. Finding a number she dialed it. 'I need a cab. Quick as you can.'

In the Honeymoon restaurant, Bruce sat waiting for his order. Chinese muzak was playing, something sounding like a flute and a zither with a tinkling sound in the background. Soothing.

Especially on a day like this. He closed his eyes in an effort to blot out the garish décor. Lanterns with golden tassels were hanging from the ceiling. Dragon designs plastered all over the walls. He suddenly remembered that dragons were meant to be lucky – a sign of good fortune?

He knew he could do with some luck at the moment, although things hadn't gone too far. He was sure he could placate Lisa and then deal with Maggie in his own time. The important thing was to stay focused and to keep the two apart. When he opened his eyes he saw a teenage boy hurrying out of the kitchen with an order. Mei checked the items and smiled again as she handed the bag to Bruce. He reached into his jacket pocket for his wallet, then suddenly hesitated. After trying his other pockets he looked back at Mei. 'I don't believe this,' he said, heaving a heavy sigh, realising the dragons had been no help. He took his mobile from his pocket.

Lisa pulled on her jacket and remembered to pick up her phone as she headed quickly to the kitchen door. She called to the dog and Bella scampered to her side. The landline rang again. She froze as she saw Bruce's number appear once more on the answerphone. What did he want now? Could he possibly know she was leaving? She recoiled as his voice filled the room.

'Lisa? Are you there?' A pause, then: 'I've just tried your phone but it sounds like you've switched it off. Maybe you've gone back to sleep. I think I've left my wallet in the kitchen.' Another pause, then: 'Lisa?'

She stared down at the phone in her hand. He was right. She had switched it off after Maggie had called. She remained frozen, rooted to the spot, until Bruce rang off. No need to worry, she told herself; he would think she was asleep. It wasn't until she heard the beep on the machine that she finally took a breath. Her eyes moved to the counter top. She grabbed Bella's lead – then saw Bruce's wallet lying beneath it. He was always so careful with his belongings – especially his wallet. He would have needed it to pay for the takeaway – unless he had some cash on him.

She stared down at the wallet again. It was stylish, expensive – and she now knew Maggie was right; it belonged to a stranger. With trembling hands she picked it up, opened it and looked inside. Nothing but notes and credit cards. She realised she would need some money too. She wouldn't have to take much and he may never even notice it was missing. She grabbed some notes and went to close the wallet before she noticed that one note had been carefully folded and was tucked into a section on its own. She took it out – just a ten pound note. Turning it over, she noticed a tiny number was written on the back in black biro. Small neat handwriting. Just like Bruce's. She stared back towards the hallway.

Bruce smiled to himself as he left the Honeymoon restaurant. It was good of Mei to let him pay by credit card once he got home. Getting into his car he carefully settled the takeaway meal in the passenger well. It smelt good; Chinese spice and black bean sauce. Suddenly he felt hungry. As he drove off, he stepped on the accelerator, eager to get home and enjoy the food while it was still hot.

There was nothing to worry about. Everything would be fine. He gripped the steering wheel tightly, feeling as though he was back in control, then he allowed himself to smile again and switched on the radio. Rounding a corner he hit the brakes sharply as traffic had stalled straight in front of him. Craning his head out of the driver's window, he could see the flashing lights of a police car attending a road accident. He took a deep breath, fingers tapping the steering wheel as he stared down at the takeaway.

Lisa was stood in front of the basement door, the dog beside her, looking up at her as if wondering whether there would be any walk after all. Lisa looked down at the note in her hand – the one she had found in Bruce's wallet – then she gave her attention to the flashing red light on the security keypad before her. Could there possibly be a connection?

The phone suddenly rang again, breaking into the silence. Bruce's voice rang out from the machine in the kitchen. This time he sounded unsettled, impatient. 'Lisa?' A pause, then: 'Look, I'm sorry, but I'm stuck in traffic. An accident. I might be a while, okay? Don't worry. Just rest. I'll be there as soon as I can.' The machine rang off. Another beep.

Lisa stared at the door in front of her, then quickly punched the numbers on the note into the keypad. Nothing. The dog whimpered, still staring longingly at the lead dangling from Lisa's pocket. Lisa gave up and moved away.

Maybe it was better this way, she thought. The main thing was to get out, to escape from the house and call Maggie while Bruce was still delayed. Then she stopped in her tracks. Something was drawing her back – a final temptation – an overwhelming need to see what Bruce had never shared with her – a space filled with clients' data – or perhaps something more? She tapped the numbers into the keypad again – this time backwards. The red light on the alarm system went out. She held her breath and opened the door.

Flicking on a light switch Lisa caught sight of a flight of steps leading down to uncharted territory. Forbidden territory. But *why* was it forbidden to her? If she left now, she would never know – and perhaps never knowing would be worse. She reminded herself that Bruce was now sitting in traffic. He had just told her so. He need never know. She fought a battle with herself and crossed the threshold.

Bruce was listening to a traffic report on his car radio. The volume was high, vying with the sound of a blaring horn sounding from the car in front of him. He stared down again at the Chinese meal in the passenger well and switched up the radio volume further: '…where an accident is currently causing delays. Drivers are advised to use an alternative route.'

Frustrated, he switched off the radio and closed his window. It was only then that he heard his mobile sounding – sending him an alert he had failed to receive until that moment; a warning that the security system for his office had been breached. He began to turn his car around.

Lisa was finally there, at the foot of the stairs, in the basement office. She glanced around. It was a large room; shelves housing a sound system, some vinyl albums and CDs – and a framed photograph – showing Bruce and Lisa on their wedding day.

She picked it up and saw only two strangers staring back at her; a bride in a white dress with a low V neckline – a dress she had always harboured reservations about wearing, in case

Bruce hadn't liked it. He hadn't liked a lot of things; drinking too much with her friends or even dancing with Kevin, and she had been right about the dress too. But why had he waited until they were alone on their honeymoon, thousands of miles away on an island in the Atlantic, before telling her? Such a terrible shock on the most important day of her life – lying there alone in a hotel room in Funchal – not knowing if he would ever return.

She had never wanted to upset him like that ever again and had tried so hard after that. To make amends she had even bought him the paperweight that was sitting on his desk right now, bought from a little shop in a back street in Funchal in which she had spent a long time just staring at the little blue wave trapped inside, mesmerised by what it signified – freedom of the waves – or perhaps the opposite; one wave, trapped inside, unable ever to become free?

One thing was certain – she *had* upset Bruce. She had put on weight... fallen pregnant. She had listened to her mum. And now she was here – in the one place he always kept for himself. His mantuary.

She set the photograph down and looked towards the main computer – and a large screen that was mounted on the wall. Then she noticed a black case propped against his desk on the floor. She knew it contained the laptop with the strange security system – the system he said he had needed to protect his clients' data. She picked up the case – and unzipped it.

Inside she found the sleek silver laptop. Opening the lid she switched it on. As the screen came to life, she expected it would again demand fingerprint I.D. – then remembered Bruce explaining that this was only programmed for when the computer was 'out of his hands'. Nevertheless, she saw now that the laptop was asking for a password. Looking away, her gaze shifted to the wedding photo. One word remained in her mind. Honeymoon. That was the time Bruce had truly shown himself to her. The time when everything had changed – almost as soon as they had arrived in Funchal…

Perhaps she had never been the cause of his anger that night. Perhaps he had always planned to reveal himself this way. On their honeymoon. She found herself typing the word into the password space. Nothing. How long did she have before he returned to discover her in his den? She consoled herself, he was stuck in traffic – and she needed to know the truth. Bella padded across and nuzzled her hand – a comfort or a warning?

Lisa tried once more. Staring again at the wedding photo, she thought back to that day. Why had he hated the dress so much? Because it was low-cut. And because she wasn't like other women – the ones in Tenerife – the *putas*, the drunken whores. He had always told her that she was special. She was his. Why? She closed her eyes. A sudden thought came to her and she turned again to the laptop screen and typed in his special name for her: l i t t l e g i r l.

Access denied.

She tried again – typing the same words in upper case – and then without a space. In different permutations….Again and again until… a second passed before the screen suddenly unfolded and displayed a number of file icons. She had finally entered the mantuary.

*

A few moments later, Lisa's attention focused on one icon among many on the desktop – Funchal.

Clicking on it, she sat back as footage starting up on the screen on the wall. A beach at night, waves rolling in and breaking to become white foam disappearing into sand... The footage continued, some night scenes; a harbour bar, a marina strung with lights – nothing more. Lisa prepared to fast-forward but stopped as soon as something else entered the frame – a young woman, her back to the camera, dancing on a beach...

It could have been Lisa herself, except for the girl's blonde hair and the fact that she seemed unsteady on her feet. Too much to drink. The girl turned, a stupid grin on her face as she stared unfocused into the camera. Who was she? A hand came into view and roughly pulled the spaghetti-strap down from her sunburnt shoulder. The girl stared back into the camera lens – confused, offended.

'What d'you think you're doing?' The girl was frowning now, still confused – but fear was written on her face as she tried to fight off the stranger's hand. Stronger than her own, it wrenched the skimpy top from her body. The girl began to back away, trembling hands trying to cover her breasts. But the camera moved in ever tighter on her face as she stared into the lens, eyes pleading, tears beginning to fall. She let out a scream as a hand shoved her back on to the sand. The camera closed in as she continued to plead. 'Please... you're scaring me now... Mike?'

Lisa shook her head, unable to make sense of this, but unable to look away – until the dog began a low growl. Bella was staring towards the top of the steps. Bruce was back. Lisa got to her feet and quietened the dog, all the while staring up towards the door. Silence. Taking Bella into her arms she climbed the stairs to the hallway – where she stopped – hearing someone in the kitchen.

Her mind raced; he must have come in through the back door. Maybe he was serving up the takeaway food. Any moment he would surely call out to her? Lisa edged her way quickly to the front door. Her trembling fingers curled around the lock – then she opened the door – and ran.

Moments later, footsteps crossed the kitchen into the hall, coming to a halt at the sight of the open basement door. A voice was sounding from below. A girl's voice. Pleading.

On the screen in the basement, a young girl continued to sob, still backing away from the camera.

'Don't. You're scaring me…' A man's hand came back into the frame and shoved her violently down onto the sand. The girl's face crumpled, eyes imploring as she begged: 'Why are you doing this?'

Maggie tried to process what she saw. It wasn't Lisa's voice, as she had first thought, but a stranger talking on the screen – a young girl, her face filled with terror, grains of sand clinging to the tears on her cheek as someone pressed her body back down onto a beach. Maggie closed her eyes, shutting out what followed. Silence – but for waves rolling up on to a shoreline.

One thought entered her head; if Lisa wasn't here – where was she? She turned quickly for the stairs but a different voice sounded, this time familiar, but slurred. Another scene was playing out on the screen. An older woman, with long blonde hair, was trying to shield her face as she pleaded to the camera.

'Please. I have a child. Let me go…'

Maggie knew the voice and recognised the accent. The butterfly tattoo on the woman's wrist became visible as she tried to get up from a bed. A hand dragged her back by her long dyed-blonde hair. A man's hand. His body entered the frame, turning the woman on to her front, pressing her face down into the bed. Rona? Leyla? Maggie shook her head. This couldn't be happening. But a voice confirmed to her that it was. It was a voice sounding not from the screen – but from this room.

'You just couldn't leave it alone, could you, Maggie?'

Looking back, Maggie saw Bruce staring coldly at her.

CHAPTER THIRTY-TWO

A biting wind was blowing as Lisa ran blindly into the woods.

Bruce would never find her here – at least not if the dog stayed quiet. She couldn't risk heading back on to the road. Bruce would surely come after her in the car, and track her down, just as he had done on the night she had gone out with her friends. But if she kept going, deeper into the wood, she was sure she could find cover among the trees – somewhere safe to hide.

Needing to catch her breath, she stopped for a moment and looked back across her shoulder, relieved to see that she had put some distance between herself and the house. Now she needed to call Maggie. Her mother would know what to do. Maggie knew everything. Maggie knew best. Maggie would find her – and forgive her.

Reaching into a deep jacket pocket, Lisa rooted around for her phone. Finding it wasn't there, she now tried the other – then the jacket's inside pockets. Nothing. Staring back towards the house, she knew she had left it behind.

There was nothing else to do, but to go on into the dark woods to find safety. At least she wasn't totally alone – she still had the dog with her. Looking around she saw Bella was sniffing at the base of a tree.

'Come on!' Lisa whispered urgently. But the dog had picked up the scent of another creature and ignored her. Lisa called louder: 'Bella…'

The animal looked up at her only once – before scurrying into the darkness.

In the basement at Woodside, Bruce eyed Maggie. 'You never give up, do you?'

Maggie considered his question and the malevolent grin she wanted to wipe from his face but she needed to play safe – for Lisa's sake. 'Where's my daughter?' she asked. 'What have you done with her?'

Bruce shrugged with feigned innocence. 'Nothing. She's asleep upstairs. But don't worry. We won't disturb her. This basement is sound proofed.' He considered her – then smiled. 'You look worried, Maggie. But you shouldn't be. Lisa's my wife. We share something very special. Something you'd never understand. A special kind of love.'

Maggie heard herself spit venom. 'You don't know the meaning of the word,' she pointed at him accusingly. 'I saw through you from the start.'

Bruce remained unmoved. 'I know,' he said calmly. 'Which is why I never wasted my time with you. Much easier to get Jeff on side. Poor Jeff,' he went on. 'So trusting.'

'Jeff was no fool,' said Maggie bitterly. 'He found out about you.'

Bruce shrugged once more. "Found out I wasn't in the Guards? I might have talked my way out of that – if it hadn't been for you.' He stared back at her. 'You planted a little seed in his mind, didn't you, Maggie? 'Seems it didn't need much to grow.'

Maggie's eyes began to narrow with a realisation. 'You killed him—'

'I didn't need to,' said Bruce quickly. 'His ticker gave out. That poor old battered heart of his? I just didn't do anything to help. Let nature take its course. But that's not to say I'm not capable of taking a life – if I have to. Outside of the army they call that murder.' He looked at her darkly. 'And if the Guards had only let me in, maybe I could've been a hero.'

Maggie realised something else: 'They... saw through you too.'

Bruce shrugged. 'Maybe. But they've got plenty of basket cases, believe me. If they're not when they go in, they are when they come out. All they ever had on me were a few complaints from some local girls. Slags. Nothing anyone could prove. But they got rid of me all the same. For the honour of the regiment.'

He gave a bitter smile. 'All I ever wanted to do was to be a proper soldier,' he gave an ironic smile, 'just like Dad.' He paused again then went on. 'It was my old mum who told me he'd been in the Guards. Killed in Bosnia. On a mission. All top secret. But guess what? Turned out she was lying.'

He was silent for a moment, then went on: 'When I got drummed out, she decided to set the record straight – and told me the truth instead. She stood there in front of me, crying, telling me how I was... just like my ol' man?' He frowned. 'I didn't understand – so that's when she came clean.' He shook his head slowly. 'He wasn't a soldier at all. Just some drunken bastard who'd forced himself on her one night. And then, nine months later here I was.' He held his arms out wide. 'Like father – like son – that's what they say, don't they?'

Looking up at the screen, Bruce considered the frozen image of himself, dominating Leyla. His head slowly tipped to one side. 'It doesn't take much,' he went on. 'Not now. And they never seem to notice. Until it's too late.' He paused, then: 'At the barracks a guy once told me all about some special plant. He'd been in Columbia. Knew all about it. 'Said that if you slept under it… you'd wake up and be able to tell the future.' He gave a smile. 'But I already knew my future. I didn't need any special plants either, not when there are drugs that do the trick, and there are a whole lot more of them now. A little bit in their drinks… and they never put up much of a fight. They never remembered a thing. Or they didn't want to.' He glanced up at the screen and watched Leyla dispassionately; her eyes tight shut, resigned to pain, fear and confusion. He gave a look that bordered on admiration. 'That one was smart,' he said. 'She didn't want to take a drink off me. But we all have our weaknesses. Hers was money.'

Maggie broke in. 'You're a sick bastard.'

Bruce looked back at her, unconcerned. 'That's what my old mum said. She told me I needed help – but who can help a son better than his mother? That's what you're there for, isn't it? To stand by your kids. Not to lie to them?' His lips tightened before he went on. 'But that's what she did. She made a fool of me – got me to look up to some pervert as a hero.' He shook his head. 'I didn't deserve that. No-one does. So I tried to explain.

But she wouldn't listen, she... just kept moving away, like she was scared of me...' He moved forward. Maggie backed away.

'I kept telling her that whatever she'd done, she was still my mum – but all I could see was fear in her eyes – just like I see in yours now.' He took another step. Maggie backed further away. Bruce went on, his voice quickening. 'And then... she must have stumbled, lost her footing just like Lisa did the other night. I put my hand out... tried to save her. But she fell... across the bannister, all the way down, looking back up at me like she was... relieved to be getting away from me.' He frowned and fell silent, then blinked. 'I could've made things right.'

Maggie shook her head. 'No. That's why you needed a wife for yourself. To cover up everything you lacked. Everything you really are.'

Bruce looked back and saw her loathing. In spite of it, he smiled. 'Me?' he asked innocently. He nodded towards the screen on the wall. 'And what about them? Tarts... slags... whores – the lot of them—'

'But not Christine,' said Maggie quickly. His head snapped back at this. Maggie went on. 'And my Lisa?' She shook her head. 'She's never been your 'little girl' – even though she's been trapped in this house, like some prisoner, thinking you're God's gift when all the while you were out there—'

'I *needed* to show them,' said Bruce. 'Exactly who I am. What I'm capable of.' He glanced again at the screen, as though for reassurance, then smiled, triumphant, before he looked back again at Maggie. 'But what do I do about you now, eh, Maggie? Tell the police how I walked in and found some... 'intruder' in the dark?' His smile remained in place as he took another step forward. This time Maggie held her ground. 'And what about Lisa?' she asked once more.

'I told you,' he said. 'She's upstairs, asleep. She won't hear a thing.'

'No,' said Maggie, taking her time before explaining. 'She knows about you now. I talked to her,' she nodded towards the screen. 'This was already on when I got here… and the back door was open,' she paused, then: 'That's how I got in.'

Bruce's eyes shifted to the screen then back at Maggie. He made a quick assessment. Shaking his head, he pointed at her: 'You're lying.'

'Am I?' Maggie's hand reached towards the silver laptop and picked up something lying beside it. 'This is hers, isn't it?' She held up Lisa's pink iPhone.

Bruce said nothing, his eyes narrowing as he focused on the phone.

CHAPTER THIRTY-THREE

Lisa continued to stumble through undergrowth, pausing only to catch her breath. After losing sight of the house behind her, she knew she had no idea where she was or where she was heading. Perhaps she had simply been moving in a circle and the house would soon reappear. She could hear her own voice sounding beneath her panting breaths, like a child about to burst into tears. Breathing deeply she tried to calm herself and quell her rising panic but it seemed impossible to regain control after seeing those images on the screen. She stared around – a hunted animal.

Was this the reason Bruce had wanted to live so far away from everyone? Was it really possible to escape from him? She felt herself shivering – from cold – and fear. The cold might take her before Bruce found her. How could she survive a night in freezing temperatures? Hypothermia would set in – perhaps it was doing so already. She was finding it hard to follow a train of thought and to think straight about anything. Her teeth chattered, echoing in her brain.

This was all her own fault. Whatever happened now could never be undone. She had made her choice – the wrong choice.

She had fallen under the spell of a monster and allowed him to take over. Bruce had never loved her – he had been using her as cover – a young fool, so desperate for approval that she had allowed him to control every aspect of her life – including turning her against her own family. He had needed to do that in order to complete the deception – the lie he had persuaded her to believe. That was his power – his ultimate charm – the spell he had been able to cast…

Eyes open, she now saw herself lost within dense woodland that seemed to reflect her own tangled thoughts. An owl hooted, reminding her she wasn't alone – even here.

Surely she could find the strength to go on – to find a route out – and into safety? She summoned all her resolve and turned to move on but took only a few steps before she walked into a thorny branch. Barbs tore into her face. She keened in pain and put a hand to her cheek, withdrawing it to find blood mixed with tears on her trembling fingertips. Then she heard something in the trees behind her.

An ice-cold wind stirred the impenetrable trees. The moon was half-hidden beneath a skein of silver cloud. Something appeared before her. A dog fox, as big as a young wolf, was blocking her path, its amber eyes reflecting the moonlight. The animal showed no fear but stared back as though admonishing her for invading its territory. In that moment, Lisa felt herself diminished as the fox bared its teeth, snarling as though it was now laughing at her weakness.

In the next instant the moon rose higher above the cloud, casting light on the reason for the animal's sense of triumph.

Something was trapped in its jaws; a small creature, barely alive, perhaps being taken off to a lair to be shared with cubs. Lisa took a step closer. The fox held its ground, its jaw re-set to clamp its struggling prey. A single feather fell to the ground to be taken up by the cold wind. A tiny bird was fighting for life – still programmed for survival. From somewhere deep inside her, Lisa found the strength to act. In one quick move, she picked up a stone and hurled it at the fox. The animal gave a shriek but in the next moment it had vanished. In its place, Lisa glimpsed its wounded prey before black wings fluttered up into the tall oaks – to freedom.

In the basement at Woodside, Maggie brandished Lisa's phone as she baited Bruce. 'She got away from you. Lisa finally escaped you. And she *knows* what you did.'

Bruce stared at her, unnerved for a moment, mask slipping, before he shook his head. 'No,' he insisted. 'The dog's not here. She took it for a walk.' He raised his hand and pointed a finger at her. 'I told you – you're lying.'

Maggie dared to toy with him. 'Am I? You'll find out soon enough when the police get here,' she waited for her threat to find its mark then chose the next moment to make her move, dodging past him in an attempt to reach the stairs. Bruce was faster. Grabbing hold of her, he shoved her roughly back on to the desk where Maggie struggled in his grasp as Leyla stared down from the screen.

'You won't know anything about that.' Bruce told her, forcing his hands around her throat. Maggie gasped, fighting for air, hands flailing, grasping ineffectually for something, anything, with which to defend herself. But he was too strong for her.

As he stared down at her, Bruce realised she was finally where he needed her to be – under his control – where he had wanted her from the very first moment they had met, when he had entered her home and she had dared to ignore him, as though he was no-one of any consequence. She had always been finding fault, nagging Jeff, interfering in her daughter's life and marriage... He found himself warning her: 'You're going to get what you've been asking for. What you deserve.' His grip was tightening on her throat, wringing the life from her. He could do it quickly – or slowly – enjoying her pain.

Maggie's hand desperately clawed at the desk behind her before her fingers finally tightened around something. She struggled to lift it but managed to strike out, smashing the sleek silver laptop against Bruce's temple. He crashed backwards while Maggie gasped for air before making another bid for the stairs. This time she managed to reach the top step, opening the door before she felt the ground disappearing beneath her, Bruce's hand was gripped tightly around her ankle, dragging her back down into his hell. She screamed out in pain as her head struck the corner of a step.

'Scream as loud as you want,' said Bruce, taunting her. 'There's no-one within a mile to hear.' He was moving in on her again when something stopped him. An animal was suddenly on the stairs, Bella sinking her sharp teeth deep into his hand. Bruce flung his arm wide, smashing the creature against a bank of cupboards. The dog yelped pitifully then cowered, whimpering in pain.

Still dazed, Maggie reached out towards the injured animal as Bruce's gaze fell on something on the desk. In the next instant, he was towering above her, arms held high, a computer cable flexed taut between his fists. He snapped it tight around Maggie's throat. Her fingers clawed at it, gouging her skin as she forced her fingernails beneath it, trying to stop the pain, the terrible choking. She heard herself gasp and saw the room beginning to fade. Bruce's features were suddenly transforming into Jeff's face – smiling before her – telling her not to be afraid. She felt herself bursting, then floating away... together with the pain... not just the physical pain all of it... the terror, the fear, the desperate need to stay alive in order to protect Lisa... everything was going to be all right after all...

Then Jeff disappeared, his image morphing into Bruce's face above her, his expression no longer fierce and terrifying but bewildered and questioning. Letting go of the cable, his hands were now reaching behind his back, before he slumped forward; a dead weight lying on top of her, pinning her to the floor. Repulsed, Maggie summoned the last of her strength to shove his body from her. As she did so, she came face to face with someone standing before her. Lisa's face was bleeding, her breath held tight in fear, as if waiting for a conclusion. Was it another vision?

'Mum?' Lisa's voice pierced the horror.

'I'm all right,' Maggie choked, struggling to her feet. She held her daughter close, feeling Lisa trembling in her embrace. As they clung to one another, Maggie stared down at Bruce's body. His eyes glared up at her accusingly as though he was still alive, but a thick dark crimson pool was spreading out across the floor beneath his skull.

Maggie felt for Lisa's hand and loosened her fingers that still clung to a heavy glass orb, the blue wave within it disappearing in a tide of warm blood. In the next instant, the paperweight fell to the floor. The screen on the wall was fading to grey but Maggie failed to notice. Her eyes had begun to close as she held her daughter tightly, seeing only a fair-haired child with cherub features whose hair smelled of sugar and roses.

CHAPTER THIRTY-FOUR

Extract 3 from the transcript of a recorded interview with
Mrs Margaret Sheild
Date: 3rd April 2024
Conducted by: Officers of Marston Police
Location: Marston Police Station, West Yorkshire

When your police officers came, they put me and Lisa in the back of a car. She leaned her head on my shoulder, like she and Nat used to do, when they were little, after one of our outings while Jeff would be driving us home from a day on the moors or a trip to 'Skeggie'. Only this time it was a sergeant who was driving us away.

As I looked back I saw the lights of that house disappearing, and I thought to myself that one day that's how all of this will be – like something in the distance growing smaller – something we'll never want to look back on ever again.

They say 'Mother knows best', don't they? And I reckon that's true – at least where Bruce Carter was concerned. When all the investigations are over, all your questions asked and a verdict reached, I still need to do something – and that's to find Rona. And yes, I know that's not her real name, but that's how she'll always be to me. You see, I need to let her know that I'll do whatever I can – that I'll be there for her and her daughter – wherever they may be.

You might say it was coincidence – Bruce finding her in that hotel? Not me. It was Fate. Fate that she met him – and Fate that my Lisa had to do what she did. Does that mean we had no choice? I don't know. I'm not asking for absolution but I know *I* had no choice from the moment that man stepped into my daughter's life.

I admit there was a time when I lost faith in Rona – but it didn't last long. Some people you meet and you carry them around in your heart. I carry that woman in mine. She once said that she was just like me; a woman trying to make things right for her family.

I knew what she meant because I felt exactly the same. I still do, because we *are* the same, the same woman, no matter what her name is or where she's from. I always told the girls at my factory that we're a family or we're nothing – and I told my daughters the same because that's the way we get to survive – together. That's one good thing about human beings, isn't it? That we can feel for each other, look out for one another – make sure we're protected?

And I know you told me I don't have to say anything – but I do. It's the only way I can make sense of this and the only way Lisa and I will ever get over it.

Can we do that? I don't know for sure but I do know that when I lay flowers on Jeff and Nat's grave, the headstone tells me they're gone, and yet they're still with me – every second of every day. I talk to them. And they answer me, in their own way. Lots of ways. Ways I can't explain. And even here, in this police station, they tell me we *will* survive this – and that we *have* to. Because if we don't, Bruce Carter will have won. And, alive or dead, I can never let him do that.

You see, after everything that's happened, and everything I've told you, Lisa will always be *my* little girl – not his.

THE END

ACKNOWLEDGEMENTS

Every book arrives with readers via a multitude of different paths. This one owes its existence to James Essinger of Conrad Press and to the continued support of my agents, Michelle Kass and all at MKA Associates who have represented me for more than three decades.

I'm also grateful to my friend, Aram Rawf, for helping me with Kurdish research.

Huge thanks also go to my husband, Kas, my family and all those who enjoy my books. An author is nothing without readers.

AUTHOR'S NOTE

The Mantuary will no doubt appear as a total contrast to readers who are familiar with my *Whitstable Pearl Mystery* series of novels and the TV series, *Whitstable Pearl*, which is based on them.

In fact, I decided to write this book during the COVID pandemic when I was confronted with various family problems including a serious health diagnosis for my husband.

It was a dark time which prompted me to reflect on how we cope with such challenges, and reminded me that writing has always given me an opportunity for catharsis in times of trouble.

Sadly, it would seem few of us are total strangers to issues of coercive control, which I have witnessed in the lives of my friends, family members and neighbours with whom I grew up in London's East End in the '50s and '60s.

Domestic abuse isn't something which is experienced solely by women, but in this book I sought to offer a view of how solidarity amongst women can help to overcome this.

If you feel you need help with these issues, the following organisations provide this:-

Women's Aid is a national charity that's been working to end domestic abuse against women and children for the last fifty years.

Refuge opened the world's first "safe house" for women and children fleeing from domestic abuse in 1971.

Men's Advice Line provides a confidential helpline and services for men who are survivors of domestic abuse.

For more information about Julie's books go to
www.juliewassmer.com

Also by Julie Wassmer

The Whitstable Pearl Mystery

Murder-on-Sea

May Day Murder

Murder on the Pilgrims Way

Disappearance at Oare

Murder Fest

Murder on the Downs

Strictly Murder

Murder at Mount Ephraim

Murder at the Allotment